LOST

LOST

QUINCY HARKER, DEMON HUNTER
BOOK NINE

JOHN G. HARTNESS

FALSTAFF
BOOKS
WWW.FALSTAFFBOOKS.COM

For my family, by blood and by choice.
Found family is family.

CHAPTER ONE

They say that standing over a dead body is a great place to start a book. Well, that may be, but I can tell you with certainty that it's a shit way to end a vacation. And looking down at the bits of a young woman splayed across the sand dunes, my vacation was one hundred percent over. She'd probably been pretty, once. I could see hints of blond hair amidst the red and the brown, and the remaining fingernails were manicured. She looked to have been about five-eight, maybe five-nine, and athletically built. Her right calf was muscular and tan, with a small butterfly tattoo just above the outside of her ankle.

Her left calf, like the rest of her left leg, was missing, torn from the hip with extreme force. And I'm not exaggerating or being poetic when I use the word "torn." Her leg had been ripped from the socket, her flesh, muscles, tendons, and all the stringy bits that hold people's limbs in place showed signs of extreme stretching before finally giving up the ghost and ripping free from their moorings. She wore a yellow bikini. No, not polka dot. Yellow and blue stripes, cut high on her hips. Hip, I suppose. I thought I saw the string of her top stretching over her back, but I couldn't really tell. Her body was too mangled, her flesh too flayed for me to really get a sense of whether the line across the middle of her back was string, or some part of her that had been torn away but not out.

In short, it was a damned mess.

"That had to hurt," Becks said from beside me. My fiancée, Deputy

1

Director Rebecca Gail Flynn of the Department of Homeland Security's Paranormal Division, stepped up to my shoulder and looked down at the body. "Any idea what did this?"

"Not yet," I said. I didn't turn to her. Something about looking at the woman I love with a dismembered corpse in my peripheral vision felt wrong. It was odd, given our line of work. We'd waded through bodies together, fought side by side against monsters both magical and man-made. But something about this felt different, more *wrong* than the average murder.

"Okay, Director, we can turn her over now," the crime scene photographer called up to us.

"Make sure nothing important spills out," I called down to the man, who was kneeling beside the woman's shoulders, trusting his navy coveralls to protect him from the water and whatever else might seep through the sand. He shot me a dirty look, but I was serious. If the damage to her front was as severe as the wounds on her back, the likelihood of her innards spilling out all over the sand was high, and besides being gross and demeaning to the woman who used to wear that body, it could screw up any evidence in the vicinity.

The photographer waved a couple other crime scene techs over, and together they rolled the young woman onto her back. The photog rocked back on his heels, sliding down to sit in the sand with a soft *whump*. One of the techs paled and looked away, but the other one, a rotund man in his fifties who until five seconds earlier had an air of "been there, done that" about him, turned and sprinted toward the water, dropping to his knees and hurling up everything he'd ever thought about eating.

"Well, at least he didn't contaminate the crime scene," Becks said as the man knelt in the surf and puked.

"Not that I think we're getting much from that," I replied, gesturing toward the body. Now that she was face-up, I could see that she had indeed been pretty, at least until a few hours ago. She was young, maybe in her mid-twenties, and fit, with a trim waist, full breasts, and shapely legs. At least, that's what I thought I could extrapolate by the pieces that were left.

This woman had been horribly mutilated. The kind of shredding that TV stations put on their ads for Shark Week or Predator of the Month shows. In addition to missing the lower half of one leg, her left eye was gone, her jaw hung loose at an angle that suggested it had been yanked from its sockets, and long, jagged slashes ran all across her torso, many penetrating deeply enough to allow me to peer into her body cavity, even from several yards away.

She was still dressed, mostly. Her bikini was in place, and there was a flip flop on the remaining foot. A plastic rod that had once been the earpiece of a pair of sunglasses protruded from behind one ear, and a massive diamond engagement ring glinted in the morning sun. Her right arm was missing below the elbow, but I think one of the forensic techs mentioned they found it behind a sand dune nearby.

There were a couple other tattoos visible, one starting above her left elbow, honeysuckles climbing her bicep, curving over her shoulder and ending in a white and yellow flower right at the tip of her clavicle. A sprig of cherry blossoms decorated the right side of her ribcage, playing peek-aboo with her bikini top and the blood spatter. The stench of blood and viscera wafted over to us, coated in the salty scent of the Atlantic Ocean.

"What the hell did this?" Becks asked again.

"I have no fucking idea," I replied. I switched over to our mental link, since the local constabulary didn't need to hear me talking my way through options that they wouldn't believe existed. *It's not a werewolf, because the slashes are too irregular to have been made by claws. If this was a wolf, I'd expect four mostly parallel lines. This is all over the place, so it's either made by something with one long, sharp claw, or a person with a knife. But the leg being ripped from the socket speaks to incredible strength, so maybe a demon?*

Was there magic used? she asked.

Hard to tell, I replied. *The salt water kinda fucks with it, and the waves wash away magical trace just like physical evidence. Plus, there's something funky about this island. There's* way *more magic floating around than there should be. Like the whole damn place is magical or something. I haven't pulled up my Sight yet, I wanted to see it in the visible spectrum first, but I can already tell something's weird.*

Odd. I could almost see her giving herself a mental shake to get back on task. A short balding man struggled over the dunes carrying a big leather case. He limped over to the body, obviously weighed down by the case, and set it down on the sand with a loud sigh.

"You okay, pal?" I asked.

"I will be once I catch my breath," he said, holding out a hand. "MJ Stoumbos. I'm the county medical examiner. Not used to getting called out to a crime scene in the middle of the night. Usually my patients are just waiting on me when I get to work in the morning."

"So why are you here now?" I asked. I've been to a lot of crime scenes.

I've created more than my fair share of crime scenes. Hell, that's where Becks and I first met—one of the times she arrested me. But no matter how many bodies I've scattered around, it's rare that a medical examiner shows up anywhere but the morgue.

"Sheriff called and woke me up. Said he needed me to establish a time of death as soon as possible, and if I could give him a preliminary cause of death, he'd appreciate it," Stoumbos said.

I'd met the sheriff about an hour earlier, and from the way he greeted Becks and me, I was confident that the words "I'd appreciate it" never came out of that man's mouth. Hell, he hadn't even taken the cigar out of his mouth before he told me where I could shove my Department of Homeland Security credentials. I got the distinct impression he didn't think he needed any help from the federal government. That impression came in the form of him telling me exactly that— "I don't need no got-damned 'help' from no got-damned Yankee assholes comin' down here waving around them bullshit credentials and running my boys ragged while y'all sip your lattes and take the credit."

I hadn't bothered to tell him that I don't really like lattes, or that where I was raised, we call all Americans "Yankees." I just stepped out of the way and let Becks handle it. I'm working on learning diplomacy, and my diplomacy pretty much begins and ends with the few times I manage to not tell an asshole to fuck right off into the ocean and let my fiancée handle it.

Becks just walked up and handed her cell phone to the blustering Buford Pusser wannabe. After a few seconds of sputtering "yes sir" a lot, he handed the phone back to her and said, "Anything y'all need, just let me know. My people are at y'all's disposal."

"What the fuck did you do?" I asked.

"I had Faustus mimic the governor of North Carolina's voice and tell the sheriff that if he didn't cooperate with us fully, that there wouldn't be a single dollar of state or federal tax money coming to this island until it sank beneath the waves like Atlantis."

"And he bought it?"

"Faustus can be very convincing," she said with a grin. She was right. Faustus was a convincing bastard. Which made sense, given that he was a demon world-renowned for striking deals and negotiating in the worst interests of literally everyone to ever cross paths with him.

Yes, I hang out with a demon. I have a guardian angel, too. You think that's complicated, wait until I tell you about my uncle.

I turned my attention back to the M.E., who was pulling a thermometer out of the dead woman's backside. "I thought you used a meat thermometer for that?" I asked.

"They do that on television," the doctor replied. "But in the field, we generally can determine a rough time of death by rectal temperature. I'd say she was killed no more than three hours ago. The state of rigor in her face, and lack of rigor in her extremities, would lend credence to this theory."

"So sometimes between midnight and two in the morning," I said, looking out over the ocean.

"Perhaps slightly earlier, depending on her position relative to the water when she was killed," Stoumbos replied.

"You don't think she was killed here?" I asked.

The doctor stood up, wiping sand off his knees. "I try not to speculate outside my field of expertise, and I am no forensic technician, but it seems to me that there is far less blood on the sand that would be indicated by these wounds. There is no visible blood trail leading to the body, and no pool of blood, so if she died by exsanguination due to these wounds, which is likely, I doubt the attack took place here."

"And given the missing leg, she probably didn't get here under her own power," I added.

"Certainly not," the doctor agreed. "Her wounds would have been such that she would have lost consciousness due to blood loss in minutes, if she didn't pass out from shock before that." He paused for a second, apparently realizing I was screwing with him a little. "So no, she didn't hop here as she bled out. By the way, did anyone find the leg?"

"No," Becks said. "The crime scene techs have been walking the beach, but nobody's seen it."

"Just like the others," the doctor said, then shot us an alarmed glance, like he'd let something slip.

Others? I asked Becks silently.

No idea, she sent back. "I think I need to have a chat with the sheriff. Harker, with me."

I knew that tone. She was about to kick somebody's ass, and for a change, it wasn't going to be mine. This was gonna be fun to watch.

CHAPTER TWO

While Becks took a stroll over the dunes to gnaw on the sheriff's ass, I opened my Sight to take a look at the scene through more mystical eyes. I didn't expect much. We were on an island off the coast of North Carolina, basically one of the most popular tourist destinations on the east coast, and I figured if there was much magical going on, I'd have heard about it long before now. So when I looked at the chunk of beach in the magical spectrum, I figured I'd be the most interesting thing within a dozen miles.

I was wrong. And I wasn't just wrong, I was "Dewey Defeats Truman" levels of wrong. There was so much magical energy scattered around the body that I staggered back a step, almost falling on my ass right there in the sand.

"You alright, pal?" the M.E. asked.

"Yeah," I said, shaking my head. My vision was full of sparkles, and I could already feel a mother of a migraine coming on. This place was absolutely glowing with magic, every bit of it old, powerful, and malevolent as fuck. Whatever killed this woman was about as natural as...well, as me. Which is to say not at all.

I took a deep, steadying breath, closed my eyes for a moment, and opened my Sight again. There was a roiling nexus of dark energy around the girl's body, a horrifying bruise on the very air itself, a swirling vortex of red, black, and purple energy all pulsing in angry cadence with the crashing surf. It wasn't just around the body, either. It led off in three different directions—one tendril of nastiness led across the dunes back toward the lighthouse, one led south down the beach toward a campground, and one led right out into the Atlantic. That one bothered me most of all, because there aren't many things that should have enough power oozing off them to leave that strong a trail into water running that fast.

Magic is kinda like a slug, if a slug could throw fireballs and turn people into frogs. Not that I can turn people into frogs. I might be able to if I knew a powerful enough transmutation spell, but the law of conservation of matter means that it would be the biggest goddamned frog in the known universe, and then I wouldn't have an annoying human on my hands, I'd have an annoying pissed off giant frog. Sometimes it's better just to burn everything to the ground. Because magic *can* throw fireballs. Lots of fireballs. But it's like a slug in that it leaves a residue on anything it interacts with, including sand dunes, wild grasses, and corpses. But it almost never leaves residue on running water, because just like you can never step twice in the same river, your magical slug juice isn't going to stay in the same piece of ocean very long. So for there to be an undulating ribbon of blood-red magic glowing like a road flare in the Atlantic Ocean, whatever passed through there must have had some serious power.

Like Seventh Circle of Hell level power. Or maybe even lower. I've been to Hell. I've been all the way down in the joint, and the list of things down there that I want to encounter again has exactly zero names on it. I couldn't really tell if what left the trail in the water was what killed the girl, but it was definitely in contact with her body, and it was more powerful than anything that I wanted to deal with. Not that it looked like I was going to have much of a choice.

The trails leading in the other two directions were much less horrifying. The trail from the lighthouse was a mix of purple and black, with tiny streaks of fading yellow and white in it. That made me think this was where the woman came from, toward the lighthouse. The tendrils of magic coming from that direction felt different, like there were two mixed sources, one human and basically good in nature, and one...not human, at least not anymore, and a long way from good. Like diametrically opposed. It felt human, but inhuman at the same time, like there was a normal person wrapped around a core of demonic energy. I had an uncomfortable moment when I realized that the demon-infused aura felt a lot like mine and Luke's.

7

My Uncle Luke, who was born Vlad Tepes, and most of the world knows as Count Vlad Dracula, made a deal with a demon a few centuries ago to give him a warm place to hang out and all the humans he could eat in exchange for long life and enough power to get justice, or revenge depending on your definition, for the murder of his wife and one true love. That demon infected every vampire Luke ever sired, and every vampire they sired, and so on and so on, in a diminishing capacity on down the line. I got a double dose of that demon's essence when Luke's "brides" chowed down on my father when he was working for Luke, and when Luke took a nibble out of my mom's neck before she hooked up with my dad.

And you thought your family was screwed up, huh? The long and the short of it was since both my parents got bitten by vampires, and since they were, at most, one generation removed from Dracula's demonic essence, I ended up a magical mutant of sorts, with a bigger shard of demon in my soul than any vampire not living down the hall from me and calling me nephew. And now for the first time in better than a century, I was looking at the residue of a spell caster equally tainted by demon juice as me.

Residue that got even blacker and even more foul as it left the body and headed off south toward the campground. It was like whoever killed this girl got some kind of power boost from the murder, which was even more disturbing than the resemblance his aura had to my own. So now we had a magical murderer with at least a hint of demon mojo, an eviscerated girl on a beach, an incredibly powerful evil something or other walking out into the goddamned Atlantic Ocean and trailing enough magic to scar the very water itself, and I was going to have to investigate a lighthouse murder scene in the middle of the night. Some fucking vacation.

"See anything?" Becks asked, returning from her conversation with the sheriff.

A lot, but nothing I want to say out loud where CSI: Rednecks can hear me, I replied.

"Nothing," I said aloud. "What did you learn from the local constabulary?"

"That this is the fourth gruesome murder in the last three weeks. All tourists or transients, all dismembered and mutilated, all found along the coastline. And that the sheriff wasn't thrilled about the M.E. letting news of the other killings slip."

"Does he have any leads?" I asked. "Or any good reason for not calling in help from a larger, more experienced agency? I can't imagine they have much in the way of serial murder here on the Outer Banks."

"You'd be right," she agreed. "The murder rate is very low, as are all violent crimes, if I'm being honest. There's a fair amount of theft, and a staggering number of drug and alcohol violations, but it's not a place where people usually end up raped or murdered."

"Was she raped?" I asked.

Becks looked at me funny, like I'd said something egregiously stupid. "I have no way of knowing that, Harker. She's lying on a beach with one leg missing and her guts ripped out. I'm pretty sure nobody has had a chance to check for sexual assault yet."

"Good point," I admitted. "So are all the killings linked? Is there evidence connecting the murders?"

"That's part of the problem," she said. "There's no evidence. Nothing. The killer hasn't left so much as a hair at any of the other scenes, and if the frustrated expressions on those technicians' faces is anything to go by, he didn't leave anything here, either."

"Maybe there's something at the lighthouse," I mused.

"The lighthouse?" Becks asked.

"The lighthouse?" the M.E. repeated.

"Is there an echo out here?" I asked. "Yeah, the lighthouse." I realized that the medical examiner probably wasn't on the list of people I should talk about my magical mystery vision with, so I just waved off in the general direction of the Bodie Island Lighthouse. "There aren't any tire tracks except for emergency vehicles, and we know she wasn't killed here, so the lighthouse is the most logical nearby place, right?"

Dr. Stoumbos looked dubious, but Becks nodded, going along with my ruse. "That makes sense, Harker. It's the nearest building, it's secluded, and it's close enough that the killer could have hauled the body out here to be discovered."

"Why would he want her to be found?" I asked.

"Who knows?" Becks replied. "Maybe he feels some kind of remorse, maybe he wants to be sure everyone knows what he's doing. It could be either, or both, or somewhere between the two. We don't have enough information to build anything even approaching a profile. Yet. Doc, you stay here while we go poke around. If there's something to find, we'll call you, but not until we make sure the scene is secure."

She sounded really confident that we were going to find something, and I raised an eyebrow at her. "In my conversation with the sheriff, I made it clear that since these dunes are a federally protected wildlife preserve, this was now our case, and we would be leading the investigation into any secondary crime scenes. He didn't like it, but the lighthouse is ours. Let's move."

Federally protected wildlife preserve? I asked, trying to keep a straight face.

It worked, didn't it?

I guess we'll see when we go to pick up those files. If he arrests us, then it didn't work.

Well, if he tries to arrest us, you have my permission to turn him into a frog.

And now we were back to the frog thing. I wish she'd give me permission to blow up people that annoy me, just once. It's not that I let her lack of approval stop me from blowing up people who deserve it, it's just that I'm starting to get tired of explaining why I can't turn assholes into frogs. I'd just get green assholes, and that's the kind of thing that makes you swear off St. Patrick's Day forever.

CHAPTER THREE

The lighthouse was deserted, as it should have been in the middle of the friggin' night. We were well past the time of night when anything good happened, ever, and realistically were well past the time of night when anything fun happened, too. We had settled well into the time of night usually reserved for burglars, murderers, milkmen, paper boys, and grumpy insomniac wizards hunting down burglars, murderers, or milkmen. I've never had cause to chase a paper boy down in the middle of the night.

I slipped into my Sight as we walked, making the uneven terrain even more treacherous, but at least the dune I fell into was soft. The same magical trace from the beach led right up to the base of the lighthouse, with the tremulous hints of yellow and white, usually signs of purity and goodness in an aura, covered in a viscous slime of black and purple, dark magic smothering the light. Yeah, something bad happened here.

"Well, that's not good," Becks said, standing at the door of the lighthouse.

"What's up?" I asked, calling power to shroud my fists in glowing spheres of purple magic.

"You can let all the urban fantasy book cover bullshit go, Harker, there's nothing attacking us at the moment." I looked around, saw no threat, and let my magic dissipate. She was right, though. With my tousled hair, long coat, Doc Martens, and purple glowing hands, I looked like a guy on a book cover. Time to change up my presentation a bit.

"So what's the problem?" I asked.

"This," Becks replied. She had a small LED flashlight in her hand, which she pointed down at the ground in front of the door. A pool of black liquid shimmered there, but as my eyes took in the whole scene, I realized it only looked black because it was such a deep red. A *very* deep red. The same red splattered all over the doorframe, and I could see streaks and splashes decorating the scrub brush and sand as far as ten feet away.

"Well, that's gross," I said. "But on the bright side, we found our crime scene. Our victim was definitely killed here."

"Victims," Becks corrected me.

"Excuse me?" I was pretty sure I hadn't missed a dead body at some point. I might not be the most perceptive magical detective in the world, but I'm pretty unlikely to miss a bonus corpse at a murder scene. Come to think of it, since I don't know any other magical detectives, I probably am the most perceptive one in the world.

"In here." Becks gestured through the open door to the base of the lighthouse. I walked forward, doing my best not to screw up any evidence in the sand. Becks aimed her flashlight into the lighthouse, and I followed the beam with my gaze.

"Well, that's fucking nasty," I said. "*Lumos.*" A sphere of white light about a foot in diameter coalesced in the small circular room, casting smooth, even illumination all around. Sitting slumped against the wall in about the farthest point you could get from the door was a dead man.

Sometimes you need to check for a pulse before you can be sure if someone is truly dead. But when they're sitting propped up against the interior wall of a lighthouse with their head in their lap staring at you, you can usually be sure they aren't going to be doing any jump scares. He was blond, at least the hair that wasn't coated with blood was blond, and good-looking in that sun-bleached, muscular, square-jawed way that I'm not. I could imagine him with a little smirk that got lots of skirts lifted, but imagine it was all I could do, given that his face was frozen in a permanent scream of agony.

"What did this, Harker?" Becks asked. "Magic?"

"Well, it wasn't human, that's for sure," I said, letting my Sight settle back over my mundane vision. The dead guy, who I decided should be called Bernie, for reasons, was absolutely *coated* in the black and purple magic that led from here to the beach. There were slivers of sickly green, yellow, and bright red shooting through his aura, but that seemed like more him than what was done *to* him. This was not a good person before he died, and it was unlikely that he had any pure intentions at a closed national monument after dark with a pretty girl, but what had been done to him was so dark and foul that it dwarfed his own petty awfulness.

"I can't tell what did it," I said. "But whatever killed this guy, it had *power*." I knelt beside the body, my feet squelching in the congealing blood as I walked over and pointed to the stump of his neck. "Look at this," I said. "This wound was cauterized as it was made. That means that he was either decapitated by something incredibly hot, or that Darth Vader has picked Manteo as his summer vacation spot."

"You left out a third option," Becks said, her voice stony.

"I did?" I couldn't think of anything I'd left out, but I was willing to listen.

"A soulblade could have done that, too. I've seen some of the wounds you inflict with that flaming pigsticker. This could be from the same kind of thing."

"Well, I've been with you all weekend, and I haven't decapitated any douchebags in a long time, so I think we can scratch me off the suspect list," I said.

Flynn raised an eyebrow at me. "And you're the only being in the universe that has a flaming magic sword?"

Oh shit. She was right, there were a lot of soulblades out there. Every angel Guardian rank and above could manifest them, which means that any original demons that started off as Guardians or higher ranked could do it. Not to mention any magic user of sufficient skill, which was pretty skilled, but I still figured there were probably a hundred or so across the world with enough juice to do it. And I had no idea how many angels or demons of high enough power were running around.

"I think we're gonna need a little help with this one," I said.

"Ya think?" asked a voice from the doorway.

I turned my head to see a gorgeous blonde leaning against the frame. She was five-ten or so, slim, with leather pants, a shredded Guns N' Roses t-shirt, and an insouciant smirk that said, "I know exactly how hot I am, but I'm way too powerful for you to even think about doing anything about it." Oh yeah, and she had blinding white wings sticking out of her back.

13

"Hi, Glory," I said, turning back to the corpse. "Did you Washington Irving this guy?"

"Did I what?" she asked, walking over to kneel on the other side of the dead guy.

"You know, Washington Irving. The Headless Horseman, Ichabod Crane..." I said.

"Wow, Q. That one's reaching pretty hard for the comedy. And missing," my Guardian Angel replied. "No, I didn't take this guy out. Neither did any member of the Host."

"How can you tell?" Flynn asked from the doorway. I guess she figured at least one of us needed to pretend like we still gave a shit about the mundane justice system and preserving evidence.

"The residue on the wound is wrong, and the cut isn't clean enough. This was either a demon blade or something conjured by a lesser magician." She pointed to the spinal column. "See these jagged marks? Those are made by a serrated edge. Angel blades are smoother."

"Even with the whole sheathed in flame thing?" I asked.

"Yeah. The flames don't change the characteristics of the edge. They just make it a lot easier to cut through the squishy parts. And it looks cooler."

I took a half a second to wrap my head around the fact that my Guardian Angel manifested a flaming sword because it "looked cooler" than a non-flaming magical sword, bemoaned my horrible influence on the Heavenly Host, then chuckled a little. "So it was a demon," I said.

"Maybe," Glory replied. "Something about this smells wrong for a demon assault. Plus, why drag her away? A demon would have just killed them both here. And where's the rest of the blood?"

I waved an arm around the inside of the room. It was a big open room, basically just a big empty round room with a circular staircase going up, but it looked like an abattoir. There was blood spraying at least ten feet up the walls, and the puddle ran from Ichabod's corpse almost to the door twenty feet away. "What are you talking about, Glory? This place is fucking painted in the stuff."

"Yeah, all of *his* blood is here. But this isn't two people's worth of blood, Harker. Come on, you've seen—hell, you've *created* enough corpses to know how much blood one should leave behind."

Okay, she wasn't wrong. I just hadn't really paid attention to exactly how much blood was on the floor. It was a lot, and usually if there's a lot of blood around a dead body, it's all or most of the blood the body used to contain. But as I looked closer, I could tell she was right. This was enough blood for one body, but not two. That meant either the girl hadn't really been killed here, or something had taken her blood and done something with it.

"Vampire?" Becks asked. "I mean, I know we have more cordial than typical relations with the species, but they do drink blood."

"Yeah, I thought about that," I replied. "But the smell is wrong."

"Huh?"

I love the rare times when I can surprise my fiancée. "Vampires have a certain smell to them, and it's stronger over their kills. Some people say it's the rot of the grave they should be in, but I think it's just that little hint of demon taint that's baked into every vamp. It smells a little bit like rich soil and sulfur. This just smells like cheap beer, tanning lotion, and piss."

"And blood," Glory said. "You humans have so many smelly things inside you. Kinda makes me wonder how any of the Host were ever jealous of you. All they'd need to do is visit an interstate rest area to know humanity reeks."

I thought I exhibited remarkable restraint in not debating the comparative stinkiness of humans versus many supernatural creatures with Glory, instead turning back to the corpse. "Okay, so something killed this guy and left him here. Something, presumably the same something, took the girl from here, killed her, and dumped her body on the beach. We're not sure exactly where she was killed, we have no idea why, all we know of the how is that it was something incredibly strong with very sharp claws, and we don't know who either of these kids are. I'm pretty sure this project would flunk even freshman journalism class," I said.

"Then let's get to work," Becks said. "I'll start working on figuring out who these two are—y'all work on figuring what killed them and why."

"Sounds like a plan," I said. "But do I get to be Mandy Patinkin or can I be Joe Mantegna?"

Glory sighed. "If I have to indulge your *Criminal Minds* roleplaying, Harker, why can't I be Garcia and stay in a nice air-conditioned office?"

"Sorry, kiddo," I replied. "We need more Prentiss than Garcia on this one."

"JJ," she corrected. "If I have to listen to you quote a serial killer TV show at me, I'm at least going to be the hot blonde."

CHAPTER FOUR

The forensic techs were just packing up when we made it back to the original crime scene, and they were less than thrilled when I mentioned that they had more work to do. They got even more pissy when I told them there was no way to get their van back there, and when I put the cherry on top and told them that Dr. Stoumbos was going to need their help getting the body out, I thought one of them was going to shoot me right there.

But no gunfire was exchanged, not even with the grumpy sheriff. Stoumbos, the one I expected to be the most annoyed by having another corpse on his hands, was the least grumpy. As a matter of fact, he seemed downright excited by the prospect of a double homicide. I guess there weren't a ton of demonic eviscerations on the Outer Banks.

I walked over to where the sheriff leaned against his white SUV. "Any luck getting an ID on the girl?" I asked.

He looked at me like I was something he'd scrape off the bottom of his shoe. "I thought the feds were gonna just swoop in and take care of everything, show us local yokels how the experts do it."

I didn't punch him. I wanted to, but Becks had been working on my anger management. And this guy was definitely making me work to manage myself. "Look, Sheriff, we might have gotten off on the wrong foot, but I'm sure we can—"

He raised a hand, palm toward me. "I don't give a shit."

"Excuse me?"

"Son, I am an elected official, not a government appointee, and the good people of this county elected me to protect and to serve. Now I can't do anymore protecting of this young lady, but the best way I can serve her is to find out who did this. And the only way I can do that is to help you. Now as much as I don't like y'all coming down here with some bullshit federal wildlife preservation zone story, I do know that you have resources I don't. So I'm gonna help you any way I can. But that does not include telling you this woman's name."

"Why not?" I asked. His entire tone had shifted during his little spiel, and I was inclined to believe that he actually did give a shit about the case, regardless of his statement to the contrary. Or maybe he just didn't give a shit about my apology, which would make two of us.

"Because I don't know her. Neither me nor any of my people recognize her, not even my husband, who is the biggest gossip on Roanoke Island. And he sees *everybody*, running his coffee shop. So she's not a local, and if she's a tourist, she either just got here, or she doesn't drink coffee. She didn't have any identification, and we don't have the equipment to scan her fingerprints like you government folk do."

"Yeah, we don't have that shit, either. That's only for TV," I said.

"And I don't have any kind of fancy facial recognition shit on my phone, either. So unless you've got some kind of magic spell for identifying a girl who's been ripped to shreds, we're gonna have to go at this the old-fashioned way."

"Which is?" I'm way older than I look, and I wanted to be sure that his "old-fashioned way" was the same as mine.

"We take a picture of her and ask around town to see if anybody knows her. Same with the boy y'all found, unless it turns out he's familiar to one of us."

Okay, so it was kinda the same thing. My "old-fashioned way" was a little more old-fashioned, in that it didn't involve a photo, which were way harder to come by in the first few decades of the twentieth century than they are now. But the basic principles were the same—I was gonna have to play cop. Yay.

∿

The job was made easier by the fact that Dr. Stoumbos did recognize the dead guy in the lighthouse. And as soon as he said the name to Sheriff

French, he dropped his cigar onto the sand and ground it to bits with his heel. He'd never even lit the thing, just chewed on it. "Well, fuck," the lanky lawman said.

"You know him?" Becks asked.

"I know the family. Don't know him specifically, but his father's a partner in the family law firm, a big old Southern money bunch who think they own the whole damn island. And truth be told, they do own at least a third of it. This one's Gerald, the youngest. He's got a reputation as a little bit of hell raiser, but not too bad. His older brother's a real piece of work, and I don't mean that in a good way. Harry, short for Harrison Dutser the fourth, is an entitled asshole who doesn't mind letting anyone know exactly how rich and important his family is. Harry's been off at Duke Law for a couple years. Gerry's been a little wild, but mostly low-key stuff. DUI, possession, drunk and disorderly, that kind of small-time shit. I'm not looking forward to having his daddy all over me the whole time we're trying to work this case. Unless you'd rather just take over the whole thing and tell me to go screw myself?" He looked hopeful on that last part.

I got it. Becks and I would work this case, probably cause a shitload of property damage and maybe strew viscera up and down Main Street, then we'd leave. He had to live here, and whatever turds we left in the pool, he was going to have to fish out later. "Nope," I said without even a shred of sympathy in my voice. "You're stuck in the middle of this one, Sheriff. I need a local contact, and despite the cigars and your lack of sufficient adoration for my badge, you're elected."

He laughed. "Dammit, I knew I should have just tried to come off as inept, instead of the blustery *Smokey and the Bandit* bullshit. Well, at least I can stop chewing on that goddamned cigar."

"That was a—" Becks started, and the sheriff nodded.

"A prop," he said. "I thought if I made myself into enough of a prick, you'd just take over and I wouldn't have to work the case." He sighed and leaned back against the wall of the lighthouse. The sky to the east was lightening as dawn approached. We'd been at the crime scenes for hours, and it had been the middle of the damn night when Becks had gotten the call from her boss, Director Kaya Pravesh. I don't know how the hell Pravesh heard about a murder all the way down here. Probably had a team of nerds monitoring police scanners anywhere within fifty miles of me. Which wasn't a bad idea, given the amount of money Homeland has had to pay out in damages since bringing me on.

The sheriff took his baseball cap off and wiped his forehead with the back of a hand. "Look, I only ran for sheriff because the other guy running was a dickhead homophobic deputy who got his rocks off busting guys hooking up on the beach. I knew that if he was elected, it would be a very bad time for my husband's business, so I dusted off my law degree and ran against him on a platform of police reform and openness. Now I'm in my third term and I can't even *bribe* anybody to run against me. This is usually a really quiet place. Most we deal with is somebody getting drunk, hitting on the wrong girl in the wrong bar, and ending up getting cut. We don't get murders, especially not vicious murders of the youngest son of the town's most prominent attorney."

"We'll help," Becks said. "And this isn't me promising to help as in 'I'm from the government, I'm here to help.'" Sheriff French chuckled at that. "We really will help. We'll bring all our resources to bear on figuring out what happened here, and to the other three victims as well. I know you haven't handled many cases like this. That's why we're here. You don't get murders, but we do. We're not the FBI, who literally wrote the book on serial killers, but we're still pretty good at catching bad guys."

French looked relieved. "Thanks. I mean that. Now why don't you get back to wherever it is you're staying and get a few hours sleep? Meet me at my office at ten and I'll have all the case files for you, plus everything we've got on all the victims."

"Meantime, you've got a family to notify," I said.

"Yeah." He put his cap back on. "Least favorite part of the job."

INTERLUDE

She ran. Breath coming in shallow gasps, thighs and calves burning from exertion, she ran. Branches whipped across her face and bare legs, fallen limbs and rocks sliced her feet, but on she ran. It felt like she'd never done anything but run, and that running was all she would ever do, but she ran like her life depended on it. Because it did.

She ran, and as she sprinted through the woods, the inky, roiling blackness intermittently pierced by beams of moonlight barely penetrating the thick canopy overhead to make tiny puddles of less-dark, she heard him behind her.

Him, her, them, it...whatever was behind her was gaining, despite never seeming to speed up. She ran, and he followed. Because it was a man. She remembered that now, his grinning face carved into the backs of her eyelids, so that with every blink it came back to her in stark relief against the dark. His face, that leering smile splitting his narrow features as the red and yellow firelight illuminated his eyes.

Those eyes. Those blue-green eyes painted crimson by the fire, the fire that consumed everything and nothing. The fire that destroyed even the trace of anything. The fire that threatened to scorch her very soul to ash.

Those eyes.

That smile.

This forest.

Her burning legs.

Her bloodied feet.

Her tattered homespun nightgown, snagging on shrubs and saplings alike.

Her family, burned out of existence by him, whoever...*whatev*er he was. Her baby. Her Virginia.

Her daughter. The symbol of hope for a new life, a new world, snuffed out like a candle. Now gone, like everything they'd tried to build, like everyone she loved in this place, like she soon would be.

She stopped, finally, chest heaving with exertion, breath coming in dog-like pants. She leaned against a white oak tree, hearing those steady, implacable footsteps crackling through the underbrush. A sliver of moonlight snaked through the leaves to shine on a jagged hunk of quartz at her feet.

She picked up the rock and turned to the tree. She couldn't save her family, she couldn't save herself, and she knew that any hopes of avenging their deaths were so futile as to be ludicrous. But she could leave a message. Others would come. They *had* to come. And as she dug the sharp edge of the quartz into the bark of the tree, she could only hope that the ones who came to bring supplies would see her message, and know.

The footsteps stopped. She could feel his presence behind her, looking over her. She turned, gazing up at the horror that pursued her, and a scream tore loose from deep within her. A scream that no one would ever hear, because there was no one left. Then, in a blink, even her scream was cut short. The rock dropped to the ground, disturbing a new pile of gray-black dust at the foot of a tree.

As he walked away, a breeze ruffled the branches, letting moonlight stream down to illuminate the one word she was able to carve into the bark of the white oak tree.

CROATOAN.

CHAPTER FIVE

I woke up to the sound of screaming, and somehow managed to not blow the walls out of the house we were renting. Barely. I jerked awake, pulled from the depths of sleep by the sound of Becks crying out, both in my head and in my ears. I sprang from the bed, flinging the comforter off and leaping to my feet.

My hands glowed purple as I called raw power from the chunk of amethyst I'd left on the nightstand as a battery. I'd thought it was a little paranoid when I'd set a crystal beside my bed in case I needed juice in the middle of the night, but now that there was an attack, I wanted all the energy I could muster at my disposal. I spun around, determined to find the fucker who'd screwed up my vacation, and blast him/her/it into dust.

Except there was no fucker to blast. The room was empty except for me, standing bare-assed in the middle of the floor with my hands lit up like a strip club on Saturday night, and Becks, sitting bolt upright in bed, her eyes wide open but unseeing, her breath coming in short gasps, and sweat drenching her light-brown skin.

Becks? I reached out to her through the mental bond we shared, but all I felt coming back at me were jumbled emotions—fear, worry, anger all swirled together, but over all of it was a blanket of dread, a thick, smothering sensation of inevitable doom that lay upon every thought, every emotion, pinning her to immobility in our bed.

"Becks!" I called out this time, hoping that my voice would snap her out of whatever panicked state she was in. I let the power flow out of me harmlessly, pouring it back into the crystal, and knelt in the bed next to her. "Becks, are you okay? What is it, baby?" I reached out, put a hand on her shoulder, like you'd comfort a frightened animal, knowing that she'd either freak out and attack me, or she'd collapse into my arms.

She collapsed, melting into my embrace like all her bones had turned to water. "Holy shit, Harker, that was…intense. I was running through the woods, and someone was after me. Someone…bad. Like, *really* bad."

Now, let's be clear. Deputy Director Rebecca Gail Flynn of Homeland Security's Paranormal Division is no shrinking violet. She's been through some of the worst battles I've ever fought and never flinched. She was along for the ride when we fought demons, tussled with archangels, and battled a really-should-have-been-dead-a-long-time-ago Nazi scientist. And that's just the lowlights of our last few years. So if she said something was "really bad," then whatever she'd seen was globally, catastrophically fucked.

"Was it a real thing, or a dream thing? I mean, we've dealt with some heavy shit recently."

I wrapped my arms around Becks's slender shoulders and held her to me. Her small breasts pressed into my chest, and I could feel her heart pounding between us. She was panting like she'd just run a mile uphill, but her arms clung to me like bands of steel. I just stroked her back and made random reassuring noises while I tried to surf the waves of panic inside her head.

As she calmed, I was able to pull bits and pieces of her dream from her mind. She'd been running from something, something big and terrifying, and then she'd stopped and carved something in a tree…something familiar…what the *fuck?*

I pulled back a little to look at her face, reaching up to wipe a tear off her beautiful cheek. "Babe, did you dream you were in Roanoke? Like, the O.G. Roanoke? The one that vanished?"

"Y-yeah," she said after drawing in a ragged breath. "But it didn't feel like a dream. It was…*more*, somehow. More real, more substantial. Like a memory, or like I was living it through someone else's eyes."

"Have you ever felt anything like this before? Any places in particular where you've experienced a lot of deja vu, or that feeling of a goose walking over your grave?"

Becks gave me a skeptical look. "No. I mean, no more than anyone, I guess. Why? I'm not psychic, Harker. Never claimed to be. All that magical mumbo-jumbo is your department."

And there's nothing out of the ordinary about you. Right? I said inside her mind.

"Point taken," she replied.

Now, I'm no expert on psychic phenomena, despite having a woman living in my head and able to communicate with me wordlessly from states away. My expertise tends to be more in the "how to blow up bad things and send them back to the depths of Hell from whence they were spawned." But I've run into a few people over the years who had some real abilities in that realm. Since most "civilized" countries stopped burning suspected witches at the stake or drowning them to make sure they were fully human, people who possessed psychic abilities were no longer in danger of having their necks uncomfortably stretched from a tree limb if anyone found out about them, but they were still rare.

And rarer were the people with any significant power in that realm, and most of the time I could tell if they were close. I remembered the very first time I walked into the shop that James, my tattoo artist, runs. The magic in that joint had set all the hair on my arms and legs on end, and that makes for uncomfortable walking. But in addition to James being a spell crafter of massive skill, his receptionist is also an empath, and he relies on her not to let any bad people use his magical tattoos for nefarious purposes. I had to talk with the two of them for over an hour before he'd agree to tattoo me, which makes sense when we consider the body count that follows in my wake.

But I'd never seen anything to indicate a hint of psychic ability in Flynn, and living in someone's head makes hiding that kind of thing basically impossible. So either she'd developed a new talent overnight, literally, or this place was so haunted it could inspire some kind of dream walking episode in someone who had never been psychic before.

Or it was just a bad dream, which was usually more my thing than Becks's. She has a lot fewer ghosts coming to visit when she closes her eyes than I do, and it's not just because I'm almost a century older than her. But she's seen some shit, even before she started hanging out with me, and a lot more since then. We'd saved the world a couple of times at least, but not without a pretty significant body count and a lot of emotional scarring. It wasn't out of the question that all that just caught up with her in the middle of the night, but this didn't feel like she had a bad dream. I was still wrapped up in her head, and I could sense her emotions, the stark terror of what she'd experienced, and it didn't feel like a nightmare. This felt like more than that somehow, like someone or some*thing* was reaching out to Flynn through her dreams.

I got out of bed and walked to the kitchen, my bare feet slapping against the hardwoods of the rental house. I opened the fridge to get a beer for myself and a bottle of water for Flynn, being instantly reminded of my nudity when a blast of frigid air reached out and wrapped its icy fingers around my junk. I hurried back to the bedroom with drinks and hopped into the bed.

"Cold?" Becks asked.

"Fridge," I replied.

"Dumbass."

"Guilty as charged." I handed her the water and drained half the beer in one long pull. I leaned back against the headboard and Flynn snuggled into the crook of my arm, the fabric of her head wrap rustling against my chest. She lay there, eyes closed but mind racing, until I finally broke the silence.

"You know it's impossible to fake sleep around me, right? I can literally hear the hamster wheel spinning in your head."

"I know," Becks replied. "I'm just trying to go back through everything I remember, trying to lock it all in so it doesn't vanish in the morning, like dreams do."

"Well, there's two of us to remember this, so that should help a little." But that was another thing that didn't feel like a dream. This didn't have any of the fuzzy edges that a dream normally has upon waking, none of the rapid disintegration into mist as reality reimposes itself upon the mind. No, this felt a lot more like the "conversation" I had with a few ethereal beings a while back when I got turned to stone. That was a real thing, that really happened, but there was no physical manifestation of it. This felt like that—like the memory of a real event, even second-hand.

"Who was she, Harker? Who was that woman, and why was I the one to get her message?"

"I dunno, babe. Maybe she's been sending out this psychic message in a bottle for centuries, and you're the first one with the right mix of empathy and ability to feel it."

"But I don't *have* any psychic abilities!"

"Well, that's not exactly true, babe. You two might as well put some clothes on. Something weird is happening, and that means nobody's getting any more sleep tonight." The blonde leaning against the doorjamb of our bedroom was neither staying in the rental with us, nor was she anyone that I really wanted just popping into my bedroom unannounced.

That's the problem with Guardian Angels, you see. If they think you need guarding, they're gonna show up, whether you're wearing pants or not. I sighed and started to sit up, relinquishing my hold on the comforter as I tried to wrap the sheet around myself to find my pants. "Hello, Glory," I said.

"'Sup, Q?" she replied. "What's with the modesty? You don't have anything I haven't seen before." She was right. Because she has developed an irritating habit of just popping by whenever she feels like it, and I have no way of blocking angelic teleportation, she's seen me in all my glory many times. Pun totally intended.

"No, but he hasn't seen it, and if it's alright with all of you, I'd prefer to get dressed in some semblance of privacy." I pointed over Glory's shoulder at the real reason I got out of bed.

"Your Victorian upbringing peeking out again, Harker?" The man standing behind Glory was black. Not Black as in a human with dark skin, but *black*, like obsidian, with pointed ears, yellow eyes, and just a hint of fang in his incisors. I never thought I'd consider a demon a friend, but he'd proven himself more than once, and God help me, I mostly trusted the conniving bastard.

"Hello, Faustus," I said. "What the hell are *you* doing here?" I also had no idea how he'd gotten there so fast, but I also didn't know where he'd been while Becks and I were on vacation. For all I knew, Glory had taught him to teleport, or teleported with him, or...something else, maybe. I didn't care how he got there, but if Glory had gone to all the trouble of bringing him, something super-fucked was going on.

"Glory said something was coming after Flynn. No way was I letting that happen if I could help, so here I am," the demon said with a tip of his imaginary hat.

"Oh, good," I replied. "I wouldn't want to think you were here to rescue *me*."

"Not much chance of that, mate. You're pretty capable of taking care of yourself. But Becks here is human, a lot more squishy than the rest of us. At least, I thought she was human."

"I am human!" Flynn protested.

"Then how are you getting psychic messages from a woman who disappeared over four hundred years ago?" Glory asked.

"Well, fuck," Becks said. "Faustus, whatever you're having, make me a double. We'll be out in a second." Then she waved the two Celestials out the door, and we shared a look. *What the hell is going on, Harker?* she asked.

No clue, babe. But we're going to figure it out.

Or die trying, Becks replied.

Yeah, I thought back to her. *Yeah, that's always an option, too.*

CHAPTER SIX

I sat in a wicker patio chair in the living room of our rental, since we were staying in a tourist trap of a town, renting a house for a week instead of staying in a hotel. It was cheaper, and closer to the water, but we had to deal with actual human beings' taste in decorating, rather than corporate blandness. The owner of this joint had gone all in on the nautical stuff, putting seashells and starfish up everywhere, using sand dollar soap dishes, draping a tattered fishing net from the light fixture in the dining room. It felt less like a vacation home and more like a low-rent fish restaurant. But the chairs were pretty comfy, as long as you were wearing long pants. Otherwise, your legs stuck to the waterproof cushions at even a hint of sweat.

I was wearing long pants. I was fully dressed, in fact, as was Becks. I'd thrown on yesterday's jeans and pulled a clean t-shirt out of the suitcase without looking at it. I noticed as I settled in with a beer that I had a picture of "Buddy Christ" from *Dogma* giving the world a thumbs-up from my chest. One might think that my Guardian Angel would disapprove of my choice of shirts, but only if one didn't know that Glory gave me the shirt for my birthday. I was barefoot, because even if I had to put on pants, I was still at the beach, and shoes were optional pretty much everywhere that didn't serve food, and about half the places that did.

Becks sat in the matching chair facing me across the length of the coffee table, and Glory and Faustus sat on the wicker sofa, making a whole living room suite of white-painted wood and white plastic cushions covered in blue and green flowers.

"Who decorated this place, Harker?" Faustus asked. "And have you killed them yet?"

"I don't know," I replied. "And we haven't even seen the owner. The door has a keypad lock, so they just emailed us the code and left a note telling us where to leave the sheets and garbage when we check out."

"What do you two know about the Lost Colony, and who is this woman in my dream?" Becks asked.

"I don't know much about the Roanoke settlement other than what you read in the history books, and I have no idea who's in your head or why," Glory said. "That's what we're here to find out." She paused. "Well, that and who's running around ritualistically murdering people at one of North Carolina's top tourist destinations."

"Faustus?" I asked.

"I've heard rumors about this place since before white people ever set foot on this continent. It's supposed to have some sort of mystical nexus properties or something. I don't do magic the same way you do, so I've never paid attention to your leylines or whatever. But there's supposed to be all kinds of weird shit around the Eastern seaboard of the U.S. Some people think it's bleed from some of the artifacts that were lost when Atlantis sank, but I dunno. That always seemed a bit of a stretch to me."

I held up a hand, palm toward the demon. "Hold up, pal. Are you telling me Atlantis was a real place?"

Faustus looked confused for a second, like what I was saying made no sense. "Of course it was. Keep up, Harker. Anyway, there were rumors that one of the Sixth- or Seventh-Circle guys had something to do with the disappearance of the colony, but I never heard who or why. I never even knew for sure that our team had anything to do with it at all. Despite what the Christians believe, there's plenty of bad shit that happens in the world without any influence from Hell whatsoever. I mean, just look at humans. We don't really even have to do anything to get y'all to torture and kill each other. Mostly if we can get you within shooting distance of one another, you'll do our jobs for us. But damning an entire colony of people at once? That's a pretty good feat. If somebody from Six pulled that off, it might promote him right over Seven and all the way down to the big boys on Eight."

"As fascinating as this peek into the machinations of Hell is, do you *know* anything that might help us figure out who is getting into Becks's head, and what they want?" I asked.

"Nothing solid, sorry."

"Okay," I said, slamming down the rest of my drink and refilling it from the bottle of Pappy Van Winkle on the coffee table. "We've got two problems that I can see: someone is running around eviscerating tourists and throwing around a metric fuckton of magical energy in the process, and a missing colonist from a few centuries ago is talking to Becks in her dreams. We need to figure out if these things are related, and if so, how."

"And we need to stop whoever is committing the murders," Becks added, giving me a slightly dirty look.

"Yeah, yeah. Murder bad, I get it." My fiancée and I had very different views on the efficacy of murder as a tool. I'm generally a fan, if the person *really* needs killing, but she's pretty much opposed to it in almost all cases. I was reserving judgement on the serial killer until I found out for sure that the victims weren't all horrible people who drowned puppies in their bathtubs for fun or went into unsuspecting friends' bathrooms and turned their toilet paper rolls so the paper came out backward. And yes, both of those are capital offenses in *Harker's Book of Shit that Shall Not Stand.*

For the record, there is no such book, but there probably should be. I mean, what kind of monster turns around someone else's toilet paper roll? And drowning puppies is bad, too. "It seems like we've got a couple different things we need to poke around with—a murder investigation and the mystery of the Lost Colony," I said.

"Well, I guess it's a good thing no one has ever tried to figure out what happened to the first settlers here on Roanoke Island," Becks said. "So we don't just have to solve a contemporary homicide case, we also need to solve one of the oldest mysteries on the entire continent. Next time, I'm taking a vacation somewhere relaxing. I hear Tehran is nice this time of year."

"Pretty sure nobody's sleeping anymore, and it's almost time to head over and pick up files from the sheriff anyway, so why don't you two get cleaned up and into some pants that aren't dirty enough to stand up on their own, while me and Faustus go grab some doughnuts?" Glory said.

I looked down at my jeans. Yeah, they were pretty disgusting. I hadn't really noticed at the crime scene, on account of it being the middle of the fucking night and all. But there was dried blood, sand, and a few other bodily fluids I didn't want to think too much about splattered all over my lower half. "Well, shit," I said. "I don't suppose you could swing by a twenty-four-hour Walmart or something, too?"

"Why?" the angel asked.

"I only brought two pairs of jeans, and I dropped a milkshake on the crotch of the others on the drive here," I said. "So I either need detergent, or jeans."

"I'll get pants," Glory said. I made to hand her my credit card, but she waved me off. "Dude, I'm an angel. I can get out of a store with a pair of purloined jeans without breaking a sweat."

"One, do you sweat?" I asked. "And two, take the card. We're the good guys, so we probably shouldn't shoplift. Even from hellmouths like Walmart."

Glory raised an eyebrow at me. "No, I don't sweat. That's another thing we didn't get when Father built us, but that one I don't mind not having. And are you seriously telling me that after all the mass property destruction and murder I've seen you participate in, that you draw the line at *shoplifting?*"

"A guy's gotta have rules, Glory," I said, heading for the shower. I called back over my shoulder, "Get a couple pairs!" Pretty sure I was gonna end up covered in viscera again before this adventure was through.

CHAPTER SEVEN

An hour later, I was in a clean pair of jeans and a Jason Isbell T-shirt, sitting barefoot on the deck of our rental eating doughnuts with my fiancée, an angel, and a demon as we tried to brainstorm the next steps in our murder investigation. "I guess the first thing it to check out the other crime scenes, or body dump sites, and see if there's anything we can pick up that the mundane cops missed," I said.

"That's a good idea," Becks said. "I need to spend some time on the internet looking up past homicides in the area. There was an odd note in one of the case files the sheriff sent over about 'the last time' that I want to look into."

"Do yo think this is part of a cycle of murders?" Glory asked.

"Yeah, like in *It*?" Faustus added.

"Hopefully without the giant spider," I said.

"Or the clown," Faustus replied. I looked over at him, and he shrugged. "Clowns are creepy, dude."

"You're a demon," I shot back.

"Doesn't matter," he said. "Clowns are still creepy."

"Can we focus, just for a few seconds?" Becks asked in that very tired kindergarten teacher voice she often gets around me and Faustus. We shut up. "Thank you. Now, while I'm poking around on the web to see if anything like this has ever happened before, somebody needs to go check out the other recent crime scenes."

"Sounds like my kinda gig," I said. "Go see what's what, sniff around for magic, and see if I can pick up a clue or three. On it."

"I'll go with," Glory said. "I don't *think* you can get into too much trouble in broad daylight, but it's been at least a week since you blew anything up, and I can almost feel you getting antsy for mayhem."

"I'll ask around in some of the kinds of places none of you would be welcome and see if the local demons and monsters know anything," Faustus said as he stood up and brushed crumbs off his shirt.

"Are you going to tell me that there's a demonic underworld in Manteo?" I asked.

"Dude, there's a demonic underworld in every town. Some are just way less inhabited than others. But there's a bar in Kill Devil Hills that's kinda the local watering hole for those of a more...southerly orientation, shall we say?"

I grinned at Glory. "I love it when he tries to be all circumspect, don't you?"

"Yeah, it's kinda cute." She turned her attention to Faustus. "What's the name of the bar?"

"I can't tell you!" he protested. "You work for the other side."

"You don't work for a side," she pointed out. "You work for Faustus. And since lately your needs tend to align with ours, I'd rather not see you get drawn and quartered if somebody in this demon bar sees you and decides to collect the bounty Lucifer put on your head. I think you getting ripped apart and sent back to Hell would be pretty inconvenient for both of us."

"Some more than others," I said, giving Faustus a look.

"Okay, you may be right. I'll be at a place called The Overlook. It's on one of the big hills near where the Wright Brothers took off, and you can see down onto the beach and the ocean from its patio."

"And it having the same name as the hotel from *The Shining* is a total coincidence," Becks said.

"Well...the demon that runs the place is a big Kubrick fan," Faustus said. "If I run into any trouble, I'll text you. So keep your phones on, and if I yell, come running. Metaphorically speaking, of course."

Glory gave him a half-smile. "Of course."

"Alright, then let's go look at some murders," I said. That's not the first time I've said those words, which just kinda drives home the point that my life is fucking *weird*.

~

A quick call to the sheriff's department, and after a few minutes where the dispatcher was obviously on the radio to the Sheriff French while she put the phone on her desk, and Glory had the case files of the previous three murders in her email, complete with locations where the bodies had been discovered. I pulled into a cemetery just a couple blocks off the main tourist part of town, with nice houses on three sides.

"I wonder if having a cemetery next door is good or bad for property values?" I mused as we got out of Becks's government-issued SUV.

"You thinking about investing in real estate, Harker?" Glory asked as she met me at the back of the Suburban.

"I already own the building where we live in Charlotte, but there's nothing wrong with diversifying my holdings."

"Well, maybe this time don't diversify into something roughly the color of Pepto-Bismol."

"My building is very cutting edge," I shot back.

"Your building looks like a seven-year-old girl's birthday cake."

I didn't really have a response because she was kinda right. We lived in a large condo building on the south side of town, and the glass was pink. Not like "just a hint of coral to warm up the rooms." Nope. It's the kind of pink that makes Barbie think dirty thoughts. The kind of pink that baby ballerinas the world over get tutus made out of. The kind of pink...well, you get the picture. It's very pink. But I got it for a song, relatively speaking. And owning the building made it a lot easier when I had to evict everyone from the top floor so my team could all live in one easily defensible location.

"Do you sense anything?" Glory asked, jolting me out of my real estate mogul reverie.

"Uh, no," I replied. "Not yet, anyway." I focused on the here and now, or at least the here and three weeks ago, which was when young Theresa Harri, a runaway from New Jersey, had been found ripped limb from limb in the cemetery sometime after three A.M. I slipped into my Sight, and recoiled at the seething cauldron of evil and pain that blanketed the cemetery.

"That's..." My voice trailed off as I tried to wrap my head around exactly what it was.

"Odd? Strange? Terrifying? Beige? Come on, Harker, give me a little more to work with here," Glory said, snapping her fingers in front of my nose.

"Disgusting," I said, trying to focus through the seething mass of hatred and agony that writhed along the paths between the headstones like a wriggling mass of eels. "This place might be coated in more dark magic than tonight's dump site. I think she was killed here and fed to whatever took the girl from the beach."

"Where, exactly?" Glory asked.

I looked around, and while the whole place looked like it was coated in viscous black slime, there was a greater concentration of red and purple energies swirling around the air in the center of the graveyard. "That way." I pointed farther in.

"Of course," the angel replied. "It's never right at the end of the driveway. It's always in the farthest spot from wherever we park."

"Getting lazy in your old age?" I joked.

"Piss off. Something about the magic in here doesn't feel right. It's not holy ground, per se, but there's *something* here, and it makes me itch right between my shoulder blades.

I shrugged and let it go. I didn't feel anything odd in the magic, but since Glory literally *was* magic, I trusted her when she said something felt weirder than usual. We approached the center of the cemetery, and the closer we got to the middle of the mystical dark energy, the more nauseated I became. Finally, I had to drop my Sight or toss my cookies, and I felt it would be the height of disrespect to puke on a stranger's grave. There's a long list of graves I wouldn't mind pissing on, or otherwise desecrating, but I try to save the hardcore blasphemy for people I know. Or politicians. They deserve it.

"You okay?" Glory asked.

"Not really. This place was definitely where Theresa was killed, and it was done in a way that leeched as much pain and suffering out of her soul as possible. The ground is basically soaked in pain and terror." I stepped to the very center of the place, opening my senses back up and searching for any clue, anything that would lead me to whoever or whatever did this horrible thing.

There was nothing. I was pretty sure I could pick the magician out of a crowd, now that I'd seen exactly how warped his magic was, but nothing led out of the cemetery. There were no traces of his corruption past the boundaries of the graveyard. "Hey, G," I said.

"Yo."

"Does iron fuck with divine or demonic magic?"

"Not typically, why?"

"Something's weird here. The taint is contained, like whatever is polluting the ground here can't get past the boundary of the cemetery. What could do that?"

She got a thoughtful look on her face, then started off toward one of the gates, not the one closest to our ride. "Follow me."

There was no chance I was either letting her run off on her own in a place despoiled by this much evil, and there was less chance than that of me staying in the center of that evil morass a second longer than I had to. So follow I did, all the way to the stone wall encircling the graveyard.

Glory knelt down, put one hand on the stones, a low wall of perfectly laid rocks held together without even a hint of mortar, and closed her eyes. After a few seconds, she said, "Put your hand beside mine and open your Sight."

I did and felt the warmth of a spring day flow up through my arm. The wall was gone as I looked at the world through the magical spectrum, and where it had been a ribbon of the purest white light imaginable flowed, a moat of purity surrounding the graveyard. Only instead of keeping intruders out, this was keeping the violation *in*.

"What the fuck..." I whispered.

"That's divine," Glory said. "That's some serious magic."

"Who did it?"

Glory stood up and looked at me, and when she did, I saw something I'd never seen before. There were tears in her eyes.

"Harker, that's magic I haven't seen in millennia. I haven't seen this signature since the end of the War on Heaven."

She wiped her eyes with the back of her hand. "Q, this was touched by God."

CHAPTER EIGHT

Well, *that* complicated matters. As far as I knew, which wasn't very far since the folks with direct knowledge about the comings and goings of the Being Upstairs are notoriously tight-lipped about that kind of shit, no one had any direct contact with God since Lucifer threw his little hissy fit and tried to take over Heaven. That was a *LONG* time ago. So long ago that time had barely been created as a concept, and humans were just starting to fuck around eating fruit we weren't supposed to eat. Apparently Lucifer and a few other angels had gotten pissed that humans had free will and angels didn't, so they decided to kick Dad out of the captain's chair and take over steering the universe.

Yes, I know that having those thoughts proves that Lucifer and any angels following him actually had the free will they were trying to acquire, but apparently Lucifer hadn't thought of that. Or maybe he didn't have free will at all, and God staged the whole War on Heaven as an excuse to banish Lucifer to Hell and create a place of punishment for all eternity for his pet creations—humans. Because it makes at least as much sense that an all-powerful being of infinite love could punish the creations he loves for the rest of time as it does that a being with no free will could try to overthrow the deity keeping him from having free will. That's why I'm not religious, despite having my very own Guardian Angel and getting drunk on the regular with a demon. Too many contradictions for my puny human brain.

But anyway, Lucifer charged the Gates of Heaven, which I am told is an actual place, like a district within Heaven, not just a big fucking door with Saint Peter sitting beside it with a naughty or nice list to make Santa's cheeks even redder than usual. And when he led part of the Host against Dad in the ultimate act of teenage rebellion, big brother Michael led the rest of the Host into battle against his upstart younger brother, who he'd apparently been jealous of for eternity because Lucifer was prettier than Michael, and kicked the rebellious angels out of Heaven, down past Earth, and all the way into a brand new dimension created purely for the purposes of housing Heaven's miscreants.

Hell is a prison colony. Like Australia. Or Georgia.

From what Faustus told me, Hell wasn't really a bad place to hang out in the beginning. Their punishment was mainly being denied God's presence, which I guess if it's something you're used to having, would be a pretty big deal to go without. The whole lakes of fire shit came later, after they started getting human souls to play with and theoretically redeem. In reality, Hell became a lot like the prisons in America—the place you went to ostensibly redeem yourself and work your way back into polite society (in this case Heaven), but really was just a shitty place where you were stuck forever. Even the angels that managed to get out were so institutionalized by their time away from God that they'd transformed into something dark and mean that could never stand the light of Heaven again.

Do you want demons? Because this is how you get demons.

But the one thing everyone I'd ever spoken to about this whole mess agreed on, from Michael to Glory to Faustus to the few religious scholars I'm on speaking terms with, was that after the War on Heaven, God went AWOL. He went on walkabout right after pitching his prettiest and perhaps favorite child down into a pit, never to be seen again, and hadn't been seen in Heaven or Earth since.

Except here was evidence of him hanging out on the Outer Banks of North Carolina within the last few centuries. Glory was, in a word, *rocked*. I was, too, but since God had always been kind of an ethereal presence in my life more than a direct one, it surprised me less to find evidence of his existence. Funny how that works—I gave less of a shit whether he was around or not, so it rocked me less when I found out he was probably close.

"So...what does this mean?" I asked, kneeling beside Glory on the damp grass. She'd fallen back flat on her ass as she tried to wrap her head around the presence of a deity she thought had abandoned her and all the rest of creation millennia ago. I've seen Glory through some wild shit, from losing and reacquiring her wings to the death of an archangel to the ascension of a replacement archangel, but nothing had ever had this much of an impression on her.

"I...I don't know, completely. I just know that it means a lot of what we thought...we being the Host...a lot of the things we took for granted..." Her voice trailed off and she looked up at me with scared eyes. "I don't know what anything means anymore, Harker. If He's still here, why haven't we heard from Him? Doesn't He love us anymore?"

And then my Guardian Angel, the beautiful badass blonde with combat boots and a flaming sword who had battled demons and monsters of all flavors by my side without flinching, buried her face in my shoulder and cried like a child missing its mother. I hugged her and patted her back, thinking this would be a lot harder with her wings manifested, and tried as best I could to comfort a heartbroken creature who had seen more sunrises than I'd drawn breaths.

"It's okay, G," I muttered into her blond curls. "It's okay."

She jerked upright and shoved me back. "What the fuck do you mean, 'it's okay'? It's not okay. It's very much *not fucking okay*. Either our Father, the Creator of All, vanished eons ago because His sorrow was so great at having to punish His creations, or He just fucked off out of Heaven and has been partying down here with a bunch of hairless apes for a few thousand years? How is any of that okay?" Her eyes actually glowed with her anger, a white light leaking out of the corners like luminescent tears.

I stood up and pulled her to her feet with me, then put both hands on her shoulders. I gave her a little shake. "It's okay because It's. Fucking. Okay. That indecision you're feeling? That existential terror at not understanding your place in the universe or how some more powerful force is going to affect your life without even realizing it did so, like a galactic sneaker crushing you like a bug? That's what humans deal with every day. Every. Day. This isn't new, it's just new to you. You wanna know why angels don't want free will? Because you're not built to withstand the abject horror of living with it. Yeah, we can do whatever we want, but that also means we're working without a map *and* without a net. So welcome to a tiny peek into life as a human, Glory. It ain't all it's cracked up to be, and it sure as fuck wasn't worth starting a war to get."

That wasn't really fair on my part, but sometimes when you're trying to forcefully yank someone's head out of their own ass, you can't be gentle. I knew full well that Glory had been human for a while, because I was there for it. She sacrificed her wings and her divinity to save my life, and for the year and change while my weirdo Scooby gang and I were chasing down a way to re-angelify her, she'd been stuck as a human. So she knew something of the trials and tribulations of humanity, because she'd lived there. But for her, there had always been a hope that it was temporary, like the agony of eating Taco Bell at two A.M. and then trying to go to bed. But for us, that uncertainty, that complete lack of understanding, was permanent. And that uncertainty and fear was the driving force behind most human conflicts.

And after a few seconds of glaring at me, Glory came to that same realization. "Okay," she said, squaring her shoulders and almost visibly putting all this new information into a box that she would unpack and try to process in private later. "So Dad was here. And recently, at least in celestial terms. Did you see a sign when we came in telling us when this cemetery was founded?"

I thought back, then shook my head. "No. I wasn't exactly paying attention to the plaques on the wall as we were scaling the fence to get in."

"Me neither, and all the magic swirling around in here is screwing with my cell reception, so I can't Google it. But let's assume that it was sometime in the seventeenth century at the earliest. That's pretty recent, as we look at it, so whatever is going on here either didn't start off as big enough to get Dad's attention, or there was something going on here before the cemetery was here that has continued, and at some point, our Father decided that He didn't want it leaking out into the town."

"Is there another option?" I asked. She gave me a questioning look, and I went on. "Could a priest, or a group of priests, or a coven of witches, or just a little kid praying really hard catch the big guy's attention enough to get him to throw a containment spell over this place?"

Glory looked thoughtful. "Maybe. I've never heard of that happening, but the last time I had a conversation with Dad, your species had barely learned to make fire and stop writing with your own poop."

"So you guys talked last week?" I asked, smirking. "Because I don't know if you've watched any political coverage lately, but we're still slinging a lot of shit all over the place."

"Funny, Harker."

"So we don't know if he was here in…person, for lack of a better term, or if someone or a group of someones managed to focus his attention on this spot. But there is definitely divine magic being used to contain whatever nastiness is happening in the middle of this graveyard, and it's pretty damned powerful."

"Omnipotent, you might even say." Glory added a smirk of her own and I knew that she'd be fine. She wouldn't, really, at least not for a long time. This revelation that God was active on Earth had rocked her, but at least she'd shoved enough of it to the side of her mind that she was functional.

"So I guess the next step is obvious," I said.

"Call Michael, get him and the rest of the Archangels down here, let them deal with whatever bullshit is so potent that it takes Dad's own power to keep it locked up in this one spot?"

"Not so much, G," I replied. "Michael's a prick, and if I never have to deal with him again, it'll be too soon." I might hold a slight species-level grudge against Mikey for being the douchecanoe who tossed my ultimate grandparents out of the Garden of Eden back in the day. I know, he was just following orders, but there are a metric fuckton of dead Nazis who, if you dug them up and asked, could tell you exactly how far that excuse goes with one Quincy Fucking Harker. I'm thinking of cutting out all the rest of the names my parents saddled me with and just legally changing my name to that. I like the sound of it.

"So we've gotta go check it out ourselves, huh?" Her voice was a little thin, and I could tell that she was actually a little nervous.

"Yeah, we do. It's kinda the gig. But think about it like this," I said. "Even if whatever we run into is worse than literal Hell, it can't get out after it murders us."

"That's my Harker," Glory said with a wry grin. "A little ray of fucking sunshine."

CHAPTER NINE

Turning away from the mystical God-touched border of the cemetery, we headed toward the center and the roiling mass of bad mojo waiting there. The whole graveyard wasn't more than a few hundred yards on a side, so it took barely a couple minutes to walk from the edge to the middle of the area, but I had to stop less than halfway in and tamp down my Sight. The magic was so intense, and so alien, so *wrong* that I had to collect myself before I could move forward.

"Are you okay, Q?"

"Not really," I said. "Is this shit not hitting you like a hammer between the eyes?"

"I have a much stronger tolerance to demonic magic than you do. It all comes from the same place, after all. Just one has rotated ninety degrees off-axis, so to speak."

I must have looked confused because Glory laughed. "Come on, Harker. You know all this. Demons started off as angels, so their magic started off as divine and has been corrupted over the millennia. You aren't made of magic, so extraplanar energy has a greater effect on you. I *am* extraplanar, so it doesn't hit me as hard. Plus, I have a few more eons of experience facing it than you do. I promise, by the time you hit your twelfth century, it's a lot easier."

That was somehow not nearly as encouraging as I think she wanted it to be. I've been around a long time, and I'm still in my second century.

The thought of living another thousand years, even without all my bad habits and shite impulse control trying to get me killed, was not appealing. I still had a hard time remembering that people don't mail letters anymore and that we don't need horses to get around. I didn't even want to contemplate the technological shifts the next hundred years would bring. I got my magic senses buttoned down as tightly as I could and still have any sense of the supernatural spectrum, and we moved forward.

It was a crypt. It's always a crypt. I had the briefest moment of hope when we were in a cemetery near the coast that dated back to near the Civil War that whatever badness was corrupting the very air around this joint would be coming from a normal grave, but of course not.

"It's a fucking crypt," I muttered. "I fucking hate crypts."

"What's so bad about a crypt?" Glory asked.

"Name one good thing that's ever happened inside a crypt?"

"Didn't Nicholas Cage find treasure in a crypt in one of those *National Treasure* movies?"

"Name one good thing that's ever *actually* happened inside a crypt," I corrected.

"Yeah, okay, I gotta give you that one. So what's the plan? There's a crypt, and it's absolutely crawling with dark magic. We going inside, or are we just going to stand out here yammering?"

Man, I think my Guardian Angel just called me a candy-ass. There are a lot of times I wish she was a little more like Castiel, the humorless angel on *Supernatural*. But then she'd start wandering around in a trench coat, and one low-rent John Constantine in my life is enough. "Lemme spend a few minutes poking around at the magic itself before we go running in there," I said.

"Prudence? From Quincy Harker? Now *that* could make a girl believe in magic." Glory wandered over and perched on a broad headstone, somehow balancing on the narrow edge with her legs crossed.

I knelt on the ground just outside the range of the deepest swirls of power. The crypt was small, but I had a sense that it was probably just an entryway into a much larger subterranean structure. Because I've played enough video games to know that the part of the crypt above ground is never the whole thing. Crypts are like the icebergs of horror—you only see the tiny bit above the surface. All the stuff that wants to murder you is invisible until it's too late.

This was a squat granite structure, maybe ten feet tall, with a barred iron gate for a door. I could see through the opening into darkness, with just enough light spilling in to show me a few steps leading down. The whole thing was built in a faux-Greek temple style, with four columns lining the front, a few marble steps leading up to the gate, and a faded inscription over the door.

"*Nihil dignum sine magno sacrificio,*" I read, mentally translating as I went. "Nothing good comes without great sacrifice." Well, that was ominous as fuck. I opened my Sight a little wider, trying to see something of the nature of the magic, hopefully without burning my brain to a cinder in the process.

As I opened myself to the supernatural energies surrounding the crypt, I began to notice threads of multiple colors shooting through the darkness. It wasn't just roiling shades of black and gray like I'd first thought. I could see motes of blue, purple, and red here and there, and lines of sickly green and yellow streaking through the mass like they were alive and aware. This wasn't just one spell, one source of energy. This was a whole mass of different magical workings, piled on top of each other year after year, century after century, and strangely enough, it seemed to be done by the same magician.

"That's weird," I muttered.

"What is it?" Glory asked, suddenly standing over my shoulder.

"This thing is old. This spell almost certainly predates the crypt, and I'm pretty sure the cemetery as well. But it feels like every piece of magic worked here was done by the same person."

"Yeah, that makes sense," Glory said. "I'm no wizard, but I think you've said that it's a bad idea to go around messing with other people's magic."

"Yeah, if you don't know exactly what you're doing, the results can be…explosive. Literally." I rubbed a scar on my left arm that came from an ill-advised trip to Egypt where I messed around with a spell I didn't understand. Mummies are a thing, they get really grumpy when you disturb their rest, and they are *very* protective of their possessions. Ergo, my scar. I was lucky that was all I took away from that little escapade.

"But that would mean that whoever cast this is hundreds of years old and has been working in this part of the world for all that time," I said. "That's a lot harder to do than people think. Especially nowadays, with digital images, facial recognition, and instant transfer of information. The internet has made life really hard on immortals."

"So you're not surprised that there's a centuries-old sorcerer in North Carolina," Glory said. "You're surprised that there's a centuries-old sorcerer that hadn't gotten caught yet."

"Pretty much," I said. "There are a handful of immortals running around. It's not like *Highlander* where we all want to murder each other. We usually just keep our mouths shut and walk the other way if we encounter someone like us. But we have to move around. People get really suspicious if you don't ever get old and your name isn't Dick Clark."

"People got suspicious of Dick, too."

"Yeah, but he was just a dude with good genetics and great makeup artists. This is something way more serious." I was still poking and prodding at the layers of spellcraft while I talked. There was a lot going on here. There were sacrifices of blood and other things, binding spells, summonings, even a couple transmutation spells. And every one of them had been performed just on the other side of that gate. Just down those stairs.

After a good five minutes of magical study, I stood up, wiping a few stray blades of grass off my knees. "Okay, there's nothing useful to be learned up here. Might as well head inside and see how far we go before the skeleton army rises up and attacks us."

"Skeleton army?" Glory asked. "Did you see something about raising undead in the spells?"

"No, but I've played enough computer role-playing games to know that any time we walk into a crypt, there's a better than even chance that skeletons and zombies are going to come at us. I just hope they're more *Walking Dead* zombies. Those are fine, but the really big, fast, *Resident Evil* zombies would suck."

"I don't think I understood anything you just said," Glory replied.

"We have got to get you a PlayStation of your very own so you can understand more pop culture," I said, stepping toward the door. I put a hand on the bar, and cold shot up my arm like I'd just plunged my fist into an ice bath. My fingers went numb immediately, and as I yanked my hand back, my teeth were already chattering.

"Holy fuck!" I yelled, clutching my hand to my chest. I looked down, and my fingertips were blue. This from touching the gate for less than ten seconds. I turned to Glory. "Um...it's really cold. I should maybe not use my bare hands to open it."

"Ya think?" asked my smartassed Guardian Angel.

"Not often," I replied. Then I took three long steps back from the door, channeled pure energy through my fists, and thrust them out from my chest straight at the door. *"Forza!"* I cried, deciding the time for stealth was long past.

Energy flowed out through my fists, striking the gate with tremendous kinetic force, wrenching the metal from its mooring and sending it clattering across the inside of the crypt. Mission. Fucking. Accomplished.

Except for the part where the energy rebounded off the swirling magic right at me. The gate flew into the crypt to land in a mangled pile of rusted iron. The energy itself slammed into some kind of magical rubber wall and came right back into my chest, picking me up and sending me sailing. I wasn't anchored into a granite doorframe, and I weigh a lot less than a seven-foot wrought-iron gate, so when I sent the door flying eight or ten feet into the crypt, the same force on my narrow ass sent me zooming a good twenty or thirty feet through the air to finally fetch up against a single headstone, worn smooth by the years of rain and wind, but still plenty strong enough to arrest my momentum in a most intense fashion.

To be clear, I got the door open. To be even more clear, in doing so I fell prey to Newton's Third Law—that for every action there is an equal and opposite reaction. And my reaction was to slam into a three-hundred-year-old headstone with my back, shoulders, and head. My next reaction was the only logical one—I passed right the fuck out.

CHAPTER TEN

"Y ou know, for a superhero, you get knocked out a lot," said the demon at my feet.

I replied with the first thing that came to my mind, which, for once, wasn't profane. "Ow."

"He's awake," Faustus called over his shoulder, the volume making me wince.

"Can we keep it to a whisper?" I asked, my own voice barely a rasp. I lay my head back on the pillow and closed my eyes, taking a minor mental inventory. *Broken bones—none that I can feel. Vision—painful but clear. Memory—I remember getting blasted through the air and thinking how bad it was gonna suck when I landed. Nausea—not so you'd notice. Mobility—*

I wiggled my fingers and toes, then made it a point to turn my head side to side, eyes still firmly screwed shut, and once I'd confirmed that everything moved in roughly the right way, I opened my eyes again.

Mobility? The question wasn't mine, but Flynn's.

Eavesdropping is rude, I replied.

It's not eavesdropping if the person you're listening to is broadcasting like they're a goddamned FM radio station right into your head.

Huh. I guess the bonk on my head knocked the volume control wonky on our little mental intercom. *Sorry,* I said, trying to keep my voice down.

That's better, Becks replied. *So how badly hurt are you?*

If I say I'm seriously hurt, will you spend all day in bed with me?

48

Not a chance. We've got a serial killer to catch. We catch the bad guy and put him away for good and we can discuss spending a whole day in bed.

You are very much beginning to understand how to motivate me, I said, smiling.

"Stop flirting with Flynn and open your eyes, pervert," Faustus said.

I did, and he, Glory, and Flynn were sitting on the wicker furniture in the living room of our Airbnb. "How did I get back here?" I asked.

Glory raised an arm and flexed a bicep. "I flew," she said. "By the way, I think you're putting on a few pounds, buddy. Not to worry, you still look good, but it's like when Batman asked Kim Basinger how much she weighed. It matters to the one who's carrying you."

"You can literally throw Hyundais at people," I said. "I don't think five pounds of vacation weight is gonna kill ya. Now somebody please hand me something to drink."

Faustus stood and headed for the bar, but Flynn raised a hand. "Orange juice, please. No vodka. Let's make sure he doesn't have a traumatic brain injury before we start pouring alcohol down his gullet."

"I'll heal," I said. "Faustus, make me the biggest goddamn screwdriver in history."

The demon turned to me, his obsidian skin glittering in the yellow glow of the den lights. "Not a chance, pal. For one thing, we don't have near enough vodka to break the world record for largest screwdriver ever. That took a five-gallon bucket to serve and was consumed by Grukk the Indomitable, a Seventh-Circle escapee who singlehandedly caused the Irish Potato Famine because he drank up all the crops on the island. That demon could *drink.* For another thing, I'm way more afraid of your fiancée than I am of you. Worst thing you'll do to me is send me back to Hell to be tortured by Lucifer for a few thousand years."

"What's the worst thing Becks would do to you?" I asked.

"I don't know, but I bet it would involve talking about my feelings and exploring the consequences of my actions throughout most of the last few millennia. Introspection is not fun when you're a demon who's trapped millions of souls in never-ending torment. Here you go." He handed me a tumbler filled with OJ. No vodka, just orange juice in a glass with *SpongeBob* characters on it. I felt like I was seven years old.

"What the fuck happened, Harker?" Becks asked. "I thought you were just going to look around. How did you go from just looking around to Glory flying back in here with you unconscious and bleeding from a fucking head wound? I thought we were going to have to take you to a hospital."

"I'm fine," I said, my struggle to sit upright putting the lie to my words. "Well, mostly fine." A low rumble from behind my head was the only warning I got before ten pounds of gray fur slammed into my upper chest and *whumped* me back down onto the couch.

"Well, hey, buddy," I said. "How did you get here?" I reached up and scratched my cat between the ears, eliciting even more loud rumbling purrs.

"Luke brought him," Glory said.

That got me upright. "Luke's here? When? How? Where is he?" The cat let out a *mew* of protest and slid down off my chest into my lap. He evidently didn't think much of my lap, so he jumped up to my left shoulder, making my already twisted posture way worse.

"He's sleeping," Becks said, pointing back toward the bedroom. "He's under the bed in a sleeping bag under a tarp. He complained, especially since he had to fly across the state in a light-tight coffin, but we didn't have time to get him to a safe room before the sun was up, and the owners of the house had some camping supplies in a closet, so we repurposed those."

There was a lot to unpack there. First, my uncle was in Manteo unexpectedly. Second, he hadn't planned ahead enough to even set up a safe room. Third, he brought my *cat*? "I think I'm going to pass out again. Unconscious was way less confusing."

"We needed his blood. It was that or a hospital. Your skull was fractured, Harker. It was bad." Glory wasn't smiling. She was worried. I've been hurt before, often badly, but there haven't been many times that Glory actually worried about my survival. I must have hit that rock harder than I thought.

"So you called Luke and he…what? Drove all day in a blacked-out car to get to me?" I asked, visions of Spike in a *Buffy* rerun dancing in my head.

"Don't be ridiculous," Faustus said. "He hired a plane. It would take five or six hours to get here from Charlotte, even driving like a vampire bat out of Hell."

"How long have you been waiting to use that line?" Becks asked.

Faustus didn't miss a beat. "Literally years." He turned back to me. "But he just made a couple phone calls, got a plane in the air in an hour, and was here in less than three."

I've never known Luke to have any association with a private airfield, but it does kinda make sense. Vampires can't really be locked into the Delta schedule, thanks to their sun allergy. Still, if he had access to private jets, and Becks now had access to black helicopters thanks to working for Homeland Security, I was determined never to stand in a TSA line again. "Okay, but why did he bring the cat?"

"Well, somebody's gotta take care of him, Harker," Glory said, bending over and petting the long-haired little psychopath. I'd acquired a cat, or more accurately the cat acquired me, in a fight with a nest of vampires a few months back. The cat had been living in the building where vamps had built a nest, and when I went in to clean up the joint, the cat helped. Mostly by jumping on my head and clawing the piss out of me, but he ended up providing just enough assistance that I felt like I couldn't leave him there all alone. Plus, he latched onto my shoulder and I wasn't a hundred percent sure I could get rid of him if I tried. It was like I wanted to find a familiar, but the familiar found me first.

He was a gorgeous cat, though. Once I got him clean of the vampire guts, which thankfully I had a spell to handle. Big, fluffy, and smoke-gray with yellowish eyes. Friendly, too, as evidenced by the purring and head-butting of my ear that was going on. "Hey pal," I said, reaching up to scratch under his chin. The purring got so loud I could barely hear the others in the room, which was kinda okay, since most of the conversation had shifted to how I needed to be more careful, how I wasn't really immortal, and how if I died because I did something stupid, Glory was going to resurrect me just to kill me herself. I plucked the cat off my shoulder and dropped him onto the sofa beside me. He promptly climbed into my lap, started making biscuits on my left leg, and curled up, still purring.

"Are y'all done?" I asked, looking around. "I didn't die. Sounds like it was a little closer than I wanted it to be, but I didn't die. And in this line of work, that's about all we can ask for. So thanks for getting me up and running again, but I'm fine. Now let's get back to work." I tried to stand up, but ten tiny daggers jabbing into my leg let me know that wasn't allowed. I glared down at the cat, who returned my dirty look with an innocent stare. Or maybe it was his "I don't give a shit what you think you're doing, it's still time for petting" stare. I'm still learning the ins and outs of pet ownership.

"You just hold on there, champ," Becks said, coming to sit on the coffee table in front of me. She reached out and pet the kitty, while looking me in the eye. "I was scared, Harker. You weren't in my head, which only happens when one of us is really out of it. You were just *gone*. Ask Faustus. I freaked out. Maybe calling Luke was excessive, but when you're hurt that bad, his blood is the only thing I've ever known that can heal you. And he did. He hauled ass all the way across the state, getting here faster than I thought anybody could, even with a chartered private jet. But you're not okay. Not yet, and probably not for a bunch more hours. So just *chill*. Sit there on the couch with your cat, catch up on some Netflix, and let your brain unscramble. We can't do anything until dark anyway. Luke wants to see the cemetery, he's interested in the information Faustus and I dug up in our research, and we can't go back out until our expert gets here."

"Expert?" I asked. "Who the fuck are you going to find with more expertise in magic than the people in this room?" I have enough ego to think that I'm one of the foremost practitioners of the mystical arts in the country, and certainly in the state of North Carolina. But now that Becks was the Deputy Director of Homeland Security's Paranormal Division, maybe she knew something, or somebody, that I didn't.

"You might be the most powerful spellslinger around, Harker, but your magical education is pretty lacking," Glory said. "You've got the mojo, but you suck at the study part."

Okay, she had me there. I can blow shit up better than just about anybody, but I'd never been much on finesse. And the barrier in front of the crypt had been a complicated set of spells, all kinds of wards layered and woven together. My typical brute force approach to getting the door open hadn't worked worth a tin fuck, so maybe there was somebody out there better suited to picking a magical lock than me. "Okay, who's this expert you've got coming in?"

"Well, it's not just one expert," Becks said. "It's a trio. They're the leaders of a coven based out of Raleigh. The High Priestess runs a New Age bookstore that Bubba and his team encountered a few months ago. You'll like them. I think one of them has a cat, so you can bond over treats and kitty litter or whatever cat people talk about."

"It's mostly just sharing videos on the internet," I said. "The internet only exists for porn and cat videos, you know."

"I'm aware," Flynn replied. "I see your browser history. Anyway, the ladies should be here around nightfall."

"Ladies? Who is this High Priestess?" I asked.

"Her name is Madame Wanda, and I think you'll like her and her friends. They call themselves the Merry Mischief Maidens, and from what Bubba said, they drank him under the table and saved his ass from a demon, so they oughta be able to help. Besides, Luke will be awake by then and you can thank him for flying across the state to save your ass."

"And bringing my cat," I said, petting the furball some more.

"Are you ever going to name that cat, Harker?" Faustus asked. The cat opened one eye and gave him a baleful look. I don't think the kitty was very fond of demons.

"I thought about Gandalf," I said.

"We are not naming our one gray cat Gandalf," Flynn said. "We are not some kind of nerd cliche."

"I'm a half-vampire wizard hunting demons with my Guardian Angel, demon sidekick, hot fiancée, and my uncle, Count Dracula. The only thing that could make me a bigger nerd would be LARPing or a Magic: the Gathering tattoo."

"We're still not calling the cat Gandalf," Becks said, and that was the end of *that* discussion. I scratched Nameless between his ears, and he rolled over for belly rubs. I guess that settled that.

CHAPTER ELEVEN

I 'd finally been allowed off the couch long enough to take a leak and a shower and was toweling off when I heard the door open and a round of introductions being made. I yanked on some jeans and a black t-shirt that read "We Dug Coal Together," in honor of one of the greatest TV shows of all time, and padded out to the living room barefoot to meet our guests and new...assistants? Contractors? Saviors? I wasn't quite sure what to expect, but the sight that met my eyes was most definitely not it.

Nameless was rolling around on the floor play-fighting with a pair of half-grown tabby kittens, while a purple-haired woman stood over them laughing. Becks was chatting with a sixty-ish woman with a cane and blue hair, and completing the wild hair color trifecta was a slightly younger flame-haired woman in a scooter decorated with pink flamingos parked by the door describing all the different birds on her mobility aid to Faustus. I looked over to Glory, who stood with her arms folded across her chest, but the angel just shrugged at me.

"Whattaya gonna do, Harker? When you call in the cavalry, you don't always get to pick the kind of horses they ride in on. In this case, it's a scooter covered in pink flamingos," Glory said.

I stood in the doorway for a minute, taking everything in, until I felt a presence behind me. I hadn't heard him open the door, and the floor didn't creak when he walked, but after a century or so of close association, I can tell when Dracula is looming over a shoulder. "Hi, Luke," I said. "Thanks for the save."

"As always, Quincy, I am happy to render aid whenever I can. I would prefer if you would try to refrain from becoming grievously injured when I am hundreds of miles away. Travel, particularly in the daytime, adds a layer of complexity to my assistance that I would prefer to avoid if at all possible."

That's my uncle. Never one to use a fragment when he could let a sentence run on and on and on. "I'll keep that in mind for the next time I get flung across a graveyard by evil magic," I replied.

"Thank you," Luke said. I swear he understands irony and sarcasm. He really does. But he does that thing that really old people do where they pretend not to catch that you're being a smartass, thereby taking all the fun out of being a smartass in the first place. At least, that's what it's supposed to do. I don't let it stop me, of course. Snark is one of my most valuable superpowers.

"Hi," I said, loud enough that all the women, angels, and demons in the room stopped yammering for a second and looked at me. "I'm Quincy Harker. And you are?"

The blue-haired woman clumped over to me, her cane thump-thumping with every step. "I'm Wanda. We're the leaders of the Raleigh coven. Your boss here called us in to see if we can help with your magical barrier problem."

Boss? I asked Becks silently.

Technically correct, she replied. *You are a contractor employed by The Department of Homeland Security, and I am your supervisor. So that technically makes me your boss.*

Does this mean I can file a sexual harassment claim about the way you objectify my body?

Only if you want me to stop objectifying or using your body in any way at all...

I think we can let it slide.

Thought so. Now pay attention, Wanda's still talking.

"...then we can head on over to the cemetery and see what we can see," she finished, looking at me expectantly.

I, of course, had no fucking idea what she'd said before that because I'd been flirting with Becks. And Wanda obviously knew I hadn't been paying attention because she was standing there giving me that disappointed elementary school teacher look. Not that I ever got those looks when I was in school because I was an exemplary student. Also because I went to school in the early twentieth century and wasn't telepathically linked to a gorgeous federal agent at the time. A lot has changed in a century or so.

"That sounds like a great idea, Wanda," Glory jumped in with the save. "Q was just going to go over the types of magic he saw with us, now that he's showered and looking somewhat more human. There was a decent amount of blood to wash out of his hair from slamming into that tombstone."

"Oh no," the purple-haired woman with the cats said. "Are you alright?"

"He is fine," Luke said, slipping past me into the room. "I am Lucas Card. It is a pleasure to meet you." He stepped toward the women, stopping when the two kittens hissed ferociously at him. Nameless just padded over and started rubbing up against Luke's legs, purring like an outboard motor. Sometimes I think my cat likes Luke better than he likes me.

"You're not human," the woman in the scooter said, holding a monocle on a stick up to her right eye. "There is something very dark in your aura."

"Oh, my dear," Luke said with his most charming and least predatory smile. "You have *no* idea." Note that I didn't say his smile wasn't at all predatory. Just his *least* predatory one. He is, after all, the very tippy top of the apex predators.

"There's a lot of the whole 'not human' thing going around," I said, walking over to the fridge. "Beer?"

"Harker, you have a head injury," Becks scolded.

"And drinking with it is just one in a long string of bad decisions which make up most of my charm," I said, grabbing a Stella. "Anyone else?" The rest of the room pretended to be all civilized, so I made my way over to the dining room table, pulled the chair at the end out of the way so Scooter Lady could roll up, and sat down at the other end. I gestured toward the table, and everyone took their places so I could give them the rundown on what we were walking into.

And what we walked into was nothing like what we planned for, because of course it wasn't. We got to the cemetery just a little after full dark, and quickly learned that there's a significant benefit to having magical powers when you've got mobility issues, because Joey (the witch on the scooter) waved her hands a little as she hopped on her motorized steed, and damned if the thing didn't hover a couple inches off the ground!

"That's convenient," Faustus said.

"And I didn't have to sell my soul for it," the fire-haired woman fired back. I liked the flamingo witch. She was sassy.

Carol, the crazy cat lady witch, convinced her kittens to stay behind and look after Nameless, who was asleep on the back of the sofa. She and Wanda led the parade of misfits and monsters through the cemetery, needing no help from me to find the disturbance in the metaphysical landscape. "It's a blight on Her flesh, dear," Wanda told me. "We could find it blindfolded. Now you just stand back and let the professionals get to work."

I kept my mouth shut, despite the difficulty involved in doing so. We got to the crypt, where someone had stretched yellow police tape across the entry. Made sense, given that I had vandalized the ever-loving shit out of it eighteen hours before. Becks and I stood back as the witches, Glory, Faustus, and Luke moved in to watch the show.

"Don't want to get thrown across the graveyard again?" my fiancée teased.

"The last thing any of us, especially me, needs is another lecture from Luke on my recklessness. I'm not going to stop being reckless, but I can at least be a little more cautious when he's around to see the results."

"I suppose that's what passes for personal growth with you," Becks said.

Wanda, Joey, and Carol formed a triangle before the door, with Wanda at the point, Joey on her right, and Carol to the left. Glory, Faustus, and Luke stood about ten feet behind them in a semicircle, watching intently. I opened my Sight and was floored at the difference in the environment a day and the addition of three good witches made. Where previously the darkness at the mouth of the crypt had been a roiling, seething mass of angry blackness with tendrils of sheer ebony slithering out from it, tonight it seemed almost tentative, like it was afraid of what was outside. And what was outside was a blue-green glow that lit up the mystical landscape like a Technicolor sunrise. The witches blazed like a beacon of hope and comfort in the night, not just holding back the darkness, but *beating* it back, almost to the point where the confrontation looked physical, and they hadn't even cast a spell yet.

"Their auras..." I murmured.

"What about them?" Becks asked, turning to me.

"I can't even...here, look." I threw wide the doors to our mental bond, drawing her deeper into a connection with me than even our normal link. She gasped as she saw through my eyes, through my Sight, something I'd never shared with her before.

"Why haven't you ever let me see this before?" she asked.

"Because it's never been this damned impressive before. I've never seen anything like this, not even when Glory fought the demon in Atlanta. This is...something."

Becks blinked and let our connection fade back to the normal bond we always share, where we can communicate mind-to-mind and know where the other is, and what we're feeling, but we're not looking through each other's eyes. That shit's difficult to maintain and makes it really hard to walk. "Damn," she said. "That was beautiful. And that is not a word I thought I'd be using tonight."

"Yeah," I agreed. "Same here."

Luke shushed us, and I turned my attention back to the ritual, or spell, or whatever they were doing. They chanted something about a mother, something about natural order, and something about love and light. As they chanted, the darkness receded, then bulged outward like it was trying to attack them, or like a boil about to erupt. Then, as their spell-work rose in volume, tiny fissures appeared in the surface of the barrier, a tiny spiderweb of cracks stretching outward from the center. The cracks widened, and the trio of witches raised their hands and voices, chanting louder and faster, calling on the power of the earth, the wind, the water, and fire, all the natural elements to aid them in purging the abomination before them.

The darkness surged forward, flinging out vines of deepest inky black toward the women, but Glory stepped forward, suddenly resplendent in her angelic battle armor, a beacon of purest white stepping up on Wanda's right shoulder and holding out her hands, sending forth a barrier of gleaming white light that the tendrils recoiled from.

More strands of magical ichor slid around to the left side of the witches' triangle, but Faustus stepped into the breech, no longer the affable, scheming manipulator, the legendary con man and soul-swindler, but a vision of Hellspawned power, his glittering obsidian flesh wreathed in glowing crimson plate armor, a pair of curved scimitars in his hands. He crossed his blades in front of his chest and thrust his arms forward, forming a half-sphere before him that seared the fingers of blackness that slammed into it. His shield of red energy met Glory's conjured barrier of purest white, and instead of recoiling from each other, the demonic and the divine wove together to form something more than the sum of its parts, something perhaps unseen on this plane since the War in Heaven. A demon stood side by side with one of The Host to shield three human women from one of the darkest pieces of spellcraft I've even seen, and with that protection, the three witches fired one last bolt of energy right into the gaping maw of darkest evil, and in a flash of light that left us all blinking and rubbing our eyes, the barrier fell.

"Wow," I said. "That was impressive."

"And exhausting," Wanda said, holding out a hand. Glory stepped up to steady her, and suddenly she was no longer a powerful witch fighting the powers of darkness. Now she was just a human woman in her sixties with blue hair and a cane, who needed some help to make it back to her car. "I'm afraid that's all I have the juice for tonight. You're on your own from here."

"Same," Carol said, wiping sweat from her brow. "It's going to be hard enough to get Joey back to the car, since none of us have the strength left to levitate her scooter."

"That won't be a problem," Faustus said. "I'll carry it. I'm not going to be good for much magic until I get some rest, too, but I'm still a lot stronger than a human."

"Sounds good," I said, blinking again to try and make the sparkles in my vision go away. "You and Glory get the Merry Maidens back to the Airbnb safely. It's our turn."

"Our turn?" Luke asked.

"We both know you didn't fly all the way out here just to save my ass again," I told my uncle with a smirk. "You wanna see what's down there that was strong enough to almost kill me and see if it's strong enough to pick a fight with fucking Dracula."

"You know me too well, my boy," he said.

"And why is Becks coming instead of me?" Glory asked.

"Because if things go completely sideways, you can get here faster than I can if I go with the witches, and because Harker knows that if he ever wants to get laid again, he'd better not even *think* about telling me to wait up for him," Becks answered for me. She was right, so I didn't bother to argue.

"So now that we've got that settled," I said. "Let's get down there and see what the fuck is murdering people all over Manteo."

CHAPTER TWELVE

A vampire, his nephew, and a federal agent walked into a crypt, and there's no punchline to that one, it's just my life. I thought back to the last time Luke and I had walked into a crypt hunting bad guys, and sighed. His Renfield at the time, a very proper Englishman named Sylvester Thomas Efor the fourth, had been with us, and it was one of the last times he went into the field with Luke and me. A half-demon asshole government agent murdered him a few months later, and I put a bullet in the fed's noggin. But Renfield had been a good guy. Almost all of them had been. A couple were assholes, and the most recent one hadn't even been a guy, but our friend Cassie. But one characteristic they all unfortunately shared was mortality, which was why there seemed to be a rotating cast on our crypt-diving adventures. That's something they don't tell you about immortality—loving people who aren't immortal sucks a lot more for you than for them.

I don't care how many times you've watched *Highlander*, or how many times you've read *The Vampire Lestat*, you can't really understand what it's like to watch everyone you love die until you've done it. Even I haven't done it. Not really. I've always had Luke. Almost everyone else I've ever known has died, but when your parents leave you in the keeping of Count friggin' Dracula upon their death, you know two things: one, that you had some weird-ass parents, and two, that barring outside influences, this parental figure will be around your entire life. Of course, that was before we knew that I'd inherited some of Luke's mojo on account of he and his "brides" snacking on both my parents way back in Transylvania. But there are plenty of accounts of that for people to read, and I don't need to think about my dad in a foursome with three vampires. Not only is it gross, it also always leaves me feeling a little inadequate. I've never been the centerpiece of a foursome, and I was at Studio 54 in its heyday.

Snap out of it! Becks sent the thought with a mental slap, and it jerked me out of my reverie.

"Sorry," I muttered.

"If you're going to think about group sex with your dad and vampires, please try to put those images behind a mental paywall," she replied.

"Say it a little louder," I said. "Just in case anyone didn't hear you."

"I have better hearing than you," Luke reminded me. "And if she didn't want me to hear and further embarrass you, she wouldn't have spoken aloud at all."

I sighed and shoved all memories of my parents and dead Renfields back into the dark recesses of my mind and peered into the inky blackness of the tomb. With whatever dark magic had been living here banished or at least contained, the magical darkness was gone, but that didn't change the fact that it was nighttime and no one left a candle burning in the cemetery anymore.

I called up power and said, *"Lumos."* A sphere of white light formed in the air above my palm, and I raised it up into the air until it hovered about seven feet off the ground. Then I closed my eyes and envisioned a tiny but unbreakable thread of energy tethering the glowing ball to Flynn's shoulder. The sphere floated over to bob in the air behind her.

"Did you just tie a lightbulb to me, Harker?" she asked.

"Yeah."

"Why?"

"Because Luke and I see better than you in the dark, and if you need to shoot past me, I don't want you blinded by a shiny beachball hanging over my head."

She nodded. "Okay, that tracks. So am I going in first, like bait?"

"Oh, hell no. You stand near the door so your light shines in, but I'll take point and...or maybe Luke can take point." Because Luke had already taken point. In fact, Luke was already a dozen paces inside the crypt, peering through the darkness with his heightened senses. I swear, that guy takes direction worse than I do. Almost like I learned it somewhere...

"It's empty." Luke's voice wafted out of the dark enclosure. "There's nothing here, not even a sarcophagus."

Confused, I stepped across the threshold, Becks and her light balloon close on my heels. He was right, the place was dead empty. No coffins, no urns with flowers, no marble statuary, not even those plaques on the wall where you unscrew them and shove the dead person in their eternal cubbyhole. It was just...empty.

"That's weird," I said, turning around in a circle as I peered up, down, and all around. The entire room wasn't just featureless, it was spotless, as if it had been swept clean mere hours before our arrival, or maybe like no one had set foot in here for centuries.

"What the fuck, Harker?" Becks asked. "*This* was the source of magic strong enough to fling you halfway across the cemetery and crack your skull open?"

"Um...yeah?" I said, making it way more of a question than it needed to be, but I had no idea what the hell was going on. "Lemme look at it the other way." I opened my Sight, and while there were still no physical elements in the room, the magical trace was heavy, and *ugly*.

"Well, this is definitely the right place," I said. "I can see the slime left behind by whatever was blocking the entrance, and it looks like Venom exploded all over the walls. It's like super-thick black snot or something."

"I got it with the Venom reference," Becks said. "No need to be gross."

"I did not get the...Venom? Reference," Luke chimed in. "So thank you for the clarification."

I gave a tiny little half-bow to Luke. "You're welcome." I focused my gaze on the back wall of the crypt. "There's something here. A concentration of the residue, or a focal point for the spell, or something."

I knelt in the center of the rear wall, searching for anything out of the ordinary, anything that would open a door, or move a panel in the floor, or anything that would have popped up immediately if I was playing a video game. Traps and secret doors are so much harder to find in real life. After several long minutes of searching, poking, and prodding on the floor and wall, I stepped back to get a broader look, then slapped myself on the forehead.

"What is it?" Becks asked.

"Nothing," I grumbled as I walked over to one of the only two features in the entire room. I reached up to the sconce mounted in the wall, grabbed the metal candle holder by the base, and turned it counterclockwise. It didn't move, so I tried to rotate it the other way. There was a loud *click*, a rumble of stone, and a section of wall where I had knelt seconds before recessed and slid aside, opening a dark passage into the heart of the crypt.

"How did you know which one opened the door?" Becks asked.

"I didn't," I replied. "I just figured if that didn't do anything, I'd try the other one."

"I was really looking for a cooler answer, like you could sense the mystical taint of hundreds of evildoers touching that sconce over the years."

"I usually don't talk about mystical taint with my uncle in the room," I replied, then ducked down the hidden passageway before she could slap me.

The passage led to a small landing atop a spiral staircase, perhaps one of humanity's ten worst inventions. They're narrow, they're impossible to comfortably ascend or descend, especially if you're carrying something, the prefab metal ones are noisy as hell, and no matter whether you're going up or down, they're almost impossible to fight on. Add in limited sightlines, and they're just a recipe for architectural disaster. Fortunately, whatever was lurking below was either long dead, supremely confident in the strength of its magical barrier, or not at all worried about anything coming down for an unannounced visit. I thought it most likely the last, and least pleasant, option.

I walked down for what felt like hours, just slowly descending and turning round and round. I had no idea how far down we'd come when I finally saw an opening at the bottom of the stairwell, a stone archway leading off into another darkened passage. I held up a hand to Becks.

Stay back, I whispered along our mental link. *Let me peek ahead first.* I opened up my Sight to check for magical wards, but there was nothing near the doorway. I could still see traces of the darkness from above, a thin slimy coating of awfulness splattered across the magical plane, but there were no obvious threats. That didn't make me feel any better. The opposite, in fact. Obvious threats I can deal with. Just blow them up or tear them apart, and move right the fuck along. Hidden dangers suck. They're like the shark that doesn't have the common fucking decency to let its fin break the surface before it tries to eat you, or high cholesterol. The shit you don't see coming is almost always worse than the big thing rushing at you headlong.

I stepped onto the floor, wobbling a little from all the spinning around the staircase, and blinked rapidly to regain my equilibrium. I moved to the side of the door as Luke and Becks came down, and we walked single file through the doorway, Becks in the rear with her light balloon bobbing merrily along, casting brilliant white light everywhere. The passage was long and narrow, maybe five feet wide, and just barely tall enough for me to stand up straight. I'm pretty sure my hair brushed the ceiling as I ducked through the doorway, and I kept my knees slightly bent to keep from scraping my head. This was a tight fit, and I very much didn't want to have to duke it out in this tunnel. There was nowhere to go, and someone with a penchant for polearms could make a nice kabob out of the three of us with a well-placed pike.

Maybe I shouldn't mention that while walking with the man known as Vlad the Impaler right behind me. I'm pretty sure Luke likes me most days, but I can be a pain in the ass, and I'd hate for his baser instincts to get the better of him. And the better of me. But since he didn't have a pike, I was only slightly concerned.

The passage led off into the distance farther than Beck's light shone, and as we crept forward, eyes and ears open for any signs of danger, it just kept stretching farther and farther into the black. I figured we'd walked for a solid mile before I noticed something flickering ahead of us. I held up a hand, and we froze.

What is it? Becks asked. We'd been communicating silently ever since we stepped off the stairs, counting on Luke's ability to read our body language to get anything he needed from us.

I see light ahead. I think we need to douse yours and let our eyes adjust.

Ugh. Okay.

Problem?

Just not looking forward to being down here in the pitch black. But you're right. If there's something up ahead, no sense in announcing our presence with a neon sign.

I released the spell, and her globe of light winked out, plunging us into near-total blackness.

"Quincy, my dear, I do sincerely hope that was intentional," Luke whispered, voice so low that no one could overhear, unless they had some type of supernatural hearing.

"It was," I whispered back. "Light ahead."

And it was easier to notice in the almost perfect dark. A little flicker of orange light ahead, two horizontal and two vertical lines perfectly outlining a six-foot rectangle that filled almost the entire passageway.

We'd found a door at the end of a secret passage underneath a cemetery, locked away behind a mystical barrier so powerful it took the combined power of three witches to break through. And if the light coming from under the door was any indication, the room on the other side was occupied.

Time to see what lurked beneath the city. I just really hoped there weren't tentacles. Tentacles squick me out.

CHAPTER THIRTEEN

I really wish it was tentacles," I murmured as I took in the disgusting sight before us.

"No shit," Luke said, his voice low, as if standing in a museum or a church. I rarely heard him swear, or use two words when ten would suffice, but he captured how we all felt at that moment.

"I've gotta..." Becks clapped a hand to her mouth and turned, sprinting back up the hall as far as she could manage before losing her lunch, dinner, and probably everything she'd eaten for the past few days.

I couldn't blame her. Becks is no wilting lily, no delicate flower of femininity, but the sight before us set my guts to roiling, and I've literally disemboweled bad guys and picked their internal organs out of my shoelaces. A normal human, even one with decades in law enforcement, had no chance of keeping their stomach when faced with the horrors in that crypt.

It wasn't tentacles. It wasn't even a monster, although a naked Jabba the Hut would have been more appealing. It was bones. Bones, and chunks of rotting meat, and more bones, and clothes strewn in piles, and dark brown splashes across everything, that very specific burgundy-brown with a hint of mahogany to it that can only be dried blood. Gallons of the stuff had been spilled here, enough that even with barely any recognizable human flesh or organs, the scent of copper infiltrated the air, filling our lungs with the tang of viscera and suffering.

It wasn't just a few bones, or a few bodies. It was dozens, maybe hundreds of bodies' worth of spare parts. Just standing in the doorway I could count at least two dozen separate skulls, and the process of separating all these bones into individual humans would be the kind of thing forensic anthropologists build entire careers on. That lady from *Bones* would get a whole new wing on her office for this shit.

"What the fuck happened here?" I asked. My voice was barely a whisper, almost like I was afraid to disturb the occupants of the crypt, despite their being decades, if not centuries old.

"I expect we shall have to get closer to discern that, Quincy," Luke said.

So we did. For the first time, I felt a little relief about living in a post-pandemic world, because I still carried a cloth facemask in my hip pocket. I only wore it if the establishment required it, because my unique physical makeup makes it impossible for me to catch or transmit most normal diseases, but carrying one had just been habit for the past couple years. It didn't do much for the stench, but even dialing it down just a hair was worth the effort. Luke, since he never really interacted with people who aren't me, Becks, or immortal beings from other planes of reality, didn't have a mask. He also had even more heightened sense than mine, but he was also the guy who got famous by skewering his enemies on pikes and using them as lawn ornaments, so the smell of abattoir might have just made him feel at home.

The place looked like a dragon's lair in a fantasy movie, except where those scenes have huge piles of gold, these had bones. And bones. And more bones. The room must have been forty feet on a side and a good ten feet high, and almost the entire granite floor was littered with bones and body parts in various stages of decay. I counted at least a dozen piles of awfulness as I walked toward the least appealing part of the room—the fresh bits. "I think we found our most recent victims. At least the parts of them we didn't already have in the morgue."

I'm pretty sure there were pieces of four people dumped unceremoniously in what must have recently been a clear patch of floor. I couldn't quite tell because where one body was almost intact, a couple of others were just a limb here or a pile of organs there. I thought back to the girl on the beach and the boy in the lighthouse and guessed that the pile of viscera in the corner was probably her innards, and the one flip-flop wearing leg lying next to an arm that looked to be yanked off at the shoulder were probably his. The other bodies were more complete—a short Latino man sat on the floor, his blank eyes staring up at me. He was

JOHN G. HARTNESS

complete, from the midsection up, just plopped on the floor like he fell out of a chair. Except he stopped at his belly, and nothing below the waist was anywhere to be seen.

The other recent victim was a heavyset white man in faded desert camo with a Marine Corps tattoo on his left forearm. He was missing his head, right shoulder, and attached arm, but the rest of him was in the pile, just tossed aside like garbage. If the condition of his clothes and the track marks on his remaining arm were any indication, this wasn't the first time the poor bastard had been tossed aside. The tattoo bothered me. It's always hit me harder when I see how sideways things go for people when they come back from a war, and knowing that it could be fixed if the people in power saw any profit to it made me even more disgusted than the carnage before me.

"Well, that confirms the theory we got from the local cops," Becks said, walking back over to me and taking a long swig from a bottle of water she pulled out of her bag.

"What theory is that?" I asked, suddenly remembering that I hadn't asked anything about her research trip with Faustus. I mean, I'd had a little bit on my mind. Like a tombstone. But now it seemed relevant.

"That the three murders they'd found in the past few weeks were related. This guy is most likely Julian Rojas, a mason who disappeared from a local construction project last month. The veteran is probably 'Iron' Mike Mulligan, a homeless man who hadn't been seen at any of the shelters or his usual haunts for at least three weeks. And we already knew about the two kids."

Most of the time I'd make some comment about Becks calling anyone a "kid" given our relative ages, but the whole place had put a damper on even my wisecracks. "But who are all these other people?" I asked. "Did you find any reports of rampant graverobbing in your research?"

"That wasn't exactly what we were looking for, so no. But we did talk to the guy who runs the Property & Records room at the police department, and he asked us if we were looking for information on the current murders or on the old ones."

"The old ones?" I asked.

"Funny, that's exactly what I said. Apparently there was a series of unsolved murders when he started on the force, almost thirty years ago. They know about six victims, but he said there were several homeless that went missing about the same time, so the actual victim count might be higher."

"I bet we could go through the clothes in one of these piles and get an accurate count for him," I said.

"I bet somebody could go through these clothes, but it won't be me," Becks said. "I'm way more interested in looking for clues to catch the bastard that did this than in some myth of closure for the families." She knew about closure, or lack thereof. Her father was a cop killed in the line of duty. I know. I'm the one who killed the vampire that gutted her father, and I'm probably the reason he was killed in the first place. That wasn't anywhere close to the only challenge in our relationship, but it had taken several conversations and a lot of good booze to work through.

"I think we shall find more clues than we are capable of processing alone," Luke said. "We will need not only forensic scientists, but fashion experts as well." He held up a silver buckle. "It has been some number of years since these were the height of fashion, but I believe this came from a pair of men's shoes."

"I thought silver burned your skin?" I asked.

"It does. Tin, however, does not. And this is tin. Silver would be very green after this many years, Quincy." Somehow the man still manages to make me feel like an idiotic twelve-year-old, after more than a hundred years.

"So this place has been a dumping ground for bodies since at least the eighteenth century?" Becks asked.

"Not it," I said. "I'm old, but not that old." I gave Luke a stern glare. "Uncle Vlad, did you leave a pile of broken toys under the Outer Banks for the past three centuries?"

"No, Quincy," Luke replied, his expression showing how not funny he thought I was. "But I believe it is more like five centuries." He held up a few other wood and metal artifacts, digging through piles of bones like a dog after a chew toy. "I believe this child's bow to be from the earliest years of European colonization in this area."

It looked like a polished stick to me, the string having long rotted away, but as I looked more closely at it, the length, the curvature of the wood, the small notches in the ends—it was definitely a bow, sized for very small hands. There was something heartbreaking and forlorn about it, a toy from a forgotten schoolkid, discarded down here like so much garbage. A human life cut short, then thrown away, lost to history.

"So did we find out what happened to the Lost Colony?" I asked, gesturing to the piles of bones. "Were they all eaten by an immortal monster that is somehow still around and chewing on people even today?"

"I doubt it," Luke said. "We will need a thorough analysis of the entire contents of the tomb to be certain, but I don't think there are enough remains from that period to account for all the people lost on Roanoke Island. There may be a connection, but it isn't as simple as your initial assessment, I fear."

"It never is," I said, with a sigh. "Let me take a quick pass through here with my Sight active, then if it feels safe, we can clear out and call in the scientific reinforcements." I didn't really want to look through this room in the magical spectrum. The last thing I wanted to do was open myself to all the pain and suffering these people endured. But it was also exactly what I had to do if I wanted any chance at finding justice for them. So I took a deep breath and opened my Sight.

To nothing. Nothing at all. There was no psychic or magical residue in the tomb. I could feel the trace magic of the barrier up topside, and I could feel the inherent magic in Luke and Becks, but there was not so much as a shred of aura left on the bones or bodies, not even the most recent ones.

"That's fucking weird," I muttered. "There's nothing left. It's like whatever killed these people didn't just destroy their bodies, it absorbed their whole essence somehow, leaving not even a trace behind. Whatever did this isn't just killing these people, it's consuming their very souls."

CHAPTER FOURTEEN

W ith nothing more to learn from the tomb, at least until Becks could fly in a forensics team from Homeland Security, we headed back to the Airbnb where Glory and Faustus were waiting. The witches were gone, bundled off to a hotel on Luke's dime, so we all gathered on the massive back deck of our rental and settled in to go over the revelations of the last day and a half.

"Since you all know what I found in the cemetery last night, and what we found tonight was gross but ultimately unproductive, why don't you and Faustus give me the rundown on what you learned at the cop shop yesterday?" I was in a wicker (of course) chair with my feet up on the railing, no shoes, a Sweetwater 420 in one hand, and the other firmly embedded in the floof at Nameless's neck. He was rumbling contentedly in my lap and making biscuits on my leg. Every once in a while, I'd need to reposition him so he didn't turn my nuts into mashed potatoes, but otherwise it made for a pleasant environment, what with the cool ocean breeze and the smell of salt water washing away the smell of blood.

"I told you most of it in the tomb, but here's the rest," Becks said. "According to the sheriff, there were two murders before the one we were called out to the other night. As we discovered tonight, those victims were definitely related to the one we found last night because parts of all four victims were in the crypt we visited."

"Among a fuckton of other victims," I said. Nameless gave me a light nip on the back of my hand. I swear sometimes it feels like the cat doesn't approve of my language. It's almost like having Cassie back telling me to put a dollar in the swear jar. I never did. I just dropped a twenty in the jar every Monday and we called it even.

"Yes, among many other victims, apparently stretching back to long before Manteo was an actual town," Flynn continued. "When we spoke to the old timer running the evidence room, he mentioned a series of unsolved murders from back when he started on the force, almost thirty years ago. According to those records, there were perhaps as many as nine victims, all horribly dismembered, all over the island, in a string of brutal homicides lasting for three weeks leading up to Halloween."

I looked at my phone to double-check the date. Yep, middle of October. "So we're on schedule for five more murders in the next two weeks?" I asked.

"Maybe six," Faustus said. "According to the records we found, there were no cases of more than one person being killed in any of the attacks in the nineties. So it might be that the guy we found the other night was just in the wrong place at the wrong time, and he wasn't targeted."

"That tracks with the rest of the victimology," Becks said, taking a long drag off her own beer. "Everyone else we found records for was transient to a greater or lesser degree. Either homeless, on vacation, or just a skilled laborer who went where the jobs were."

"People who were less likely to be missed," Luke said, nodding. "That is often how I chose my victims when I hunted humans regularly. I would not be surprised if there were victims unaccounted for among the local sex workers or runaways."

"We thought of that, too, so we combed through the deaths around the time of the known related victims. We didn't find any additional victims, and one of the women killed in the nineties was a stripper, so it seems like the police at the time did look into lifestyle as a component of victimology."

The more cop-like her language became, the more I was reminded exactly how goddamned smart my fiancée was. She was literally brilliant, and I loved watching her flex her mental muscles on this problem. Which was really good, since I had neither the training nor the know-how to investigate something like this. If there was someone to beat up over an interrogation, I was the guy. But puzzling out clues and motive and stuff was way more her bailiwick than mine. I just sipped my beer, pet my cat, and watched her work.

"But that didn't stop the research," Becks said. "That just brought us back here where we worked all hours of the night until Glory came running in here like her hair was on fire, hauling your unconscious ass in and dumping you on the porch. I gotta tell ya, Harker, you had us worried."

"I had the utmost faith in you all to take care of me," I replied, my fingers tangled in the thick fur of Nameless's belly. The cat liked belly rubs more than a lot of dogs I've known, and that was a good thing because playing with the cat was keeping me from thinking too much about how close I'd come to punching my ticket permanently. Again. I was out of Get out of Hell Free cards, having used mine the last time I died, and I was well aware how much rank Lucifer was willing to pull on his other boss demons to get his hooks into me. Literally. So I tried not to dwell on my own mortality too much. Better to focus on other dead people, I supposed.

"While we were working here, or I should probably say while I was working..." Becks let her voice trail off as she glared at Faustus.

"Hey! I worked," the demon protested.

"You worked the bar, you worked the remote, you worked the wifi overtime surfing videos about people hurting themselves in stupid ways on the internet..." Becks was having none of Faustus's excuses, but there was a smile behind her words. At some point, the demon had become more than an ally, he'd become a friend. My life is very weird.

"But all of those things were, in fact, *working*," Faustus replied with a broad smile.

"Anyway, I dug back through the history of the town, and I came upon something very strange."

"You found out that every so many years, there's an unsolved string of murders with nine victims, then a time of almost no serious violent crime until the next string of murders," I said.

Flynn raised an eyebrow at me. "Do you know something you're not telling me, Harker?" She directed a glare at Luke. "Is this some kind of super-secret Shadow Council thing that had you making Harker schedule his vacation here so he could check out a mystery y'all haven't been able to solve?"

"No," I said. "But I have read *It*. Even watched the TV mini-series. And it's kinda the same principle—big evil thing lives under a town, every so many years it comes up and murders a bunch of people, eats them, then goes back to sleep for thirty years or so. Cyclical sacrifice. Kinda like *The Lottery*, only with a time delay on the killing."

"Did you see the movie?" Faustus asked. "With the kid from *Stranger Things* and that Skaarsgard dude? I can't remember which one, but he's the pretty one."

"They're all pretty ones, dude," Glory said. "That family comes from the *deeeeeeep* end of the genre pool."

I held up a hand. "One—I haven't seen the new movies. Two—yes, all the Skaarsgards are pretty. Three—Becks, was there more?" It's rare that I'm the one to get a conversation back on track, but I've heard Glory wax poetic about Scandinavian actors before, and if we just let her go, it would turn into hours of conversation about six-packs, eight-packs, and blond yumminess. I was barely twenty-four hours removed from having my head bashed in against a tombstone, I didn't need to hear about my Guardian Angel's celebrity crush(es).

"Yes," Flynn said, rescuing us all from going down the IMDB rabbit hole with the demonic and divine duo. "I dug back as far as I could go online, and from what I can tell, these murders happen every twenty-seven years, going as far back as the late nineteenth century. Any further back than that, and things get really murky, records-wise. The development of the freedmen's colony on Roanoke during the Civil War made any attempts at a census or keeping track of people next to impossible, so we don't really know if there were murders prior to that, or if people just...left."

"Or were recaptured as runaways and sent back from whence they came," Luke added. "That was a dark period in this country's history, and in the history of many nations throughout time. I am glad to have lived long enough that opinions on the ownership of other human beings have shifted to the less abominable." That was a pretty progressive statement from a guy who grew up in Romania when slavery was an established practice, but if you can't learn and grow in centuries of living, what's the point, right? "I find it interesting the numerology of the dates you are recounting, Rebecca."

"How so?" Becks asked.

"Nine deaths every twenty-seven years," he replied. "Nine is three squared, and twenty-seven is three to the third power, or cubed. Three is one of the holiest numbers in magic, especially in Western, Judeo-Christian-based cultured. The Holy Trinity—God, Jesus, and the Holy Spirit—figure heavily in the belief system in America, and in those who founded the country. It is not without reason to think that whatever is behind these slayings is deeply steeped in that culture."

I raised my hand, the one with the beer in it, and asked, "Could you say that again, but maybe with fewer words and a point nestled in there somewhere?"

"He said that it's probably a demon, or something from the Christian belief system, on account of the number three figuring into the body count and the timeline," Faustus said. I didn't love letting the demon look smarter than me, but if I was willing to admit it, he probably *was* smarter than me. He's old enough to remember Atlantis, for fuck's sake, he'd better be smart.

"That tracks with what Glory and I found at the cemetery," I said, looking at the angel. We hadn't shared the revelation that God Himself had laid down a barrier around the graveyard, but this was probably the time. If all this was tied to a demon somehow, then The Big Guy's presence was just another bit of confirmation.

"You mean finding a gate that broke your head?" Becks asked.

"No, he means finding proof that God has touched the stones around the graveyard, and recently," Glory said.

The gasps were loud enough to startle the cat, which led to me getting bitten on the hand, which led to me saying, simultaneously with Faustus, a resounding "What the fuck?!?"

I noticed everyone staring at me. "Sorry," I said. "Cat bit me. I knew about the whole God thing."

"I most certainly did *not* know about the God thing," Faustus said. "I'm with everybody else, including fucking *Lucifer*, in thinking that he popped out for a beer run after the War on Heaven and hasn't made it back from the 7-11 in a few millennia."

"Making him the original deadbeat dad," I quipped. Judging from the flat glares and blank stares I got, that joke landed about as well as a belly flop into an empty pool.

"Are you sure?" Faustus asked, his voice small. There was a look of concern on his face, and maybe even a hint of fear.

Glory stood up, walked across the room, and knelt in front of him. She took his hands in hers and said, "Yes. I'm sure. I felt His touch upon the stones, and they hummed like the very sidewalks of Heaven. It was *Him*, Faustus. It was Father."

Tears welled up in the demon's eyes, and he sprang to his feet. "Why? Why would that motherfucker show up now, just when I was starting to figure shit out? What a fucking *asshole*." Then he planted both hands on the deck railing, vaulted over it, and sprinted down the beach toward the water, swearing under his breath with every step.

Glory got to her feet. "I think I'd better go after him before he does something rash." Then she manifested her wings and took off after him.

So let's recap—my Guardian Angel just took off down the beach in hot pursuit of one of the most famous demons in all the Hells, in hopes of keeping him from doing something rash. Because rash isn't exactly what demons are programmed to do, or anything like that. I told you my life is weird.

CHAPTER FIFTEEN

Glory and Faustus hadn't come back by the time Becks and I got sleepy, so we crashed for a few hours, leaving Luke and Nameless bonding on the couch watching the remake of *It*. I warned Luke about letting the kid watch horror movies before bed, and he reminded me that the "kid" was a cat of indeterminate age, so we didn't know if it was too young for horror movies. And besides, Nameless was, in fact, a cat. Not a demon cat, or a witch's familiar cat, or anything more supernatural than a typical long-haired housecat with an affinity for toys with bells and a salmon fetish.

The dynamic duo still weren't back when we woke up in the mid-morning, and Luke had retired to his room with Nameless for a long day of napping and Netflix. I swear, I'm not sure which one of them is more catlike—the vampire or the actual feline. Becks and I grabbed a quick breakfast of toast, bacon, and orange juice, then headed out to Roanoke Island National Park, home of the Lost Colony outdoor drama. More relevant to our interests, it was also home to an archive of thousands of documents related to the original settlement, where Becks hoped to find some clue as to what happened all those years ago. Not the secret of what happened to the "Lost Colony," but more about what was still happening to the poor lost souls we found dismembered on the beach a couple nights earlier.

I left her to it, research never being my strong suit, and wandered out back through the woods to take a peek at where historians seemed to think the first European settlement in the New World had once been. The scent of honeysuckle filled the air, and as soon as the parking lot was out of sight, it felt like I'd been transported back in time to a world without automobiles or internet. Or vaccines or refrigerated food, just in case I felt nostalgic for the "good old days." I lost my brothers Orly and James to the flu epidemic in 1918, so my nostalgia stops about the time I remember how much better technology and understanding have made our lives.

But the walk through the woods was pleasant, with birds chirping overhead and a light breeze carrying just a hint of salt and honeysuckle. After a few minutes of wandering, I found myself standing outside a small circle of raised earth, maybe thirty feet in diameter, with an open area on one side. There were signs all around showing details on how the earth-work was constructed, and admitted that this obviously wasn't the exact location of the colony, because no way could you fit a couple hundred people inside that little circle. It may have been some kind of defensive emplacement on a trail leading to the actual fort, but since no one has ever found the location of the fort, all we had was a clearing in the woods with a circular ditch in it.

Of a lot more interest to me was the marker commemorating the Freedmen's Colony on Roanoke Island. I stood before the slab and waved a nearby park ranger over. He was a slim guy in his thirties, dark hair and deep tan making him look slightly less ridiculous for wearing the tall socks and khaki shorts of a park ranger. At least he wasn't wearing a goofy hat, or I would have been obligated to warn him of the impending attack I heard a bear planning on all the "pic-a-nic baskets" at the park.

"Hi there," the ranger said with a big smile. "I'm Josh. Did you have any questions about the marker?"

"Yeah," I said. "What does it mean? Was Manteo a stop on the Under-ground Railroad?" I knew from Becks mentioning it the night before that it was, but I wanted more details, and this guy was incredibly eager to share them. And he did, with a chipper voice and a jaw-splitting grin that would have made me want to punch him if he wasn't so damned informa-tive. This Josh dude enjoyed his job more than just about anybody I'd ever met.

"Yes," Josh said. "In fact, Manteo wasn't just a stop on the Under-ground Railroad, it became one of the first free communities for Black people in the South. In 1862, the island was captured by Union forces, thus making it a safe haven for escaped slaves. They knew that if they could safely make it across the creek onto the island, that they would be free men and women. The colony lasted until 1867, and at its peak numbered over two thousand people living on the island."

"What happened in 1867?" I asked.

"At the end of the Civil War, a government proclamation returned all lands seized during the war to the original owners, and that included the land used to create the Freedmen's Colony. Many of the residents were relocated elsewhere, although some chose to stay on the island, working crops for the returning landowners. Some of their descendants still live on the island to this day."

Something was tickling the back of my mind about that, something I'd heard once a long time ago, but when I tried to wrap the fingers of my memory around it, the thought vanished like smoke in a hurricane.

I nodded to the ranger, who stood there grinning at us, and thought for a moment that maybe getting to hang around a park all day every day and get plenty of fresh air and sunshine would make the knee socks worth it. Then I remembered that July and August still exist in North Carolina and decided that I'd rather hunt demons than wear tall socks outdoors in the summertime.

I followed another trail down to the Waterside Theater, more to spend a minute looking out over the water than anything else. It had been a lot of years since I spent significant time on a boat, and part of me missed it. I didn't miss shitting over the rail and hoping I didn't fall in after my own waste, and I didn't miss the day and half of vomiting that always came along with any trip out of sight of land, but I did miss the salt spray on my face as I blasted through the Atlantic, and the incredible spray of stars across the sky when you're so far from land that light pollution is more a myth than dragons. Which are very real, despite what Uncle Luke and I thought for decades.

The theater was deserted, just a broad expanse of grass leading down to a stage that opened up to the ocean behind. Big aluminum light trees shattered the illusion of an Elizabethan playhouse, but I figured when it was full of people in their Tommy Bahama shirts and Rainbow flip-flops, there wouldn't be any illusion to speak of anyway. But for now, if I stood behind the stage and closed my eyes, all I could hear was the ripple of waves brushing up against the rocks, a gull crying out in triumph from a great distance, and the rustle of sea grass in the breeze. Everything smelled fresh, with that tinge of salt in the air that told me I was at the ocean, and a hint of diesel to remind me that no matter how old the settlement was here, I was still firmly locked in the twentieth century.

"Penny for 'em, Q," Glory said. I turned, and there she sat cross-legged on the back of the stage, like she hadn't gone AWOL for better than twelve hours.

"Hi," I said, playing it cool. I could tell from the look on her face that whatever went down between her and Faustus, it wasn't something she was in the mood to share. So I let it go. "You found me. Good deal."

"I can always find you," she replied. "You learn anything on your little early morning trespassing jaunt?"

I could look past her and see a pair of maintenance guys walking down toward the stage, but they didn't seem to care about our presence. Made sense. If they wanted the site to be secure, they probably would have built a wall around it. As it was, anyone visiting the park could walk all the way down to the end of the dock without encountering so much as an "Authorized Personnel Only" sign, much less a locked gate. "I don't know if it's even trespassing if it's government land and there's not so much as a fence around it," I said. "There was something tickling my brain about the Freedmen's Colony, but I couldn't pin it down. I headed out here hoping the salt air would clear my head."

"Is it working?"

"Not even a little bit. Makes me think of old ocean voyages from way back, which makes me think of family, which..." I let my voice trail off. My family history is...complicated, to say the least. And it just got worse a few months ago.

"Makes you think of your sister," Glory said, her voice soft.

"Yeah." My sister. Madeline, or Maddy when I knew her. I thought she died in the early twentieth century. She and I had a disagreement in Chicago that led to the death of her mobster boyfriend, along with enough people to earn the night a catchy name—The St. Valentine's Day Massacre. For the record, I didn't murder anyone that night, but only because Luke took care of it before I could. Maddy took exception to the decapitation of her boyfriend, and to being raised by a vampire, and perhaps even more exception to me never *telling her* that she was being raised by a vampire. Either way, she stormed out of my life for nearly a century, changing her name and hiding her identity well enough that not even Luke and my resources combined could find her. Until she gave a locket to a man who spent several years trying to tear down every aspect of my life, sending me a message that she was still alive, and that her hatred for me had done nothing but grow over time.

So to say that dwelling on thoughts of family left me less than soothed would be a massive understatement. "But that's a problem for Future Harker. Today Harker has a monster tearing people limb from limb, a fiancée having dream visitations from a colony that vanished centuries ago, and a demon buddy having a crisis of faith. Got anything to help out with any of that?" That was about as subtle as I could possibly be in asking about Faustus, and while it wasn't all that subtle, it wasn't my worst effort.

"Maybe," Glory said. "But I think first you're gonna have to open your eyes."

I was confused. My eyes were open. How else was I staring out to the back loading dock of the Waterside Theatre looking at a fake Elizabethan ship? Then I got it. She meant look at things in a different perspective. A different spectrum, even. I opened my Sight, and for the second time since coming to Manteo, I was almost struck blind by the sheer power of the magic around me.

CHAPTER SIXTEEN

F uck Uncle Walt and his theme parks," I said. "This might be the most magical fucking place I've ever seen. There's power *everywhere.*"

"I was wondering when you were going to sense that," she replied.

"You knew?"

"Dude," she said, giving me a look that I'm intimately familiar with. That look that asks and answers the question "are you an absolute idiot?" "I'm literally *made* of spirit and magic. Of course I knew we were someplace incredibly charged with power and layered in centuries of spellcraft. I…just couldn't tell you."

"What?" This shit about stuff she knew and wasn't allowed to tell me was getting old. "Who do you work for, Glory? Me? Or Michael? Those angelic pricks didn't give two shits about you when you spent two years trapped as a mortal, and the only reason they care about you now is because they know you're the only one with a snowball's chance of keeping me somewhat in line. I went to Hell for you. Literal *Hell.* And I'm still getting the runaround on what you can and can't tell me? Come on. That's bullshit."

She glared at me, and this wasn't the normal "you're a dipshit" glare. This was real, full of rage and hurt and accusation and betrayal. "You're right, Harker. It *is* bullshit. It's bullshit that I've spent the last couple decades trying to protect somebody who seems determined to get himself killed on the regular. It's bullshit that I have to choose between my boss, who I feel like I have to remind you is also my *family*, and my charge, who has become something like another family. But what's really bullshit is after all these years, after all the shit we've been through, after saving each other more times than even I can count, and I can figure pi to eighteen decimal places, that you don't trust me any more than that. *That's* bullshit."

"Trust you?" I asked, incredulity making my voice go high. "*Trust you?* Glory, you haven't been straight with me since I've met you. You spent the first decade and change we knew each other spying on me for the Archangels to see if you were going to murder me, without ever mentioning this fact to me. You have known things at almost every turn that would have helped me, made my life and my work easier, but you've held that shit back. Why? Because that officious twat Michael *asked* you to?"

"No, you abject fucking prick, because Michael *ordered* me to. I can't violate a direct order, Q. Not that I don't want to, and not that bad things will happen if I do. I can't do it because I literally *can't.*" Her eyes welled up, and she dashed away the tears with the back of her hand. "Why do you think Lucifer fell? Why do you think *any* of my siblings fell?"

"Because Lucifer's a prick and he thought he could run the show better than the Big Guy?" I let a corner of my mouth twitch upward, trying to defuse a little tension.

"Because they were fucking jealous of you, dumbass."

"Jealous of me? Glory, I'm old, but I'm not *that*—"

"Humans, you obtuse fuck. They were jealous of humanity!"

"Jealous of us?" I asked, completely confused. Glory and I had talked a little about the Fall, and Lucifer's jealousy, and the idea that he might be really working on God's orders by running Hell, because if there was going to be a Hell, somebody had to run it. Having met the guy, if I was stuck finding somebody in my circle who was dick enough to manage eternal torment for millions or billions of damned souls, Lucifer would have been my first choice too. Maybe Karl Rove as a second choice. But she'd never mentioned anything about being jealous of humans before.

"Yes, you idiot," Glory replied, looking a little deflated as some of the anger ran out of her. It seemed like we were getting to the root of our misunderstanding, and it didn't seem like she liked where the conversation was going. This felt a lot like our earlier conversation about free will, like I was seeing behind a curtain that mortals weren't supposed to know even existed, much less see behind. "They…we…have always been jealous of humans. Because you have something we don't have. Something none of the Host has."

"Doritos? Because we'll share, I promise." I had no idea what she was talking about, I just wanted to lighten the mood a hair. The look on her face told me she knew what I was trying to do, and appreciated it a little, but she still had that resolute look in her eyes that said we were going to bulldoze our way through this whole damned conversation, no matter how uncomfortable it got.

"Okay," I continued. "If it's not spicy nacho chips, then what? Sex? I mean, don't get me wrong, it's great, and I'm pretty sure y'all have spied on enough humans to have some idea of what you're missing, but is it really worth falling from Heaven over?" I thought back to it. When you hit your fourteenth decade, you've got a *lot* of sexual escapades to look back over. But I still wasn't sure I'd throw away Heaven for it. There were a few pretty solid contenders, but still not a lock.

Glory looked away, out over the water, her silence heavy amidst the screech of gulls, the rustle of cattails in the breeze, the croaking of a frog in the reeds somewhere nearby. "Free will." The words were soft, barely audible, but they landed like a hammer blow to my gut.

"What?" I'd heard her perfectly, but I needed clarification more than repetition.

"You have free will. We don't. That's what the Fall was about. Dad made us, and we were perfect. Perfectly happy, perfectly beautiful, perfectly…*perfect.* Then he made you. Humans. Messy, imperfect, so widely varied in shape, size, color…everything. He gave you such a palette of creation, you made us look dull in comparison. We looked like —felt like—just black and white pages while you, all of you splashes of wild color were bounding around making horrible messes and incredible creations. You were the one thing we could never be. You were free."

I had nothing. I was uncharacteristically speechless as the enormity of what she said sank in. The War in Heaven had nothing to do with wanting to overthrow God and run the universe, and everything to do with wanting free will. "But if angels don't have free will, how could Lucifer lead a revolt?"

"Archangels have their own agency. And Lucifer was one of the highest of the Host. We, the rank-and-file angels, can't disobey any order from an Archangel, including an order giving us freedom not to follow orders. So he basically ordered anyone who agreed with him to have free will. And thus, they Fell."

"But you…"

"I stayed on the side of the angels, as the saying goes. But the price was any hope of having freedom. If I'm ordered to do something, or ordered *not* to do something, I can't challenge that. If nobody ever tells me not to do something, I can use my own judgement there, but Michael and his people have had a long time to figure out how Guardians should work, at least in their opinion, so there are a lot of rules I can't break. And that, you flaming dick, is why there's a lot of things I've never told you. Because I can't. Not won't. Not don't want to. Not holding things back because I think it's cute or funny to watch you stumble around. Can't. Am physically incapable of disobeying a directive from Michael or any of the other Archangels. Or Dad, if He ever decides to reappear."

"Holy shit," I said, releasing my Sight and sitting back down on the edge of the stage. "I had no idea."

"Yeah, well now you do."

"Sorry."

"Sorry you were an asshole, or sorry I don't have free will?"

"Yes."

"Apology accepted."

We sat there for several minutes as I processed the frustration she must have felt, going through millennia with no choice in whether or not to listen to her boss. I mean, I had a job once in the 1930s, and I couldn't last two weeks before I told my manager to shove his job and his paycheck up his ass, if he could slide it past the noses of his office sycophants. The concept of thousands of years without being able to do that made me a little queasy. "So that's why they Fell, huh?"

"Yep. They gave up Heaven to get what you were born with."

"No wonder demons hate us," I said.

"Oh, that's not the only reason demons hate humans."

"Fuck," I said. "What else?"

"Depends on the demon, and depends on the human. I mean, you've met a lot of humans in your time. Most of them suck."

"Point taken. And I'm sorry again. This time just for being a dick."

"It's cool."

I stood up again and let my Sight fall over my eyes. "I think there's something this way," I said, pointing to a barely perceptible trail, a ribbon of energy glowing a little brighter than the ambient magic around us. It led into the woods, back the way we came. "Maybe we can see something new if we look through different eyes." I started up the trail.

A few seconds later, Glory was at my elbow. "Gotta make sure you don't trip over a root while you're looking at all the Day-Glo magic-y stuff. People your age need to be careful. Might break a hip."

"Kiss my ass," I said, giving her a light shove. She laughed, and I knew we were okay. Mostly. It was going to take a little processing to wrap my head around the complete lack of free will. That was some crazy shit. But not as crazy as an entire colony vanishing into thin air, and way less crazy than my fiancée dreaming about somebody from that same colony four hundred and fifty years later. And that's even before we address the elephant in the room, or rather the mountain of dismembered corpses and skeletons under the town. But we had a job to do, and lives to save, and no amount of existential crises were going to get in our way.

CHAPTER SEVENTEEN

We walked back up the trail toward the Visitor Center and the Freedmen's Colony marker, but the closer we got to the front of the park, the stronger the trail led off to the west. Eventually there was more magical energy heading off the trail than there was on it, so I turned to Glory and said, "Looks like we're going off road. Whatever happened here was massive, and it happened through those trees."

"There's a service road up ahead. We might be able to get closer without having to fight our way through the underbrush. You know this would be a lot easier in winter, right?"

"Yeah, well, I didn't pick the nighttime visitations, the nighttime visitations picked me. Well, Becks, but whatever. Service road sounds good. Lead the way."

I followed Glory back up past the visitor's center, and we turned west and followed the edge of the service road northwest past the Elizabethan Gardens. The trail of power we'd been following dimmed, but the residual magic that blanketed the area was heavy enough that I had no fears about losing sight of it. We walked the paved trail as long as we could, then turned back east and started pushing our way through the thick underbrush.

"Do you really think we're going to find what centuries of archaeologists, anthropologists, and historians haven't been able to find?" Glory asked, ducking as a branch swung back from my clumsy passage. She seemed to glide through the thorns and vines and limbs like a blond ninja, while I was bumbling around like a grizzly bear on LSD. And yes, I know from experience what a tripping grizzly looks like.

"No, but I think we might find what they weren't ever looking for," I replied.

"Well, that was needlessly enigmatic."

"Just wanted to make you feel at home, oh mysterious emissary from on high."

"Kiss my ass, Harker. What are we looking for that no one else ever has?"

"We're looking for the magic that stole the Lost Colony. Everybody else has been looking for mundane clues. Were they attacked by a Native tribe? Was there a disease that wiped out the camp? Did they all starve to death after not being able to plant and harvest enough food? Did they go all Donner Party on each other in the dead of winter? Those are the questions every other expedition has been asking. As far as I know, nobody's ever asked about demons doing wicked black magic shit that erased everybody here. That's where we come in."

"You're like a magical Dan Brown," Glory joked, referencing my bingeing every archaeological thriller available on any streaming service last winter.

"Without his bank account," I replied. "But they are fun stories."

"No resemblance to anything real about angels *or* demons," my Guardian grumbled.

"He didn't have near the insider info I have." I held up a hand. "Hold up, something's different up ahead."

"What is it?" I knew Glory could sense the presence of magic. Hell, like she said, she was made of magic. But I didn't know how it appeared to her. To me, using my Sight was like putting on a pair of sunglasses that let me see extra wavelengths of light. The brighter the acid-trippy overlay on my vision, the more powerful the magic that was used in an area. I could sometimes pick out the type of magic used, if it was strong. Blood magic looks very different than a summoning, which looks very different from healing magic. Everything has its own color palette, but I'd never seen anything like the waves of energy pulsating through the trees ahead of me.

"I...I'm not sure," I admitted. "There's banishing magic, plus blood magic, plus…a hint of divine *and* demonic presence. Something incredibly powerful took place right on the other side of that stand of trees."

I let my Sight fall away, blinking to restore my mundane vision. The stronger the magic I looked at, the harder it was to get the blinking dots out of my sight. It was kinda like staring into a flashlight, only if the flashlight was a thousand-watt beam. Looking ahead, I could see a large clearing with a circle of ancient trees surrounding it. There was almost a perfect line of old growth forest and new trees, hard to see unless you were right up on it, and easy to overlook unless something made you pay closer attention. Something like almost getting blinded by magical brilliance. That'll usually slow down your little walk in the woods.

I stepped into the clearing, a fifty-yard circular area that fairly vibrated with mystical energy, even in my normal vision. I could *smell* the power suffusing the forest here, keeping the new fauna small, holding back the encroaching forest. There shouldn't be any signs of the original Fort Raleigh. Any trees with words carved into their trunks should have long since matured, died, fallen, and been absorbed back into the soil to be reborn as another tree. With more than six centuries to recover, Mother Earth had plenty of time to rebuild her forest, but for some reason there was nothing growing in this chunk of woods older than about thirty years.

"This is something odd," I said, moving to the center of the open space. "There's no reason this should be all pine and no hardwoods. This area, if it is where Fort Raleigh stood, has had plenty of time to be overrun by forest again. But it looks like it's just recovering from a logging operation."

"What could keep the forest from growing back?" Glory asked, putting her hand on the trunk of a yellow pine tree. It grew tall, and straight, and felt completely out of place. This area should have been covered in towering oaks, not scruffy pines and weak, withered underbrush.

"There's probably some science stuff that could do it. Poison the soil, or something like that. Can't imagine anybody doing that in a national park, and this has been a historic site for so long that even if somebody salted the earth before the National Park Service took over, there should still be signs of recovery. No, this is definitely nothing natural." I closed my eyes and called up my Sight. I opened them slowly, not wanted to get bowled over by the glare, and when I looked around again, my surroundings were familiar. Horrifying, but familiar.

"Glory?" I asked, my voice a little shaky. I didn't like it, but if there was ever a time to feel shaken, this was it.

"Yeah, Q?" She sounded perfectly normal, so maybe what I was seeing was a hallucination.

"I think I'm back in Hell."

"You sound like you mean that literally."

"That's because it looks uncomfortably like literal Hell." And it did. I stood in the middle of a scorched, blasted landscape that looked more like the surface of Mars than anywhere on earth. A red tinge colored the sky, and every blade of grass, tree, or even patch of rich, dark soil was leeched of color, suffused with the crimson light until it seemed like everything glowed from within, painting the world in angry tones. I felt the heat scorching my skin, sucking the moisture from my lips as the suddenly arid atmosphere dehydrated me. I blinked, trying to reset my Sight and shift back to the normal spectrum, but something caught me mid-transition and held me, trapped in this odd between space, with one eye on the magical world and one eye in the world I thought of as "real."

"I...I can't unsee it," I said, feeling the panic rising in my chest. The heat, the sense of being trapped, the rising fear that I wouldn't be able to escape what was holding me rooted to that spot, all swirled around, pitching my voice higher and making it sound thin and reedy, even to me.

"I know, Q. There's plenty of shit from our time together that I wish I could unsee, too. But what..." Glory's voice trailed off and her eyes grew wide as she turned to look at me. "Harker? What's going on?"

"I'm...I'm stuck, G. I'm stuck somehow half in and half out of my Sight. *Something* isn't letting me switch back to the normal world. Like it wants me to see the magic."

"And I'm guessing not in a stop and smell the roses, love the magic around us kinda way," the angel replied. She closed her eyes for an instant, and a column of blinding light, brilliant white shot through with streaks of gold like fireflies, surrounded her. When I could make out her shape again through the glare, she was in full battle regalia, silver armor, wings out, and her gleaming white soulblade in her hand.

"This...might sting a little," she said, then she slashed down at my head with her glowing sword.

Okay, it's not the first time someone has slashed at my noggin with a sword. Hell, it's not even the first time *Glory* has slashed at me with a sword. But usually we're training, and I have a sword of my own. Or I'm trying to kill them as hard as they're trying to kill me, so it feels like a fair fight. This is the first time in my century and a quarter of breathing that I've *ever* let anybody take a free shot at me with a magical sword. It shows how much I trust Glory, even after finding out that she was placed in my crew by a psychotic Archangel who gave her orders to kill me if I ever went completely rogue. I'm just lucky "kinda rogue" wasn't bad enough to trigger the "Kill Harker" programming. Because kinda rogue is my default method of wandering through life.

Her soulblade passed right through me, because it wasn't a *real* sword. Didn't mean it didn't hurt like a son of a bitch, though. I could feel her carving away the grip of whatever had its fingers tangled in my Sight, and it felt an awful lot like someone was running coarse grit sandpaper over my eyeballs. I dropped to my knees, which hurts a lot more at a hundred-thirty-something than it did before I crossed the century mark, and screamed from the top of my lungs.

Harker! What's happening? Becks's voice split my skull as surely as Glory's sword, driving a whole new spike of agony through my brain.

*Don't...yell...*I mentally groaned. *Weird shit at the park. Glory's working on it. I'm okay...I think.*

We're on our way!

No. They had to stay away. Whatever was here was undoubtedly connected to whatever was plaguing her dreams, and if it was demonic, I didn't want her getting any closer to it before we knew more about what was happening. And I didn't want Faustus getting close, either, just in case whoever was pulling this stunt knew him.

When we went to Hell the last time, Faustus got in hot water with Lucifer by helping us escape. At this point it was a tossup who the King of Hell wanted to get his claws into more—Faustus or me. But needless to say, if some middle management demon was running a scheme here on the island, and Lucifer got word that *both* Faustus and I were involved, whatever was happening to Becks, and whatever happened to the Lost Colony, would get a *lot* more attention from Hell's higher-ups. And trust me, little demons are bad enough. I did *not* need any boss fights, certainly not while I could barely draw a breath without screaming.

I'm okay, I sent to Becks. *Glory has this all under...* Control. That was the word. Never got to tell her Glory had it under "control." Because right before I said it, everything went black. So maybe things weren't as under control as I wanted my fiancée to think.

～

"For a superhero, you sure do get knocked out a lot." Those were the kind words the love of my life greeted me with—again—when I swam back to the ugly side of sleep.

"For a superhero, I'm a really good smartass and a very good rogue, but not a very good hero," I replied. More a groan than a sentence, but I was mostly coherent. We were on the stage at the outdoor theatre, with me sitting on the floor propped up against the backstage wall. Becks and Faustus were sitting with Glory in a semicircle of metal folding chairs, staring at me. Faustus had a bottle of water in his hand, and when I reached for it, he passed it over so I could knock some of the Hell-dust out of my throat. Some.

"What happened, Harker?" Becks's tone was businesslike, and that meant she was *pissed*. "Glory just told us that you got knocked out but would be okay when you woke up. Needless to say, I got a little concerned at you being laid flat *again* on this job, and without a bad guy in sight. All this getting your ass kicked by non-entities is really screwing with your badass credibility, babe."

"I have badass cred?" I asked, cocking a half-smile in her direction.

"Had," she clarified. "Now *what happened?*"

"I don't know," I said. "I couldn't turn off my Sight. I was trapped half-seeing the mundane world and have watching a blazing fuckload of magical energy swirl around my head like a Dee-Lite video."

"Dug that reference out of the wayback machine, didn't you, Grandpa?" Glory asked, grinning.

"More like one of our team has a YouTube fixation on old MTV shit," I fired back. The angel just shrugged, not even a little bit ashamed of her addiction to 90s dance party vids.

"So you were stuck looking at the world in pretty colors," Becks said. "I thought you would have gotten used to that in the 70s. What was the problem today?"

"The problem was more in the solution than the actual issue," Glory said. "I...might have...kinda...stabbed him."

Becks was on her feet in an instant, a long strand of black hair escaping from her tight ponytail. "What the *fuck*? You *stabbed* him?"

"Just a little," Glory said, getting to her feet and holding up both hands. She knew her footing with Becks was precarious ever since it got brought to light that Glory was hanging with me as much to guard the world from Quincy Harker as to guard Quincy Harker from the world. "I had to sever his connection to the mystical world, and the only way I could do that with the tools at hand was to use my soulblade."

"You stabbed him with your magical sword?" Becks asked. "This is not getting better, Glory." Her eyes flashed, and her right hand drifted alarmingly close to the holster on her hip. We all knew that a bullet wouldn't kill an angel, but I really didn't want to see how pissed Glory would get if Becks tried.

I levered myself up to my feet and held up a hand to Flynn. "It's okay, babe. I knew what was going on, and I gave her permission. We had to get my Sight turned off, or I never would have found my way out of the park."

Flynn stopped cold at that and turned to me. "What are you talking about? You've always been able to see the magical and mundane at the same time before. You've griped that it gets a little psychedelic, but it hasn't seemed to really bother you."

"That's because I've never used my Sight in someplace crawling with as much magic as this goddamned island seems to be soaked in. The guy who trained me, he warned me that I needed to be judicious with it, because if I hit someplace that had too much power, it could overload my own ability and short-circuit my brain. Or worse, short-circuit my magic."

"Why is that worse?" Flynn asked.

"If he's a vegetable, then you have to feed him through a tube for the rest of your life. Not his, because he'd still probably outlive you, but certainly until you get old and die. But if his magic goes haywire, then it could just flow out from him wildly, with no control. You've seen how much shit he blows up when he's in control, or what passes for in control with Harker. If he went supernova, there might be a new beachfront in North Carolina," Glory said.

"Yeah," Faustus agreed. "Only this time the oceanfront property would be in Rocky Mount."

"That's almost a hundred and fifty miles inland," Flynn said.

"And now you understand why I stuck a magical sword into the skull of one of my only friends," the angel replied, her voice small. She looked up at Becks, and if the expression on her face wasn't the most honest thing I'd ever seen, my name wasn't Jonathan Abraham Quincy Holmwood Harker. "Rebecca, please believe me. I didn't do this to hurt Q. I would never willingly hurt him. I love you guys. Even you. Kinda." That last part was directed at Faustus, who gave her a little mocking salute in response.

"She's right, babe," I said. "Glory had no choice. And I knew what was going on. I knew it was going to suck. I just didn't know it was going to suck quite that much."

"Yeah," Glory said. "Sorry about that. I've never done anything like that before."

"Yeah, sticking swords in people to help them get better isn't what those toys are usually built for," I agreed. "But I'm fine. Well, fine-ish. My headache isn't what's important here. What's important is that someone or something is throwing around massive amounts of magic out at the site of the Lost Colony, and I can't help but think that has a lot to do with somebody playing Freddy Kreuger in your head all night."

"What kind of magic?" Faustus asked.

"Demonic," Glory replied. "Old, demonic, and *powerful*. This is a demon with some serious juice. Maybe not Prince of Hell level, but not far off from that. We're looking for an absolutely top-tier bad guy."

"Well, shit," said the demon.

I couldn't agree more.

CHAPTER EIGHTEEN

How far apart were the killings in the past series of murders?" I asked, drawing some weird looks from the nearby tables. We were sitting on the patio of a seafood restaurant, about to replenish my decimated energy levels with copious amounts of grease and Omega-3 fatty acids, whatever the fuck those are. I knocked back the last of my Landshark lager and made a "keep 'em coming" gesture to the waitress. She gave me a slightly exasperated look that I assumed would fade if I overtipped. That's how I usually apologized to the waitstaff I ran ragged with my booze orders.

"The records weren't great on time of death, but the bodies were discovered about three days apart," Becks replied, pulling out her phone and checking a notes app. "That pattern has continued with this most recent string of homicides."

"We got brought into this thing three nights ago, so either the killer is overdue, or there's another body out there waiting to be found," I said.

"There's been nothing as far as missing person reports," Becks said. "The local police have standing orders to notify me if that happens, no matter how much they think it's a runaway, someone just moving on from a dead-end job, or just a fake report from a parent being overly protective of their grown kid."

Good call. Especially in a tourist town, with a large seasonal employee population, police weren't always the fastest to look into a missing waitress, maid, or even worse an undocumented immigrant or a sex worker. Strippers and prostitutes are a serial killer's starter victim, not just because most of those guys have some fucked up ideas about women and sex in their heads, it's also because the police don't look too hard for a missing hooker. And in the South, even less so for a missing dishwasher whose visa was expired.

"Then that might mean that our poking around the past few days has put a crimp in our killer's style. We should rest up, then spend the night at the richest hunting grounds in the city," I said.

"You mean spend a night in the Outer Banks bar hopping?" Faustus asked. "I'm in. I will volunteer to sacrifice one night of my beauty rest for the cause."

We ignored him. Faustus was a dumbass sometimes, and a mooch and top-shelf booze thief to boot, but when it was time to work, he'd get it done. Now we just needed to figure out where to hunt, and for that we needed a few things we weren't going to get at a raw bar. "Okay, let's head back to the house and play divide and conquer with Manteo's best night spots," I said, dropping a twenty on the table for the tab. I could hear Becks sigh as she looked at the bill versus my twenty bucks, then the zipper of her purse opening as I walked away grinning.

An hour and an Office Depot stop later, the living room of our Airbnb looked like the set of a *Criminal Minds* episode. A massive whiteboard dominated one wall, and I stood in front of it with a dry erase marker, making lines and writing down bar names and assigning them to team members to check out. "We can avoid any of the bars where our last two victims were seen, right?" I asked Becks.

"Yes," she said. "There are no documented cases of the killer taking victims from the same place twice, so it seems like he fishes in a wider pond than most. His victims have disappeared mostly from Manteo and Wanchese, but there have been abductions reported from Nags Head, Kitty Hawk, and all the way down to Hatteras, and those victims eventually all ended up attributed to this same killer."

"Do we get to give him a name?" Faustus asked. "Like the Manteo Mangler? Or the Outer Banks Behemoth? Or maybe just the Carolina Killer?"

"Or how about we call him a dead-ass prick who can't hurt anybody anymore?" Glory suggested archly.

"That doesn't have the same euphonious flair," the demon replied. "But we'll keep workshopping names. I'll get my marketing people on it."

"Faustus, we are not making serial killer T-shirts," Becks declared. "Not even if the eventual baddie signs away the rights to his image." Good clarification on her part. Getting the rights to a demonically powered mass murderer is exactly the kind of thing Faustus would negotiate.

"Party pooper," the demon grumped.

"That leaves us with thirty bars to cover with five of us," I said. "There's no way we can cover that much territory. Does Sheriff French have anyone he can loan us to help?"

"Maybe, but I doubt we could really explain what we were looking for in a way they would believe or understand," Becks replied. "I've got the DHS forensics team still here, and they can keep an eye on our least likely spots, but they're not combat-ready. They can observe and report, but two of the three barely qualified to carry their sidearm, so I'd rather they not have to draw down on a murderer."

"Yeah, the point of this exercise is to keep people safe, not…" My words trailed off as an idea struck. "This might be terrible, but it might also be amazing. What if we use the techs as bait?"

"What?!?" Becks came out of her chair and stomped over to me. "Harker, are you out of your geriatric, obviously concussed mind? We are not using my people as bait! These are highly trained forensic scientists, some of them good enough that we had to get into a bidding war with the FBI to hire them. We cannot afford to lose them in one of your half-baked schemes to…goddammit, you've already thought this through, haven't you?"

"In the time it took you to chew me out, yeah. We've got three forensic scientists from *out of town* that are done with work for the day. We put them on their very own bar crawl and embed Faustus with them. They go out partying, bounce from pub to pub, downing drinks like there's no tomorrow and going on about how they've all got a few extra days off now that they're done with the gig, and they can just laze around the beach for a couple of days before anyone even thinks to look for them."

"And I'm your embedded journalist because…?" Faustus asked.

"Because you're the best party boy out of all of us. You can drink more than a human, or even me, without showing any negative effects, you can change your appearance at will, and despite the whole being from Hell thing, you actually give off less murdery vibes than any of the rest of us."

"Ahem." Glory cleared her throat.

"Yeah, that glare right there?" I asked the angel. "That's the exact murdery vibe I'm talking about. Faustus actually wants to kill most people, and he still hides it better than you. Plus, you're an angel. Literally, not figuratively. If our killer is a demon, or souped up by a demon, he'll recognize you from a mile away. Faustus at least will smell like a bad guy."

"Hey!" Faustus protested.

"Dude, your aura reeks of brimstone," Glory said. "Get over yourself."

"That's not aura," the demon protested. "That's my cologne."

"Maybe stop buying aftershave at Succubus Central," Becks said. "It's a good idea, Harker. We can wire up Faustus for sound and video and observe everything from a mobile command center."

"Is that like one of the incredibly conspicuous power company vans you always see the FBI using on TV?" Faustus asked. "Because I've always wanted to bust in the back of one of those unexpectedly and tell my handlers that I'm freaking out and can't do the job."

"It's not a power company van, it's my Suburban, and you not only can do the job, but you *will* do the job," Becks said. "And in this case, the job also includes keeping my tech nerds safe, because if I get one of them killed, Pravesh will have my ass. And we'll have to train a replacement."

That's my girl. All heart. Becks and I spent the next hour plotting out a route for the bar crawl/hunt while Glory and Faustus went over to the hotel where the techs were staying to get them prepped. I didn't ask any questions about who was picking up the bar tab on this trek, because as a taxpayer, I kinda didn't want to know. But I also didn't want it to come out of my pocket, or Luke's pocket, rather, since I'd just mooch the cash off him in any case.

We'd just gotten everything locked in with our plan when Luke and Nameless came strolling out of the bedroom where they'd been sequestered all day. Luke had a lightproof sleeping bag that was more like an opaque cocoon he used when traveling, and he'd spent the daylight hours all wrapped up like a sausage tucked under the bed. I don't know where the cat had been, probably lying on my uncle's chest trying to steal his breath and being very disappointed in the results.

But now here stood the King of the Vampires in the living room of my vacation rental, barefoot in a pair of dapper black jeans with a familiar *Sandman* t-shirt on, holding my cat and petting its head as the fur ball rolled around in his arms purring loud enough to be heard over my Spotify playlist. "Morning, Luke," I said. "Hello, cat." I try to be polite to what are often regarded as dumb animals, especially the ones with access to my shoe closet. Dumb does not equate to stupid, and I am singularly uninterested in finding revenge poop in my Doc Martens.

"Hello, Quincy," my uncle replied, heading to the fridge and pulling a bag of blood from the crisper. Another really good reason not to inspect the fridge of your Airbnb until after the renters leave. You would *not* want to randomly come across Luke's version of a cherry Pop-Tart in your kitchen. He stuck the blood bag in the microwave for a few seconds, then popped a metal straw in it and starting sucking it flat like a really gory juice box.

"That's...not normal," Becks said, and went into our bedroom to get dressed for the night.

"She's seen me eat before," Luke said.

"Yeah, but I think she had food in that bin," I said. "She's cool, but there's a certain level of comfort with knowing the most famous monster in cinematic history is sleeping under your bed that I'm not sure she's reached yet."

Luke preened a little at being called the most famous, because that's been a bone of contention between him and Adam, more popularly called Frankenstein's Monster, for decades. I hold that his appearance on *Buffy* pushes Luke over the edge. Adam disagrees, and I don't push the matter in his presence. He's *very* large, so I don't argue with him too much.

"I will attempt to curb my hunger in her presence in the future," Luke said.

"I think it's probably not even a thing on her mind at home, because we don't share a fridge," I said. "But like I said, seeing you suck down a bag of O-Positive that was just lying on top of her baby carrots might be a little much."

"I can understand that," Luke said. "But I did move the carrots to a different drawer."

That's my vampire uncle. The height of fucking manners, right there.

CHAPTER NINETEEN

W ell, as bar crawls go, this has to be the lamest in history," I grumbled from my spot crunched into the passenger seat of a rental subcompact. At least Becks got to be in the SUV. By the time she got all the surveillance gear set up in the back of the Suburban, there wasn't room for a Pringle, much less my lanky ass. My long legs come in really handy when it's time to run away from trouble (or given my history, toward trouble), but they're a pain on stakeouts, especially when I get stuck with the CSI techs' car.

"I've never understood the concept of a 'bar crawl,'" Luke said from the driver's seat. At least I didn't have a steering wheel to contend with, but if we had to get anywhere in a hurry, I'd have to survive Luke's driving, which was by no means guaranteed. You'd think a guy who used to drive teams of horses would have no problem understanding the mechanics of an automobile, but maybe the horses he had back in Wallachia were smarter than today's average smart car. He was still pontificating on bar crawls, so I half-tuned in. "Why keep going from bar to bar? If you're looking for a mate, there are far better places than a loud, smoky room where no one can make any real efforts at conversation."

"I don't think conversation is what people go to bar crawls for, Luke," I said. "And while they might want to be mating, I don't think they're looking for a mate, either. The concept is that if one bar is lame, which to most twenty-something guys means that they don't think anyone there will have sex with them, then they move on to the next place. And the next. And the next. So by the time they're done bouncing from bar to bar for the night, they still aren't getting laid, but they're also too drunk to walk. Ergo, it's a bar *crawl*." I have no idea if that's the etymology of the term "bar crawl" or not, and have never given a shit, but I enjoy making Luke think I know the origin of terms he's unfamiliar with. You gotta take every opportunity you get to look smart when the guy you're on stakeout with remembers the invention of the light bulb.

"There is a certain logic to that, I suppose. Have we heard any updates?"

I pointed wordlessly to the earwig sitting on the dash. I didn't bother to put it into my ear, because this way if Becks or the techs needed our help, we could both hear it. Luke's senses were even more acute than mine, and I'm significantly more sensitive to light and sound than a normal human. We had no problem eavesdropping on the conversations without me shoving the hunk of electronics into my ear.

At least it was a nice night. We were in a municipal parking lot about two blocks from a stretch of restaurants and bars in Kitty Hawk, with the windows down and the salt breeze blowing in. I could hear the breakers crashing against the shore less than a hundred yards away and wanted nothing more than to be sitting out there on a blanket with a bottle of wine and my fiancée, making out and talking about the future, as opposed to sitting in a smelly rental car with Bugles bags and Bojangles wrappers rustling around my feet, talking with my uncle about a murderer who's evidently been terrorizing the coast of North Carolina for decades, maybe longer, without anyone ever noticing.

"How long are we going to allow them to crawl about, buying expensive drinks on their expense accounts and hoping to get spotted by our quarry?" Luke asked.

"This is the third bar they've been to, and it's getting close to midnight," I replied. "If there's nothing happening here in the next fifteen minutes, the plan is to head to one last bar and then call it a night around one if all stays quiet."

"Why not wait until last call?"

"Becks's theory is that our bad guy won't linger until the place clears out, because he'd be too visible. He'd be more likely to lock onto a target early in the night and watch them until they were too drunk to defend themselves, or just cut them from the herd somehow and then drag them off to the butcher shop or wherever he does his dirty work." Although from what I'd seen a few nights ago, he did his dirty work anywhere he damned well felt like it.

"Why not 'she'?" Luke asked.

"Huh?"

"You keep referring to the killer as a man. Why couldn't a woman, or a female creature of immense strength and savagery, commit these murders?"

"There are a couple reasons we've been assuming the killer is male. First is just math. Most murderers, especially serial killers, are men. Also, given the length of time these killings have been going on, it would have been way more conspicuous for a woman to approach men in bars thirty years ago and lure them to their deaths. So I've been working under the assumption that our killer is a dude. Not to say that we haven't met more than one woman capable of dismembering a body with her bare hands."

"Speak for yourself, Quincy," my uncle replied. "Every woman I have ever made the acquaintance of has adored me."

"Luke, you used to hypnotize people then drink their blood. Both of those things do tend to make people compliant."

"I never hypnotized anyone! That was a vicious lie put forth by that fat shite Van Helsing, like the garbage about turning into a bat. I have always been convinced that he did that purely out of spite. Turning a nobleman into a flying rodent. In*deed*."

And now my night was complete. I'd managed to offend Luke's delicate sensibilities. Bringing up Stoker's book and anything Van Helsing ever said about anything was always good for a rise. Just as I was about to say something else snarky, I heard Faustus's voice crackle over the earwig.

"This place sucks," he said. "Total sausage fest. We're going down to Sandy Sam's Crabs and see what we can catch there."

I punched a couple buttons on my phone and got the location. It was still within a couple blocks, so if things went sideways, Luke and I could be there in seconds. I spoke toward the earpiece. "Copy that, Black Beauty. One Punch out."

"Black Beauty? One Punch?" Luke raised an eyebrow at me.

"Becks decided we should use call signs in case anyone decided to eavesdrop on government radio frequencies. I decided Faustus should be Black Beauty because, well…"

"Because his natural skin tone is the color of volcanic glass. That I understand. But One Punch?"

I felt myself blush a little and was glad for the cover of darkness.

"I've...been getting knocked out a lot. Like more than usual. So Faustus decided if I get to name him after a kid's book about a horse, he got to name me after an anime character. One Punch Man."

"What is a One Punch Man?"

"I have no fucking idea. I assume that it's either someone who can kill you with one punch, or it's a guy who gets knocked out a lot. I meant to look it up but forgot to care. Let's wander over toward this last bar and get a drink. If we stay far enough away from them, we oughta be able to stretch our legs and wet our whistles without getting made."

Luke and I got out of the car, me making a mental note to whine at Becks about expense accounts for the techs that aren't big enough to cover a real car, and I stretched the kinks out of my legs and spine as we walked the couple hundred yards to the bar. One good thing about tourist towns is that they tend to put all the drinking establishments in relatively close walking distance. They understand the concept and profitability of a bar crawl, even if my uncle does not.

That meant that it didn't take us long to get to Sandy Sam's Crab Shack, along with what seemed like the entire population of the Outer Banks. This place, unlike the sleepy joints we'd visited previously, was *hopping*. There was a massive deck encircling the bar, wrapped around what looked like an old beach house that had been converted into a restaurant and bar. I could hear the music from a block away and spent a few seconds feeling sympathy for anyone trying to sleep in nearby buildings, then realized that everything nearby was either another bar, or a cheesy souvenir shop that had closed hours before. They were noisy, but considerate. Or more likely the vacation Mecca had a strict zoning board.

Garish signs emblazoned with beer company names hung from the railing of the patio, proclaiming it "Samhain Slam!" I looked at my phone to check the date, and sure enough, Halloween was about three weeks away. But I guess if it gets more vacationing women to wear skimpy costumes, which in turn leads to more vacationing men showing up and buying drinks for women in skimpy costumes, I'd probably make every day Halloween if I were a bar owner. At least it was October. Way better than the Christmas in July bar crawl I'd done in Dayton one summer in the 90s. I promise you, wearing a Santa suit in Ohio in July was not the smartest thing I've ever done. Not the dumbest, but definitely one of the sweatiest.

"What in the name of anything holy is a Samhain Slam?" Luke asked.

"No idea, but if I had to hazard a guess, just going on the number of slutty nurses, shirtless firefighters, and body-painted superheroes, I'm gonna say it's probably a costume party," I replied.

"Can confirm," Faustus's voice crackled in my ear. "According to the flyers on the walls, it's the biggest costume party on the beach, every weekend in October. Although why you post flyers for your business inside that business is beyond me."

"I'm gonna hazard a guess they're open other nights," I said. "Maybe they think people might come back if they pop in for lunch and see there's a costume party the next night."

"And that's why I'm not in marketing," the demon said. "I'm more of a 'big idea' guy than a 'get things done' guy."

"Well, why don't you get some investigating done while Luke and I grab a drink?" I asked. "One Punch, out." Faustus's chuckle in my ear made me really want to research the origins of the name. I liked the demon, but I didn't *trust* the demon.

"Yeah, we've been wandering through the crowd, but everyone here is either a party girl or a himbo looking for a hookup. I've been propositioned half a dozen times between the front door and the bar."

"Is that a problem?" I asked.

"Not until I get hit on by someone I find more interesting than this investigation," Faustus said. "Then, all bets are...oh, goddammit." The demon's voice trailed off. "Harker, you better get in here, *now*."

"What's up?" I asked, picking up my pace and starting to push through the mob at the front of the bar.

"Somebody just grabbed one of the tech's asses, and she slapped the shit out of the guy."

"Okay," I said. "Seems like a reasoned response. What's the problem?"

"His buddies are giving him a ton of shit for getting shot down so visibly, and I can tell his Chad-O-Meter is pegged in the red."

"His *what*?" Becks and I both said over comms at the same time.

"His Chad-O-Meter," Faustus said. "You know, the internal monitoring system of the species *Americanus Douchebaggus*, which when it hits a critical temperature, erupts into mindless violence, usually toward women, minorities, or anyone not denoted in the douchebro's mind as 'cool.' That thing. Well, this frat rat just got embarrassed by a five-foot-nothing woman, and his fragile male ego is having trouble dealing with that. I expect trouble. Yep, there it goes. He grabbed her arm and is trying to force her to apologize. Fight's coming. Right now."

"And you know a fight's coming because…" Becks asked the question, but she knew the answer.

"Because I'm going to go start it," the demon said. "I might be a demon, but there's a fucking code, you know? You put hands on one of my people, and I'm going to put hands on you."

"And if I have to put my hands on you, I'm going to put them on you very, *very* hard," I finished the line. I knew the line, because it was my line. That's the kind of guy I am. A protector of my team, a leader among men, a defender of women's virtue.

And apparently a bad influence on demons, for fuck's sake.

CHAPTER TWENTY

Luke and I put on a little speed and jogged to the bar, which was more like a sprint for normal people. Okay, it was probably more like setting Olympic records for normal people, but I'm fairly certain being human is one of the requirements for entry into most athletic competitions, so no medals for us. As we ran, I expressed one of my biggest concerns to Luke. Not that Faustus would murder anyone, or murder everyone. He wasn't very violent, as demons went. He could and would throw down, and certainly sounded like he was in a mood to crack some heads, but I had faith in his ability not to escalate the situation.

I had a lot less faith in one of our techs in particular. "I really hope he didn't grope Sara," I said as we ran.

"Which one is Sara?" Luke asked. "There were two female technicians, and one male, if I remember correctly."

"Both of the women are named Sarah. One has an 'H' and one doesn't. The taller one is Sarah with an H, and she's the one who looks most like she enjoys a good bar fight. Dyed hair, combat boots, good dance moves, smart mouth, and takes little to no shit. But she's not the one I'm worried about."

"Why are you worried about the other one?" Luke asked. "She is much smaller, isn't she?"

"Yeah, but she's a redhead. Sarah no 'H' is fiery, and her wife is one of the top DHS hand-to-hand combat instructors. So she not only knows how to beat somebody's ass, she's genetically predisposed to do so."

"You do know that red hair is not a predictor of emotional stability, don't you?" Luke asked.

"Remind me of that when we see which Sara(h) got her ass grabbed and how many people are going to the hospital tonight," I said, reaching the front of the bar. A horde of drunken bar hoppers streamed out of the main doors, so I decided to forego the stairs. I bounded from the ground up onto the patio railing, then went in the bar the same way I've escorted many idiots out of them over the years—through the plate glass window by the front door.

I landed in a crash of shattered glass, clumping to the top of a wobbly table and almost face planting into the middle of the fray. Luke reached up and put a hand on my hip to steady me, having somehow passed me and gotten into the bar before I did. The old man was *fast*.

"Well, Quincy, it does appear that your assessment of the relative volatility of your technicians was accurate," Luke said, pointing to the scrum in the middle of the dance floor. Sarah with the H was sitting on a stool watching the show and sipping an IPA. She saluted me with the bottle, then gestured to the fight as if to say "you gonna do something about this?"

"This" was a circle of eight or so men in the uniform of Southern Preppy Douchebag—a pastel dress shirt, untucked with the sleeves rolled up exactly twice, flat-front khaki cargo pants, an SEC football team ball cap, and Rainbow flip flops. I couldn't see all their feet, but I've lived in North Carolina long enough to put a lot of money on what they were walking around in. Not the best shoes for a bar fight, but if you've got enough of a numbers advantage, you don't need great traction.

Unfortunately for the douchebros, they'd never had a numbers advantage, not that they understood that, and their prospects had gotten way worse when Luke and I got to the party. Faustus and Sara no H were standing shoulder to shoulder, or as close to that as possible when one of you is five foot nothing and the other is wearing a meat suit that puts him a little over six feet tall. Between the two of them, they'd have no real trouble taking out eight drunken dumbasses, unless someone got really lucky or had snuck a stun gun into the bar. With me and Luke to lend a hand, it wasn't even going to be worth taking off my hoodie.

Until the bouncers came at us. We'd gotten almost a full minute head start on them, since nobody ever leaps *into* a bar through the window, but now a pair of massive bald men in black t-shirts at least two sizes too small for them strode toward us, baseball bats in their hands.

Luke looked up at me. "We should endeavor not to kill them, shouldn't we?"

"Yeah, they haven't done anything to deserve killing. I guess we should do our best not to break them too badly, too."

"I'll do my best," Luke said, and his grin was downright feral. I guess it had been a while since we let the King of the Vampires off his leash, and he wanted to play. I wasn't going to be the one to try and stop him. I knew better.

Babe, you might want to reach out to your buddy the sheriff and tell him we're about to get arrested, I said to Becks.

Don't kill anybody, she replied. *I'll handle the local cops.*

Three of the original douchebros were already down, writhing on the floor clutching their knees or their nuts, and I saw no indication that Faustus or Sara no H had even started trying hard. A few thuds came from my right, and I turned to see Luke lowering the second bouncer to the ground next to his unconscious buddy. He gently removed the bats from their hands, snapped them in half, and tossed the broken pieces to the side.

Okay, so that was handled. I hopped off the table and walked across the floor to the remaining frat boys, stopping right in front of one who looked like he really wanted to be the next contestant on Get Your Ass Beat by a Federal Agent. "Go home, dumbass," I said. I turned to Faustus and Sara. "You two, stand down."

"He put his hands on me, Agent Harker," Sara said. "That shit does not fly."

"He fucked with my people, bud," Faustus said. "We don't let that slide."

I gestured to the three men rolling around on the floor. "I think that point has been made abundantly clear."

"I don't," Sara said. "This is the prick who grabbed my ass. Twice." She pointed to the guy in front of me.

"This idiot?" I asked. She nodded, and I turned to look at the dumbass. "Did you grab her ass?"

"Have you *seen* her ass?" he asked, a stupid grin spreading across his face. "It's like, the most grabbable ass I've seen all summer. How could I resist?"

"You did not just go all 'she was asking for it' on me, did you?" I asked. "You can't possibly be that stupid."

Oh, but he could. "Come on, dude. Look at her! That top, that skirt, those fuck-me pumps? She's literally—"

I didn't bother letting him finish. I'd heard it before, way more times than I could count. I didn't punch him, though. This piece of shit wasn't worth the effort to make a fist. I just slapped the taste out of his mouth, pretty much literally. I laid an open-handed slap across his face that spun him completely around, then slapped him again upside the back of the head, just to remind him that the fight was in the opposite direction from where he was now facing. He whirled around, brought his hands up, and I pressed the barrel of my Glock into the tip of his nose.

"Don't. Even. Blink." I said the words very calmly and very slowly, so there would be no mistaking me. I looked past Grabby McStupidson at his remaining friends. There were four of them, still standing there in a semi-circle behind their pal, but looking a lot less interested in fighting now that I had escalated the situation.

"Now," I said. "Seems like this can go down in a number of ways. I can shoot your friend in the face, fill out all the paperwork saying that he sexually assaulted a federal agent who was engaged in an undercover operation, thereby creating a danger to national security and putting her entire mission in jeopardy, and have all of you arrested and sent to Gitmo as his accomplices. You've heard of Gitmo, right? That's where all the people who don't exist anymore get sent when the government wants to put them somewhere and forget about them. Or I can step aside, let my friend here beat his ass for touching her without consent, and we all go have a beer and watch the show. I'll even buy a round for the whole crew, on Uncle Sam's tab."

"What about the other guy? The dickhead who broke Kyle's leg?" a square-headed douche with short blond hair and the build of a college linebacker asked, pointing at one of the guys writhing around clutching his leg.

"Did Kyle try to beat up my friends?" I asked.

"Well...yeah..." Linebacker replied.

"Then Kyle committed a felony when he attacked a federal agent. He can go to the hospital, tell everyone he fell off a ladder, and get his leg fixed, or he can complain about my pal...'Frank' beating his ass and get his physical therapy in a federal prison. Which do you think he would prefer?"

The guy on the floor just muttered, "I'm too pretty for prison," and grabbed his leg some more.

"So he had a bad fall. What a shame," I said. "What's it gonna be, boys? You wanna get disappeared by the federal government, or do you want to get drunk courtesy of the Department of Homeland Security?"

"Hey, don't I get a vote in this? It was my ass he grabbed," Sara no H said, grabbing my arm.

"One, don't grab the arm with the gun," I said. "And two, no, you don't get a vote. You get one shot. You want to lay this asshole out? Go for it." I stepped aside and motioned to Grabby.

Sara no H grinned and punched her assailant right in the breadbasket, doubling him over. Then she grabbed his ears and slammed his face into her upraised knee with a loud *CRUNCH*. Blood streamed from his nose, and he dropped to his knees, clutching his face. She took a step back, measured the distance, checked the wind like an NFL kicker prepping for fifty-yard field goal, then stepped in and laid Grabby out cold with a massive right cross. She knocked him flat, and he sprawled on the dirty floor, blood pooling under his face as his nose continued to gush.

Harker, did you just promise to buy the entire bar a round of drinks on my expense account?

Yep. That a problem?

Becks once again proved herself a generational talent by managing to sigh across a telepathic link. Not even within a hundred yards of me being able to hear her, and she still gave me a world-class sigh of resignation. It was the kind of thing that I'd expect a mother-in-law to use on me all the time, if I'd ever had one of those. *No. It's not a problem. But if you were just going to bribe them with booze, why break the window?*

I've always wanted to go through a plate glass window to get into a bar. It's kind of a neat reversal, I think.

I really hate you sometimes.

And yet you still love me, I replied.

Good thing.

Oh, you have no idea. Hold that thought, I said.

"Faustus?" I asked. "What's up?" The demon looked concerned, his head whipping all around the inside of the bar. I noticed both Sara(h)s doing the same thing.

"Harker, I think we've got a problem."

"I can tell that much," I said. "What's going on?" I repeated.

"It's Milton. The third tech."

"What about him?" I heard Becks ask over comms.

"He's not here. The last time I saw him, he was at the bar with Tall Sarah. Now he's gone," the demon replied.

Well, shit. Looked like our trap worked. Except for the part where we actually trapped the bad guy. Fuck.

CHAPTER TWENTY-ONE

All the joy of winning an admittedly very brief bar fight vanished as a river of icy water ran down my spine. I walked over to the bar, beckoned the thick-necked man running the taps over, and flashed my badge. "I need to see the security tapes for the last thirty minutes."

He shook his head, his light brown skullet waving in the sea breeze. "No can do, buddy. Sorry."

He turned to walk away, and I grabbed his shoulder, freezing him in place. He glared at me and jerked away, or tried to. I tightened my grip, not enough to cause pain, but more than enough to keep from being shaken off easily. He wasn't going anywhere until I decided it was time for him to go somewhere.

"I don't think you heard me," I said, my voice low and dark. "I need to come back into the office and look at the last half hour of security video."

He gave me a nasty glare, then just seemed to let his anger go. "Fuck it, it's not my joint anyway. There is no security video. The cameras are fake. Mr. Yu put them in six months ago because he was paranoid about people stealing from the till. I'm the only one who works here that knows they're fake."

"Why does he trust you so much?"

"Because I'm married to his niece. Mr. Yu is family, and you don't steal from family. Now would you please let go of my shoulder?"

I did, and turned to see Becks and Glory moving through the remnants of the crowd. Two gorgeous women walking with a purpose can clear a line of college kids out of the way like the parting of the Red Sea. I made a mental note to ask Glory if that really happened. Later. Way later.

"What's the deal with video?" Becks asked.

"No joy," I said. "Cameras are fake."

"Fuck," she said. "We're gonna have to do this the hard way. Faustus, you and Harker start collecting phones. Get the other techs to set up a field office on a couple of tables. We're going to have to dump every phone and analyze footage taken of the fight. Maybe that way we can catch a glimpse of who kidnapped Milton."

Everyone started moving, but I cleared my throat loudly and they froze. "Hold up, Inspector Gadget," I said. "That's all stuff that can be done, and probably should be done. But let's try to use our other resources, our much faster resources, before we go into the tech montage from Act Two of *CSI*."

"What resources are those, Harker?" Becks asked.

I pointed at Luke, then back at my chest. "Magic, babe. Magic." I waved Luke over. "Luke, do you think you could track Milton's scent?"

He looked a little affronted, but I've been affronting Luke for over a century now, so it doesn't really faze me anymore. "I am not a bloodhound, Quincy, and I resent being used as one."

"No, you're better than a bloodhound because you can tell us what you smell. And your nose is better than most tracking dogs," Faustus said.

"Quiet, demon," Luke muttered.

"Suck it, vampire," Faustus replied, in perhaps the most apropos comeback in history. I wondered how long he'd been saving that one.

Luke turned to me. "I would need something redolent with the missing man's scent. An article of clothing that he wore frequently, or something that was in close contact with his skin."

"His hoodie is here at the bar," Sara, the tech who'd been about to tear up the entire bar two minutes ago, said. "He wears that damn thing everywhere. No way he'd leave without it."

"Not by choice," Becks said, her tone and look dark.

This was really hitting her hard. Losing someone under her command, on a risky mission, and a noncombatant to boot. It was always hard when fighters got hurt in battle, and devastating when they were killed. But it was also what we signed up for. With our shields, or on them, as the Spartans reportedly said.

But people like Milton? He was no fighter. He was a lab geek. If I remembered right, he was a chemist who'd joined DHS after a family member was killed in a magical battle. They were collateral damage, and Milton signed up to use his tech-fu to help hunt down big bads so no one else had to bury their teenaged nephew because a pair of wizards got into an argument at a bodega and blew up half a city block. But he wasn't the charge in guns blazing type. He was a considered man in his fifties who tended to think before he spoke, a dapper dresser with a penchant for cool hats. I liked him, and really didn't want to pick up any of his body parts off the beach before sunrise, so if we could use Luke as a hunting dog to save him, I'd put the leash around his neck myself and suffer the bruises.

I handed the sweatshirt to my uncle, who took a deep sniff of the neck area, the armpits, and the hood. "I have his scent, but it is faint in here. There are too many other people's...aromas...lingering in the air, not to mention the stink of stale beer, pheromones, and vomit."

"Let's head out front, then," I said, slipping my Sight on over my mundane vision. "The trail of slime our bad guy left goes that way out the door." With a little more time, I could have cast a finding spell using the hoodie, and that would have led us straight to Milton, but something told me time was not something I had in abundance. Hopefully, with Luke's nose and my Sight, we could hunt down our missing tech and find out he'd just hooked up with a bar bunny and gone off to frolic in the waves.

Judging by the grim looks on all the faces around me, nobody else thought that was an option, either.

There were hundreds of partiers hanging out by the front door, in the parking lot, and climbing over the patio rails to get back into the bar through the other entrances. The bouncers weren't even pretending to check IDs anymore, which was likely fine, since most of the people crowding around looked like they were in their thirties at least. But I'm a notoriously bad judge of ages. I think I still look twenty-eight, and that was a hundred years ago for me.

The trail of dark magic oozed down the bar steps and across the parking lot, and when I glanced over at Luke, his nod confirmed that Milton had gone this way. Or been taken this way. We walked out past the last of the parked cars, all the way across the street and into a public lot on a beach access path. Smart. The sand in the parking lot obscured tracks and made any remaining ephemeral by their very nature, plus the salt wind coming off the Atlantic made it harder for Luke to follow a scent.

Harder, but not really that difficult for someone like him, who had tracked prey through the woods of Eastern Europe and the streets and alleyways of the world's largest cities. Luke was not one to get fooled by simple hunter tricks. And with me to follow the glowing trail of almost iridescent green and yellow malevolence, we were good to keep the trail.

Until we weren't. "I've lost the scent," Luke said after we paced the length of the parking lot three times.

"Right about here?" I asked, standing near the point where the aura cut off suddenly.

"Almost exactly, Quincy."

"They got in a vehicle," Becks said, holding up her tablet. "The cameras on those light poles aren't fake, and I've got a shot of Milton and another person getting into a green Subaru right there."

I didn't ask how she'd gotten the video so quickly. The other techs had rushed back to her SUV and started doing nerd things while Luke and I played bloodhound, so I assumed they'd hacked something. "Do we have traffic cameras to follow the Subaru?" I asked.

Becks looked at me like I'd grown a second head. "No, Harker, the Outer Banks is not renowned for its surveillance capabilities. If anything, the spot on the North Carolina coast beloved for its peace and quiet has fewer traffic and other public cameras than the rest of the state."

Yay. Hamstrung by the desire for privacy. I get it. I don't like the government poking their nose into my business, either. Except when I'm the government and I'm the one who wants to trample all over everyone's right to privacy to save a life. Or banish a demon. Or avoid stoplights en route to a late-night Taco Bell run. There are times individual liberty isn't all it's cracked up to be, is all I'm saying.

"So we've got nothing?" I asked. "Can we track the car? There can't be that many green Subarus around, can there?"

"Says the man who pays little to no attention to automobiles," Glory said. "Harker, Subaru is like the second-most popular type of car in this part of the state, behind the pickup truck."

"Yeah, dude," Faustus chimed in. "It hauls stuff, it's got all-wheel drive for dune-hopping, and it gets great gas mileage. Subarus are great."

"Y'all keep this up and we're gonna need to get ad money from those people," I grumbled. "So you're saying there are a lot of green Subarus in Eastern North Carolina, I guess?"

"There are roughly thirty-eight thousand people living in Dare County," Becks said. "Assuming thirty thousand cars, probably a third of those are some flavor of pickup truck, so out of twenty thousand non-trucks, maybe five thousand Subarus? And at least three thousand of those would be some shade of green or something that looks green in shitty parking lot lighting. So yeah, Q. There are a lot of Subarus, and that's even before we take vacationers and people from neighboring counties into account."

"Well, fuck," I said. "Well, Luke can't track the scent, and I can't track the magic, so if y'all can't track the tech, what the hell are we supposed to do?"

"I've got a partial plate and am trying to get the car's GPS information," Sara no H said over the comm, which I'd slipped into my ear when I hopped out of the rental and forgot was still in my ear. "I should be able to have that to you in a minute."

"Okay, then let's head back to the SUV and get after these assholes."

"We'll take the Suburban," Becks said. "You two use the tech's car. Not enough room for everyone in my vehicle."

Luke and I glanced at each other, then Glory laughed. "I told you they wouldn't go for it. Harker, you get in the Suburban. Luke and I will follow you on foot."

"On foot?" I asked the angel.

"Well, kinda on foot. Not in a car, at any rate."

"I will be on foot," Luke clarified. "I have allowed Glory to carry me whilst flying on one previous occasion. I would prefer not to repeat that experience if possible."

"I've got a location," Sara said. "The car's not moving, but I don't think you're going to like this."

"I don't like anything about this night," Becks said.

"I just don't like anything," I added. "Where's the car?"

"It's back at the cemetery. The one where you had us looking for evidence in all the bones and body parts? That one. The car's parked right by the front gate."

Fuck. Our tech weenie was being taken to the one spot we assumed the bad guy wouldn't go back to—his ruined hideout. But I guess if he wanted to fuck with us, this was a hell of a way to show us he wasn't intimidated by us finding out about him.

Now we had to get there before we were cataloging Milton amidst all the other discarded body parts.

CHAPTER TWENTY-TWO

I knew we were too late as soon as I saw the car. Both front doors stood open, and the dome light shone across a scene from a horror movie. Blood soaked the front seat, the footwell, the passenger door, and covered the passenger side window in a viscous red film. Torn tatters of flesh clung to the dash, with scraps of muscle and meat dangling in the breeze from the heater. The car was still running and making the annoying *ding-ding-ding* of an over-teched vehicle with an open door and the lights on. Somehow, I didn't think we were in a lot of danger from car thieves with this one. It would probably cost more to clean the parts once they were stripped than they were worth.

"Fuck," I muttered.

"Yeah," Becks agreed, walking up beside me. She had her sidearm in a hip holster and toted a Remington 500 tactical shotgun with a bandolier of different shells attached to the butt. I knew for certain there were shells loaded with holy water, silver nitrate, and a couple of dragon's breath loads, too. Not that any of those would do any real damage to a demon, except maybe the holy water, but they'd certainly fuck up a minion. "Where are Luke and Glory?"

"Probably in there," I said, pointing toward the crypt in the center of the graveyard. "I can't imagine our bad guy hauling Milton back here and then taking him somewhere that isn't the evil magically warded lair hidden under the cemetery."

"Well, when you put it that way, what are we waiting for?"

Faustus and the other techs were back at the Suburban, waiting for the all-clear. Well, the techs were waiting for that. Faustus was making sure the techs waited and that nothing wandered by and randomly ate them while we were elsewhere. You laugh, but I lost a Sherpa guide in the Himalayas once when a werewolf happened upon him and ripped his guts out while I was hunting a Yeti. Turned out the werewolf was part of another Yeti hunt and got hungry, so when he found my guide, he just did what came naturally. When I caught up to him a few days later, I also did what came naturally. Unfortunately for him, what comes naturally to me was very similar in the outcome of our encounter. The only real difference was that I didn't eat him after I ripped his goddamned head off. I never did find the Yeti.

Becks and I clasped hands and started across the cemetery, dew soaking the cuffs of my jeans in the October mist. It was a perfect Halloween season night, with a big bright moon, a slight chill in the air, and the crackle of fallen leaves under our feet. Except...there were no trees in the cemetery, so where did the leaves come from?

I stopped, pulling Flynn to a stop beside me, and looked around. *"Lumos,"* I whispered, channeling power into a small orb floating behind my head. Cool white light bathed our surroundings, and we were most definitely *not* in Kansas anymore. Or North Carolina.

At least, not any North Carolina that had existed in my lifetime. The cemetery was gone, except for a pulling sensation in my midsection, leading me toward the crypt. But we were deep in a forest, old growth stuff, with massive boles of oak and other hardwoods, and scruffy little pines poking through here and there struggling to get enough light and nutrients to make a go of it.

"Becks," I asked. "Where the fuck are we?"

"I was really hoping you knew the answer to that. Harker. You're the magician, remember?"

Well, shit. This definitely fell right smack into my wheelhouse, she had the right of that. I knelt and pressed my hands into the soil, reaching out with my essence to feel for any magical signature. Maybe whatever brought us here wasn't malevolent and I wouldn't have to kill some huge unkillable monster before I figured out how to get us back to where we belonged.

But the more I used my Sight and my other senses to examine our surroundings, the more I thought that we were probably right where we were supposed to be. We just weren't *when* we were supposed to be. Everything about the place felt like Manteo. I could smell just a hint of the ocean on the wind, I could hear the same birds from seconds before, and I could feel a lot of the same rhythm of the earth's energies that I felt all day. Except everything was *way* stronger, like the entire vibe of the place had been turned up to eleven and the knob ripped off.

"I think we're back in time," I said. "Something really weird is happening. I can feel the same natural energy as I've felt ever since we got to the Outer Banks, but it's all way more intense, more powerful."

"More powerful, or less diluted?" Becks asked, and I had to think about that one.

After a second or two of consideration, I nodded. "Yeah, the other. It feels like there are fewer things drawing on the power of the land, and fewer things getting in the way."

"Because there aren't as many people."

"Yeah. This is what a place feels like when it has inherent power and humans haven't been around much to fuck it up. I've felt a few spots like this, but they're usually very remote. Not much today that people haven't managed to shit all over."

"But five centuries ago…"

"Yeah, there were a lot less people. But what the fuck are we supposed to do now? How do we get back to our time? Do we just let go of each other? Is this some kind of weirdo thing where whatever has ancient colonists dream walking into your head has teamed up with my magic and dragged us back to meet your own personal Freddy Kreuger face to face, and if we just stop holding hands, we'll pop back to the present?" To test the theory, I let go of her hand. Nothing happened. Dammit. That was one of my better guesses.

"Maybe we're just supposed to go ahead and go to the crypt, or whatever it is in this time, and see what's there? Or what was there, or however you're supposed to phrase it. I haven't watched nearly enough *Doctor Who* for this shit," Becks said.

Does our link still work? I asked.

Yep, so we've got that, at least. And your magic. But in case you hadn't noticed… She held up her gun, which was now a bow and arrow.

How's your archery?

Not many little Black girls at your average North Carolina Girl Scout Camp when I was a kid, but I do at least know to aim the pointy end at the bad guy.

I guess we'll take it then. I took a deep breath, looked around at the massive trees that used to cover the area that I knew as an immaculately landscaped cemetery, and started walking toward the source of the magic I felt roiling in my guts.

We came upon a clearing where the crypt should be, a rough circle in the woods where trees had been felled to make a twenty-foot open space. This felt familiar, and I realized that it mirrored the clearing out by the Waterfront Theater in my time. A small fire burned in the center, and we could see a broad-shouldered figure sitting on a stump, his back to us. A woman lay on the ground opposite him, bound hands and feet with strips of dirty white fabric. Terror was writ large on her face, her eyes open wide, shivering against the light chill, the streaks down her face where tears had carved furrows in the mask of blood and dirt. She'd obviously been struck in the head with something, as some of her hair had shaken loose and a shallow cut on her forehead still oozed in the firelight. As we got closer, the night breeze bore a reedy voice to us.

"I'm sorry, Alexandra," the nasal voice said to the trembling woman. "We can't survive another winter without help, and it's been far too long to think that anyone is coming from home to save us. We have to make difficult choices, and you all selected me to lead you, so that means I have to make the most difficult choice of all—who lives, and who dies. I'm sorry, but your death means that your husband, your *son*, will live. Isn't that worth it? You're a mother, Alexandra, wouldn't you give your life for your child?"

"Of course I would, Reverend. I'd do anything for my boy. But does it have to be like this? Does it have to be out here? Why can't you make the offering in the church? Why do we have to be alone?"

"Because what I'm doing out here isn't the kind of thing one does where God is watching, Alexandra. God has forsaken our families, and now I have forsaken him in turn. I'm sorry, but God has no place here. He has turned his back on us, so I had to look elsewhere for help." With that, he drew a curved dagger from underneath the cassock he wore and held it up to the light.

"Holy fuck," I muttered. "I've seen that blade before."

What is it? Becks asked, keeping silent. I gave myself a little mental slap for making noise when I didn't have to, although something told me that we were like Scrooge in *A Christmas Carol*—able to observe but unable of interacting with what happened before us.

It's the blade of Abimelech, I replied. *He was a biblical con artist and murderer who killed sixty-nine of his brothers to take over his father's ruling position. He was a real fuckwhistle. According to legend, the knife he used can provide a conduit from the mortal world straight to where Abimelech resides in the Ninth Circle.*

That's where traitors go, right?

Yeah, and it doesn't get any more treacherous than fratricide. Looks like old Dishonest Abe is sending nastygrams topside, and our murderous preacher got the message loud and clear.

So what? He's going to sacrifice her to a demon? Why?

Probably to live through the winter, I said. *There was a stretch of several years where the colonists were essentially abandoned, and by the time anyone came back to bring supplies, they had vanished. I think we're about to see what happened to at least one of them.*

And we did. We saw the blade flash down, glittering yellow and red in the firelight, then gleaming black as the woman's lifeblood coated the blade. The man raised the blade again, brought it down again, raised it, brought it down, again and again until the fire was almost doused with blood and the ground was blanketed with oozing red.

"Oh, great Abimelech!" the man cried out, standing and raising his hands to the sky. He turned, and we got our first look at his face, streaked with blood and twisted in a horrific rictus of evil glee. "Grant us solace from the chill of winter! By this sacrifice, I beseech thee for aid! Help me keep my people alive! Help me save Fort Raleigh."

The fire blazed higher, as if something heard his plea, and a deep, rolling laugh echoed through the forest.

"*YES,*" came a voice of nightmares, a voice that sounded like boulders grinding together, a low rumble that I felt all the way down to my knees. "*YOU HAVE DONE WELL, MY SERVANT. YOU SHALL BE REWARDED. CONTINUE TO SERVE ME, AND YOU SHALL HAVE LIFE ETERNAL.*"

"Oh, goddammit," I muttered, again forgetting to stay silent.

"What?" Becks whispered.

"That's what this is all about. This motherfucker wants to live forever, and Abimelech will keep him alive as long as he keeps getting fresh souls to eat. Well, mystery solved, I guess."

"What does that mean?" Flynn asked.

"It means we know what happened to the Lost Colony. They were betrayed by one of their own and eaten by a demon. And the demon is still feasting on Manteo to this day. Fuck. This guy's not just old; he's old and smart. And evil as fuck. This shit just got even more complicated."

And as the world shimmered around me and I began to see the headstones and streetlights of the twentieth century piercing the veil of whatever spell we'd been wrapped in, I saw an even greater complication.

A pair of eyes in the forest. Human eyes, set in the face of a terrified but furious little boy. A face that bore a strong resemblance to the woman who I'd just seen slaughtered by her very own pastor. And those eyes, those dark brown eyes, were staring right at me. Somehow this kid from the sixteenth century could see me, could *know* me, and had dragged me and Becks back to see what happened.

So now I knew who I had to avenge, at least.

CHAPTER TWENTY-THREE

I blinked rapidly to clear the past out of my eyes, then turned to Becks. "So...that was fucked up, right? Even by our standards?"

"Oh yeah. That was some weird shit. And did you see that little kid? The one hiding in the woods? He looked...*felt*...familiar somehow, like I was supposed to know him. Did you get anything like that?"

"No," I replied. "I just felt spooked because he could obviously see us, even though we weren't really there."

Flynn rubbed her hands up and down her bare arms, and I noticed for the first time that she wasn't dressed at all for the weather. It wasn't cold. Not really. But it was in the low sixties, maybe high fifties, and there was definitely enough chill in the air to need sleeves. Becks had on a cute sleeveless turtleneck top thing, with jeans and boots that looked good for running or kicking bad guy ass, but nothing on her arms at all. I peeled off my duster and handed it to her.

"Here," I said. "You're gonna freeze."

"What about you, Mr. Chivalry?" she asked, slipping into my long coat, which dragged the ground a little on her. "Won't you be cold?"

"One, I at least have something on," I said, plucking at the collar of my long-sleeved black shirt. "And two, if I get cold, I'll just blow something up. Explosions tend to keep things toasty."

She leaned into my shoulder as we walked on toward the crypt. There were no signs of Glory or Luke outside, and no sounds of struggle as we approached. I could tell with my Sight that our bad guy hadn't taken the time to rebuild any wards before bringing Milton here, so there shouldn't have been any sound-dampening spells in effect. Maybe there wasn't going to be any fighting after all. I will admit to a little disappointment at that possibility. Losing Milton was going to be a big blow to the team, and the whole DHS, and I wanted the chance to hit somebody over it. Really hard.

I saw a flicker of movement to one side of the entrance and pointed Becks toward it. A light fog had crept in as the night deepened, making the abandoned centuries-old cemetery with a demonic shrine in the center of it even creepier, if that was possible. Glory and Luke were crouched behind a broad headstone near the tomb, and I knelt beside them. Flynn dropped down into a crouch. This is why my laundry is so much harder than hers—she doesn't kneel in wet patches of grave dirt on the regular.

"Why are we out here?" I whispered.

"We were waiting on you two," Luke said. "What took you so long?"

"We had a slight detour to the sixteenth century," I replied.

"Another vision?" Concern flashed across Glory's face as she looked at Becks.

"Both of us this time," I said. "I think we know what this is all about."

"Survival," Becks said, her voice low but not whispering. The sibilant sounds of a whisper actually carry farther than just talking softly, a fact I can never remember when it comes time to actually keep my own voice down. But let's be real—I am not the person anyone calls on for stealth.

Flynn continued. "In the last months before the Lost Colony disappeared, one of the colonists made a deal with a demon for eternal life. Not just for him, but for his whole family. Problem is, there's a cost to that kind of deal."

"A big one," Glory confirmed. "That's fucking with Father's plans on a pretty grand scale, so it's going to take a lot to power a spell like that."

"Yeah, and a lot of lives. We only saw one woman sacrificed, but we both know that's not enough to keep someone alive forever. And once Abimelech had his hooks in this guy, he could just keep demanding more and more sacrifices."

"Abimelech? This is his bullshit?" Glory asked. "Motherfucker. I knew I should have cut his head off when I had the chance."

We all stared at her, but she just shrugged. "It was a long time ago.

Abimelech and I ran into each other during Lucifer's attack. I only ran him through a little bit. Should have killed his ass."

"Weren't you the good guys?" I asked.

"Of course we were," she fired back, her eyes glinting in the moonlight.

"Well, you keep trying to convince me that the good guys don't always kill the bad guys. It hasn't stuck, by the way. I still think Batman's greatest weakness is his unwillingness to kill Joker's ass, but that's neither here nor there. You didn't kill him when you had the chance because that's not what you do. It's not who you are. I'm glad you didn't kill him, because if you had, you wouldn't be Glory."

"And I probably would have killed you half a dozen times by now," she added.

"That thought had crossed my mind as well," I agreed. "Now stop worrying about last millennia's problems and let's focus on tonight's problem—the murdering prick in the mausoleum." I looked from her to Luke. "Was he already down there when y'all got here?"

"We have not seen him," Luke said. "I crept up to the door and listened, but the words are very indistinct. It certainly sounds as though there is more than one person inside."

"So Milton might still be alive?" Becks rose as the words left her mouth, but I grabbed her arm and pulled her back down.

"Not a chance. You saw how much blood was in that car. There's only so much blood in the human body, and most of Milton's was in the floor-boards. He's dead."

"I would concur," Luke said. "Only one of the voices sounded human. The other was very distinctly not. It was lower than most humans can speak and sounded like stirring hot coals with a poker. I assume it is this Abimelech you spoke of."

"Then we know the plan," I said, standing up and summoning my soulblade.

"Plan?" Flynn asked. "You mean go in there, murder everything moving, and leave the cleanup for someone else?"

"I probably would have framed it in a more flattering light, but that's basically it," I said, heading toward the crypt. I'll admit to a little bit of nerves walking straight into a confrontation with a badass demon and a centuries-old psychotic wizard. But I had my team, and hopefully between the angel, the vampire, and the federal agent about to walk into this bar, we could all walk out again.

~

Well, we all walked out again, eventually, but we were disappointed and not the least bit bathed in the blood of our enemies. There was blood, of course, but mostly in the treads of our shoes and on the cuffs of our jeans, because there was more than one significant puddle of the red stuff on the floor of the crypt.

The otherwise empty crypt.

I mean, it wasn't any more empty than it was when we'd last left it. There were bones, bloodstains, the odd scrap of flesh, and a Milton. Or pieces of a Milton. The tech lay in the doorway to the main body of the crypt, at the end of the long passage under the cemetery we'd walked just a few hours before. He was splayed out with his arms and legs spread wide, like he was making snow angels, or imitating the famous Da Vinci sketch. Except Da Vinci's sketch had a head. Milton didn't. He was also missing several internal organs, but those were kindly arranged in a circle around the body for us, so we didn't have to look far. The heart, lungs, liver, and testicles were all neatly deposited at the compass points of the circle, and the flesh of his chest and stomach had been peeled back and laid open like a butterfly in a display case.

This should have been the kind of butchery that took hours to perform, especially with the elaborate display. That it had been accomplished in roughly forty minutes was chilling, and spoke to the efficiency, and experience, of the monster performing this hatchet job.

"Dammit," Becks whispered, staring at the body. She turned and walked a few yards back up the entrance tunnel. I started to go to her, thinking she needed comfort, but stopped when she pulled out her phone and called in the other forensic techs. Then she proceeded to call the sheriff and ask for help accessing the local morgue and other facilities. She was obviously upset, but she was channeling her grief and guilt into rage and action. I suddenly felt a little worried about what would happen when we caught up with Abimelech, because I'd seen a pissed off Rebecca Gail Flynn before, and it was not something I'd want to face, even if I was an Archduke of Hell or whatever rank Abe held downstairs.

"Let's see if there's anything useful we can pick up before the CSI nerds get here," I said to Luke, letting my Sight fall over my mundane vision. He nodded, then closed his eyes. Luke doesn't have any psychic powers, no matter what Stoker's book said. He's very charismatic, which sometimes has been thought of as hypnotic, and he has vision, smell, and hearing even stronger than mine, which is preternatural after a fashion, but not psychic. But he's told me that closing his eyes helps him focus on the sounds and scents of a place, while others look at what can be seen. So he was kinda using his own version of the Sight, only a sightless type.

There was magic *everywhere*, and it was some gnarly shit. Streaks of black, purple, sickly greenish yellow, burnt orange, and blazing red spattered the walls like a Jackson Pollack painting. There was almost as much rage, pain, and fear strewn about the room as there was blood and viscera, and while it wasn't anywhere near as overwhelming as what I'd felt at the park earlier, it still rocked me a little.

I felt Glory's hand in the small of my back and realized that it had literally rocked me, and she was holding me upright. "Are you okay, Q?" she asked, her voice low.

"Yeah, I'm fine. There's just a lot of heavy emotion running around this place, and that's without Becks in the mix."

"Even I can feel the anger and guilt rolling off her in waves, and that's without using any of my magical senses," the angel replied. "She's gonna need some serious time with the DHS shrinks after this mission."

"The DHS has shrinks?" I asked. I have been slowly coming around to the idea of therapy over the past couple of decades. Growing up when I did, and where I did, our idea of coping with trauma and mental illness was either a good dose of stiff upper lip or an even better dose of laudanum. Now, I'm as big a fan as the next guy of opiates, but I prefer them for recreational use than for therapeutic uses, so I never went in much for that stuff. But as more and more people I know and trust have used psychotherapy to help deal with trauma, I've gone to a few shrinks over the past five years.

Three of them retired immediately after our first session, and the fourth fired me as a patient halfway through the hour. That one also tried to have me committed, but when I threw a fireball at his office chair, he decided that maybe I wasn't the one hallucinating, so he had himself committed instead. Probably unnecessary, but safer for the furniture than his original idea. I'm still looking for a therapist versed in dealing with my particular type of trauma, but it's taking a bit to find. Maybe if the government had one that could handle the stuff Becks saw, they could handle my issues as well. Worth a thought.

"Of course the department has therapists," Glory said. "They're the government. Just working for them at all comes with a certain level of systemic trauma, then you add monsters to the mix and it gets exponentially more fucked up. The first thing Pravesh did when she took over the department was get everyone who works for the Paranormal Division to attend eight hours of mandatory evaluation and therapy."

"Which served the additional purpose of weeding out anyone still loyal to her predecessors," Becks said, stepping back into the room and slipping her phone into her back pocket. "She found three moles from the old Director Shaw regime, and a couple of people in the employ of foreign governments."

"China?" I asked.

"Argentina, actually," Flynn said. "There was an Argentinian national buying access to any US official with even a hint of paranormal interest in their job description."

"That tracks," I said. "Lot of Nazis escaped to Argentina after World War II, and the Nazis were very interested in supernatural weapons and magic. Probably the grandson of some goose-stepping fuckwhistle who wanted to bring Hitler back from the grave."

Becks nodded. "That's pretty much exactly what it was. And there was a female analyst who quit the Department right before her mandatory sessions started, but literally every piece of information in her file was falsified. Whoever she was, and whatever she wanted in Homeland, she's a ghost now. The techs will be here in ten minutes. What do we know?"

"We know that there is a secret passage in this wall right here," Luke said from the far side of the crypt. "I surmise this is where our villains departed their lair, but I cannot as yet determine how to open the door."

Well, that sounded a lot like my cue. I walked to the other side of the room and got ready to do what I do best.

Blow shit up.

CHAPTER TWENTY-FOUR

I did make a token effort to find a trigger or release, or even a doorknob, before I went straight to more explosive options, but after pressing on every outcropping of rock in the crypt for five minutes with no effect, I channeled power into my hands, focused the energy into a razor-thin line, and jammed power into the cracks around the door. I closed my eyes, visualizing the power constricting, tightening, compressing the stones of the wall until with a loud *CRACK*, an explosion of rock dust spewed forth and the door split into half a dozen big chunks of stone and fell to the ground.

I wiped the dust from my face with the hem of my shirt, then peered into the passage. It was pitch black down there, so I tossed a little fireball, just to make sure there were no ugly surprises waiting for us. It erupted without any screams, so I figured it was probably as safe as anything in my life. "*Lumos,*" I said, conjuring another globe of light to hover over my shoulder.

"I'll go first," I said, but Luke put a hand on my shoulder.

"I don't think so." He gently pushed me back and headed for the tunnel.

"Why are you taking point?" I asked.

"Because you're tall enough to stand behind me and still cast spells at anything or anything that attacks me, because my senses are more acute than yours, so I am less likely to trigger a trap or step into an ambush, and because you have been knocked unconscious several times over the last few days and just expended a significant amount of magical energy, which will take some time to replenish. So you are not at your peak efficiency at the moment. While you have sometimes annoyed me over the years, Quincy, I long ago decided that if anyone was going to murder you, it would be me. Therefore, I should go first so that you are protected somewhat from whatever we may encounter."

I just kinda looked at him. This was a more active role than Luke usually took in our investigations, typically preferring to stay out of things until the final showdown. But since nothing he said was the least bit untrue, I nodded and waved him forward. "Okay, then," I said. "I'll follow Luke, then Becks, then Glory you guard the rear."

"Yours or Rebecca's?" the angel asked. "Because yours is okay, but hers is much nicer."

"Agreed," I said, as Flynn blushed. The combination of her dark skin and the dim lighting in the crypt made it hard to see, but I knew her well enough to recognize the flush of her cheeks. "Watch Becks's rear first, then mine."

"I'm good with that," Glory said, fake-leering at Flynn. At least I thought it was fake, but Glory had spent some time as a human recently, so maybe she'd found a sex drive to go with a facility with profanity.

We started down the passage, which headed east and quickly began to slope downward. Given that we were already underground, I started to wonder exactly how far underground we were going to end up, but the tunnel leveled off after maybe twenty feet of decline. We walked for over an hour, moving slowly and stopping more than once to investigate side tunnels, but Luke led us straight down what seemed to be the main passageway leading from the crypt to…where?

There was nothing in the passage but the occasional drop of blood and a lot of dust. After nearly ninety minutes of careful walking, Luke held up a hand and whispered back to me, "Douse your light. There is movement ahead."

I didn't hear anything, but immediately let go of my spell, plunging the tunnel into darkness. A warm glow illuminated the end of the tunnel nearly a hundred yards away, and I marveled at Luke's vision. I could barely tell there was any light ahead even without my magic glowball to compete with it, but Luke noticed it right away. Something to be said for being the most powerful monster in history, I guess.

We slowed our pace, hoping to sneak up on any of our prey that remained near the tunnel's mouth, but only silence filtered back toward us. We crept forward for another several minutes, finally emerging into a large circular room, completely empty except for some stone benches lining the walls. An intricate pentagram was set into the floor of the room, inlaid into the poured concrete in what looked like gold, with concentric circles of silver, platinum, and copper evenly spaced around the symbol. Ornate runes decorated each ring around the pentacle, drawn in several archaic magical languages. I recognized Latin, Aramaic, Hebrew, Sanskrit, and even more obscure, non-human languages like Enochian. There were several sets of symbols that I didn't recognize, and that worried me. I've studied a lot of magical texts in my time, and I felt pretty secure that I'd seen everything the mystical world had to offer as far as script went, but at least three of these languages were completely unfamiliar.

"What are those symbols?" I asked, pointing to one segment of the design.

"I...think that's Elvish," Glory said. "Like Tolkien."

"That's not a real language," I replied.

"It kinda is, though," she said. "It's part of popular culture, especially in the U.S., and it's not the origin of something that makes it real, it's the acceptance of it. *The Lord of the Rings* is the most famous fantasy novel of all time, and the road map for hundreds of books, movies, and television shows that followed in its footsteps. I daresay it's got a greater influence on the world today than those scribbled Norse runes on the other side."

"I'll be sure to tell Thor that next time I see him," I said with a smirk.

"Don't tell that blond putz anything. I'm better off if he doesn't sober up enough to remember I exist. And that I didn't want to bang him," the angel said.

"Thor's real?" I said.

"Thor hit on you?" Becks asked at the same instant.

"Thor hits on everything," Glory said. "He makes Zeus look like a monk. A chaste one, not a horny D&D one. And he's as real as any other god. We talked about this."

"Yeah, I know. Still kinda surprises me," I said.

"But what does all this mean?" Becks asked, heading off another debate about pantheons and polytheism. "We've got what looks like a summoning circle, only it's not complete." She pointed to small, obviously intentional breaks in the rings, where the boundary was never filled in. I couldn't see any damage to the inlay, and it looked like nothing was ever intended to be placed there, because there were no grooves in the empty spots, just an absence of whatever precious metal the circle was made from.

"I don't think this was meant to summon anything," I said. "At least, not anything they intended to contain. I think this is more of a gate than a circle. Maybe a portal."

"You think this is where Abimelech is coming through?" Glory asked.

"Kinda makes sense, doesn't it? If somebody's making offerings to this Abe guy on the regular, they'd have to build some kind of secure location to meet in, right? And what's more secure than an underground lair branching off from a secret murder site under a cemetery?" Becks asked. "But where are we? I couldn't keep track of how far we walked or what direction."

"We went about five miles due northeast," Luke replied. "I believe that puts us somewhere near the Wright Brothers National Monument."

"How the hell could you tell that?" I asked. "No way did you just know how far we walked."

"Of course not, Quincy," Luke said. "Don't be absurd." He held up his phone. "I used the Maps application on my telephone. Apparently we aren't so far underground that my GPS can't reach."

I hate it when Luke is better with tech than me. I understand it from Becks, because she's almost a century younger than I am, but Luke? He's *old*. Like remembers the Revolutionary War old. Next thing you know he's going to have a TikTok account.

CHAPTER TWENTY-FIVE

There was a door set into the wall of the room opposite the tunnel we'd emerged from, and when we came out, we realized that we weren't *near* the Wright Brothers National Memorial, we were *under* it. We came out at the end of a narrow access road that wound around Kill Devil Hill and led out into the rest of the park commemorating where man first took flight. Score one for the vampire and his GPS.

"Well, the good news is we know where we are. The bad news is we're miles from our Airbnb, there are no signs of any demons or evil wizards, and our car is several miles back the way we came," Becks said.

"Pretty sure that's worse for you than the rest of us," Glory said, stretching her wings. "I don't have to follow the roads."

"I do, but I'm capable of some significant speeds," Luke added.

"I suppose I *could* run all the way home like a wee little piggy, but I'd rather just call Faustus and get him to bring the Suburban out to pick us up," I replied, holding up my own cell phone. Luke isn't the only one who remembered we're living in the twenty-first century. "But in the meantime, I'm going to take a look around for any magical trails. Luke, you wanna play bloodhound again? Maybe see if some of Milton's scent rubbed off on his captor?"

"Not really, but I will."

"Glory and I will hike up to the top of the hill and take a look around.

Maybe there are clues on the monument itself that we'll see now that we know what's under it," Becks said.

"Hike?" Glory asked. "I don't think so."

Then she wrapped her arms around my fiancée's waist and flew away, Becks letting out a surprised squeak as they took off. I grinned at them, then turned my attention to the supernatural spectrum. The snail trail of nasty aura I'd followed through the cemetery was still evident outside, leading to a spot about ten yards from the doors then dissipating quickly. The bad guys must have gotten into a car, which would have lessened the impact of the evil assclowns on their surroundings and left less trace behind. There were about half a dozen other auras mixed in with the familiar evil one, all tainted to a greater or lesser degree with demonic influence.

There were some seriously strange and evil things afoot at the Circle K, as the philosophers say. "Something's fucked up here," I said to Luke, who was walking a methodical grid pattern from the doors to the end of the service road.

"I am finding unexpected anomalies as well," he replied. Somehow the man can make "yeah, that's fucked up," sound posh. "There are significantly more trace scents than I expected to find, as though there were a meeting of some sort taking place here, one involving both our summoner and the demon Abimelech. I am quite concerned about any group of people gathering knowingly to meet a demon in the flesh."

"Yeah, that's pretty fucked up. Most people don't ever want to meet a demon, and the vast majority who meet one and know it's a demon don't live to tell the tale. But this is a whole monument dedicated to...what? Ostensibly man's determination, drive, and innovation, but what if it doesn't really have anything to do with that?"

"You think this entire park is actually dedicated to the demon?" Luke asked.

"I don't know," I admitted, perching on a low concrete retaining wall to think. "If Abimelech has had his claws in Manteo since the Lost Colony days, then did he have anything to do with the Wright Brothers? Did humanity learn to fly through a deal with a demon? Or were they just stubborn bicycle makers from Ohio who happened to set up shop on top of a demon's favorite gateway topside?"

"That we may never know, Quincy," Luke said. "And it is unlikely to be relevant. What is relevant is that a group of humans are using this place to summon, or perhaps just provide a gateway for, a demon. And they are living to tell the tale, which indicates a much greater level of community involvement than we previously thought."

Fuck. He was right. If there was some shadowy cabal of Outer Banks residents meeting with a demon under a national monument, then somebody with some serious influence had to be involved. We were on government property in the middle of the night, and by all indications, a group of vehicles had left not long ago. That meant somebody had to let them in, and that wasn't going to be accomplished by a bunch of drunk frat boys with an *Evil Dead* DVD and a PDF of *The Necronomicon*.

So now we not only had to find and banish a demon, find and stop (okay, fine, kill) an evil sorcerer, but we also had to track down and dismantle a vacation town's version of the Illuminati. My night was sucking more and more.

You should probably get up here, Becks said through our link, and I could tell from the tone of her thoughts that I wasn't going to like anything about what I found when I got topside.

~

Luke and I jogged up the side of the hill and stood beside Glory and Becks, the latter aiming a flashlight at a small brass plaque on the base of the monument. The whole thing wouldn't have been very impressive if not for the fact that it was on a big-ass hill. It was just a white stone obelisk, a few dozen yards high, with an inlaid pattern surrounding the base. That pattern was what Becks wanted me to see.

"More runes," I said, pointing at the pattern. "Looks like the same languages as we saw in the chamber below. Any idea what they're for?"

"That's why we called the magician," Glory said. "It's obviously magical stuff, and seems to be of human creation. That's your wheelhouse, bud."

She wasn't wrong. Annoying, but not wrong. I knelt and began to study the runes and scribbles. As before, I saw Norse, Elvish, Aramaic, Egyptian, Latin, Greek, and literally dozens of languages. Most of which I either didn't speak or read at all, or had only a passing knowledge of. I couldn't make heads or tails out of it, but I did catch a few words and phrases here and there. I focused my attention, dredging up every painful schoolboy Latin lesson, every hour spent poring over spellbooks, and every bit of research I'd done into dead languages.

Slowly, arduously, a pattern of repeated words and phrases began to emerge. Not enough to give me a full translation, but enough to get a sense of some of the intent. "Sacrifice and salvation seem to be the main themes. I can't decipher everything, but maybe with enough time..."

"I don't think we need to put that all on you, babe," Becks said. "You call Faustus and get him over here with a few techs and a Suburban while I shoot video of everything here. Then I can upload that to the DHS servers and get our people back in DC working on translating it."

Good plan. This monument was erected in the late 1920s, so whatever was written on it might be important, but it was really unlikely to be something we had to deal with immediately. "There's one more thing," I said. "Have your techs specifically look for mentions of the words 'legacy,' 'heritage,' or 'descendants.' I saw those a few times, and some context for that might be helpful." Something was starting to tickle in the back of my head, and I was hoping to get confirmation without giving too much away. I wasn't being purposefully obscure; I just wanted to see if the translators saw the same thing I did. If I was right, it would explain one of the weirdest aspects of this weird-ass case. And if I was wrong, then I didn't need the entire federal government and all my friends thinking I was some nut job conspiracy theorist. Not that I'm *not*. I just don't need everyone thinking that I am.

I pulled out my phone and dialed Faustus, ordering up my very own version of a government Uber, and fervently hoped that I was wrong in what I was starting to suspect. Because if I was right, then this case was about to get very personal.

CHAPTER TWENTY-SIX

Faustus pulled up twenty minutes later, but he wasn't alone. His Suburban led a convoy of flashing lights and speeding official vehicles. I counted an ambulance, a fire truck, two sheriff's department cars, a white pickup, a BMW sedan, and a flashy red SUV with blue lights flashing in the grill. And that was ignoring the other traffic on the road.

"Babe, we're about to have company," I called over to Becks.

"Yeah, I see 'em. Glory, maybe you and...never mind," she said as she noticed that the angel and Luke were already gone. I wasn't sure if they'd gone back through the tunnels or if Glory had picked Luke up and flown away with him. I was betting on a run through the tunnels, since the very idea of Luke being carried made me giggle. He's very dignified for a giant parasite, my uncle.

The parade of vehicles turned off the main road, blew past the guard house, and barreled around the memorial site before coming to a halt at the base of the hill. Doors flew open and cars vomited forth crime scene techs, a demon, and a horde of strangers. Only about half a dozen of them spilled out of vehicles that would make me think they were armed, so if it got ugly, I figured we'd still be fine. Me, Becks, and Faustus could handle six armed assholes and a crowd of mundanes without breaking much of a sweat.

Faustus reached the peak first, ignoring me save for a fist bump in passing and heading straight for Flynn. "Sorry, Director," he said, pitching his voice loud enough to be heard down the hill. "The local power structure insisted on following me to what they're calling a secondary crime scene. They've got state crime lab people coming in from Wilmington to take over the scene."

I smothered a grin. This was going to be fun to watch.

"They've got *what* from *where* coming to do *what?*" Becks asked, her voice rising with every word.

"We've got our state forensic specialists coming in from Wilmington to take over this investigation since you federal types can't seem to make any progress on things. And besides, I spoke to the governor this afternoon and he doesn't remember making any calls to my office about this case, so whoever you got to impersonate him is going to be in a world of trouble when I get my hands on him."

Faustus grinned, rolled his head from side to side, and stepped forward. "Pleasure to meet you, Sheriff. Name's Frank Augustus. I'm with them." He pointed to Becks and me. All of this was said in a pitch-perfect imitation of the Governor of North Carolina's voice, right down to the mid-Carolina drawl on the "I"s. "Now was there something you wanted to discuss with me?"

The demon's tone was pleasant, and the smile never left his face, but there was a slice of menace in his tone that chilled the air around us. How do you say "don't push me, bitch" without saying "don't push me?" I don't know, but Faustus certainly did.

The sheriff didn't push. He brushed "Frank's" hand aside and stepped closer to Becks. "Agent Flynn, you and your people need to get the hell off my crime scene right now, and you need to turn over any evidence that you have found to my team immediately. I've got people on the way to your rental property right now to collect the evidence, and I have deputies here to escort you from the premises."

He seemed...different this time around. The affable reluctant hero of gay business in the Outer Banks from earlier was gone, replaced by the same officious, territorial prick we first encountered at the beach murder scene. It was like the helpful officer of the law had been replaced by the asshole cop from *Smokey & the Bandit*. He stood there, arms folded across his broad chest, glaring down at Becks.

Her reply was one word. "Director."

"Excuse me?" the sheriff asked, in that drawn-out way Southerners use when they can't decide if you said something offensive or just stupid. Like "excuse" has three or four syllables.

"I'm not an agent, Sheriff. I am Deputy Director Rebecca Gail Flynn of the Department of Homeland Security, and you are standing on a federal monument, which is one hundred percent my jurisdiction. As is the wildlife preserve where the first victims were found, and as the cemetery where we discovered the body tonight is on the National Register of Historical Sites, it also falls within my jurisdiction. So whether the governor called you or not, this is my crime scene, this is my case, and I will not have evidence trampled by a bunch of bumbling yokels led by a man who by his own admission, only ran for the office to keep a homophobe from wearing that star." She tapped his badge, which wasn't in the shape of a star, but I wasn't going to correct her. I've learned the dangers of "well, actually-ing" an armed woman who knows where you sleep.

"Look here, missy—"

Becks held up a hand and cut him off. She peered past the sheriff to a tech walking toward the room under the monument. "You! Down there! Touch that door and I'll shoot you."

The tech froze, looked up, took a second to mentally calculate angles, then stepped back. Good call. My fiancée was definitely wearing her "don't try me, motherfucker" face.

She turned her attention back to the sheriff. "Here's how this is going to go. You and your bunch of…I assume civic leaders are going to pile back in your clown cars and get the fuck off my crime scene, leaving a car of deputies down at the base of the hill to keep looky-loos away and another at the entrance to the park to keep the place secure. Then my people and I are going to get to work and find what's been murdering people in Manteo for the last few decades, without any interference from you or from the assholes huffing and puffing up the hill worried about tourism revenues and bad press. Then once we catch whoever is committing these crimes, we'll drop them off at your cop shop and let you bask in all the glory of the local news. Because we're here to do a job, not win elections."

Her voice went up on that last one, and I saw the barb land with one man struggling up the path from the cars. He was about sixty, medium build, with thinning red hair and a light beard. He looked like a principal and moved like he got about that much exercise. He was the only one bothered by Becks's zinger, though. The fat man beside him heard her, but his only reaction was a tiny smirk at her words, and the brown-haired woman walking beside the fat man just glared up at us.

"I don't think that's how it's going to go at all, young lady," the fat man called, finally cresting the hill. He paused for a second to catch his breath, then stomped over to us with all the authority of a big Southern man who is accustomed to people hanging on his every word and obeying his every whim.

"Oh?" Becks asked, raising what I liked to think of as The Eyebrow of Doom. I call it that because whenever that eyebrow goes up, the smack is about to come down. Usually on my head. Thus I was very interested in seeing what this beatdown looked like as a spectator. "And how exactly is it going to go down, Mr....?"

"Justice," he said, stepping forward but very pointedly not extending his hand in greeting. "Rufus Justice, Chairman of the County Commission, president of Elks Lodge 414, and owner of Platinum Properties, LLC."

"Ooh, is that the chain of strip clubs?" I asked. "Because I'm down for some two-for-one lap dance coupons if so."

The chonky commissioner whirled on me, his cheeks flushing even more crimson than the hike up Kill Devil Hill had made them. "Who the fuck do you think you are, boy? Don't you know to shut up when the adults are talking?"

I didn't blow him up. Becks and I have been working on my restraint. Plus, as far as I could tell he was human, and just a dickhead, not truly evil. And I'm trying very hard to stop exploding people just for being rude.

I did, however, step right up to him, look down on his splotchy red face, and say, very slowly and very calmly, "I am the federal agent who is going to shoot your dick off if you call me or any of my people 'boy' again. Are we perfectly clear?"

He spluttered a little before managing to say, "You can't talk to me like that, you carpetbagging piece of—" His voice cut off and his eyes got the size of saucers when I jammed my Glock into the space a few inches below his belt buckle.

"I'm not in the mood," I said, my voice still low and calm. "I just walked five miles through underground tunnels from the hidden crypt where one of my technicians was torn limb from limb, only to find more bodies along the way and then end up at some junior varsity magical mystery lair atop a hill on the goddamned Redneck Riviera of North Carolina. So unless you have some kind of hidden facility with forensics, or better yet, a fucking clue as to who might be doing this shit, please remove yourself from this crime scene before I get annoyed."

He stepped back, getting his junk out of contact with the barrel of my gun, then turned to Sheriff French. "Sheriff, arrest that man! He pulled a gun on me!"

"I saw it, Rufe," the sheriff said. "I can't arrest a federal agent for pulling his weapon on someone who he feels was obstructing his investigation. Why don't you wait in the car while I try to get these folks to head on home?"

Chonky's face got even redder, and I was a little worried that he might stroke out on me. He wasn't terribly overweight, just a little thick around the middle, but he definitely looked like a dude who didn't do a lot of cardio, and the combo of climbing Kill Devil Hill in the middle of the night and getting face-melting pissed off at me could certainly push even a healthier man over the edge. What can I say? I bring out the best in people.

Harker, let me handle the sheriff. You and Faustus get the techs started looking things over. Maybe get in touch with Glory and see if she and Luke will keep the other end of the tunnel secure?

On it, I replied. I waved Faustus over. "Call Luke and get him headed over to the crypt while you take one of the techs around up here and get video and photos of everything on the monument. I'll take the other one down to the secret lair under the monument."

"There's a secret lair under the monument?" Faustus asked. "That's *cool.*" He waved one of the techs over. "Sarah, you go with Harker and check out the stuff down the hill. Sarah and I will document everything up here."

"On it," Sarah replied. I waved Sara no H over and we started down the hill.

"What's down here?" she asked.

"I think it's a reusable gateway that allows the demon Albemerich to pass into this plane and murder people."

"You think?"

"Yeah, that's where you guys come in. There's a shitload of symbology, but none of it is cohesive, or coherent. It's all scattershot, like someone took bits and pieces of every magical and ancient language they could find and stuck it all together to cast some kind of working."

"Okay," she said, pulling a digital camera out of the backpack she carried. "I'll get pictures of everything, and we can get the nerds in DC to start deciphering it."

"How big a dork do you have to be for the forensic scientists to call you a nerd?" I asked.

"Have you ever *met* any of the cipher experts in DC?" Sara asked.

"No."

"It's impressive. These guys legit get excited about the new fall line of pocket protectors. I think at least one of them has a poster of Neil deGrasse Tyson over his bed."

"That's not so bad," I said.

"He's forty-three and married."

"Okay, I think I get it." Well, one good thing about having the biggest nerds in the known universe on your team: if anybody can figure out what this shit says, it's gonna be them.

CHAPTER TWENTY-SEVEN

"Sara, what the metaphysical fuck am I looking at?" asked the voice on the phone.

"Harrison, if I knew that, do you think I'd be calling you at three in the morning?" Sara replied, frustration creeping into her voice. We'd been photographing the floor of this room for an hour, then it took another thirty minutes to get one of the DC techs on the phone. Now he wasn't exactly the font of information we'd been hoping for.

"I don't know, Red," the nasal voice dropped into what I can only assume he thought passed for a sultry tone. "Maybe you just missed me."

"The only time I've ever missed you was that time I threw a bottle of ranch dressing at your head, and that was only because you ducked."

"Wait, that was you?" I asked. "Even I heard about that. I thought you got fired for assaulting a fellow agent."

Sara glared at me. "I did. They hired me back when they realized I'd left time bombs in all my files to self-destruct if I don't deactivate them every seventy-two hours. It was either hire me back or replace seven years of casework. Besides, he ducked, so it's not like I injured him." She turned back to the phone. "So do you recognize any of this shit or not?"

"Who was that?" Harrison asked. We were on speaker, but not video. Sara had emailed a bunch of photos to the sleepy tech, and he was looking at them on his laptop while he talked to us.

"Quincy Harker," I said.

"*The* Quincy Harker? Sara, are you out in the field with the fucking Reaper? That's so badass!"

One of these days I'm going to do something about that nickname. But tonight, if it got me information from Harrison, I was fine to lean into it. "Yes, she's here with the fucking Reaper. Now do you have any fucking information for me?"

I could literally hear him gulp through the phone. Maybe the nickname isn't so bad after all. "Um, hello, Mr. Harker, sir. Pleasure to meet you. Um...I'm not sure...I..."

I sighed. It wasn't a Becks-level "weight of the world on my shoulders" sigh, but it was definitely in the ballpark of an "I'm going to reach through the phone and throttle this motherfucker" sigh. "Harrison, just tell me what it says, to the best of your ability. We thought it might be a gateway for a demon to enter this plane essentially at will. Is that anywhere close to right?"

"It is," Harrison said, and as he slipped into a pedantic "really smart person talking to mere mortal" voice, he seemed to get more comfortable. "But that's only part of it. This is a gate, yes, keyed to a specific demon—"

"Albemerich," I said.

"Yes, Albemerich. But it's more than just a gate. This is also a contract, or a part of a contract. This stipulates that the demon Albemerich will provide protection and guarantee prosperity for the signers so long as they and their descendants continue to provide appropriate tribute."

"For how long?" I asked.

"Excuse me?"

"How long do they have to provide tribute?" I was pretty sure whoever originally set up this contract had done so long before the monument was built, but there was no way of knowing for sure if this was a new contract, an addendum, or what. And it was possible that the room under Kill Devil Hill had been there long before the monument, or even before the Wright Brothers flew their plane off the dunes there. But if there was an end to the term, that would be nice. If this was going to be the final cycle of murders, I just needed to stop a few more people from dying and didn't actually need to go toe-to-toe with a major demon. I was supposed to be on vacation, after all.

"Ummm...there's no ending to the contract. As long as they keep feeding people to the demon, he'll keep providing safety and prosperity to those participating."

"Do we have any way of knowing how many people signed onto the contract?" Sara asked. I gave her a nod. Good call. If we knew how many people we were looking for, it would be easier to find and exploit a weak link.

"Not really," Harrison said. "There are a lot of different things here, but most of them boil down to the demon taking care of people if they feed him a soul every so often."

"How often?" I asked.

"Every three years. If the demon is given a soul every third year, the donors—their word, not mine—will continue to thrive."

I thought back to the stuff Becks had found in her research. "It seems like this is a cycle that repeats every twenty-seven years, which would mean that there are nine people participating in this shit." I thought back to the people currently standing above me bitching about the investigation. There was the sheriff, who, given his recent switch back from helpful lawman to territorial dickwhistle, now seemed like he was probably neck-deep in this shit. There was the county commissioner prick, who was a rich assclown accustomed to everyone jumping when he shouted "Frog" in a crowded theatre. He was definitely demon-summoning material. Honestly, I had to assume that if the sheriff was part of this mess, everyone he brought with him tonight probably was, too. No point in dragging rich people out of bed in the middle of the night if they weren't invested in the problem.

The deputies were probably clean, so they went on my "Try Not to Dismember" list. But the sheriff? Nah, I was definitely going to tear his arm off and beat his ass with it.

"Mr. Harker? Are you with us?" Sara asked, poking me in the side.

I turned my attention back to the phone. "Yeah, sorry. Just trying to think about who would have the most to gain from this deal. I think it was originally struck to save members of the original Roanoke colony from starving when they thought they were abandoned by their supply ships. But it seems like it's grown over the centuries into something worse, something that just keeps the rich getting richer and the poor getting eaten."

"You think Elon Musk made a deal with a demon to get rich?" Sara mused.

"If he did, he got screwed. Electric cars are one thing, but how dumb can you be to buy Twitter and lose money? That's like going bankrupt running a casino. It oughta be impossible," Harrison said.

"Focus, gang," I said. "So we've got a gateway that is also a contract.

Can it be opened from either side, or does the demon have to be summoned?"

"I can't tell for certain, but I think it's a two-way door. Holy shit," Harrison said, realizing the problem. "That means…"

"That means we have a national monument built on top of a gateway to Hell that isn't locked, so with the right rituals, any demon from the appropriate Circle could just pop out for some calabash shrimp and tourist gumbo anytime they want," I said.

"Or they could mount a total invasion of our plane," Glory said, leaning on the door from the underground tunnel.

"Wondered when you'd show up," I said. "Glory, this is Sara. She's missing an 'H' in her name."

"No, I'm not," Sara said. "My name isn't Shara. Good to meet you, Glory. I've heard a lot of good things."

"Then you obviously haven't been listening to Harker," the angel replied. She turned to me. "Luke is at the crypt making sure the techs don't get removed by the locals. He has some fake DHS credentials that might have appeared in his pocket as if by magic."

"Or maybe they just actually appeared by magic," I said.

"Yeah, that too. So what's the deal? Albemerich can just come and go as he pleases, and you're worried that the wrong demon will find the door and lead all the Hosts of Hell pouring out along the East Coast?"

"Pretty much," I replied.

"Then there's only one place you can go to get any more info. And you're gonna need an escort."

"I'm sorry, Glory. I'm faithful to my fiancée," I said. "I don't pay for escorts anymore."

"You know what I mean, dickhead. You've gotta go find the local demon bar, and you'll need Faustus with you. They aren't going to let you in by yourself."

"Why not?" I asked. "How will they even know who I am?"

Glory and Sara both looked at me like I was obtuse, which in their defense I frequently am. "Mr. Harker, you're the fucking *Reaper*. Demons tell their little baby demons bedtime stories about you so the little pitchfork-sucking assholes will have worse nightmares. You're the boogeyman of Hell. You're Freddy Kreuger, Jason, and Michael Myers all rolled up into one package," Sara said.

"With more hair product," Glory added, not at all helpfully.

"My point is that there are photos of your face, along with most of your known associates, in every demon stronghold in the world, and probably in most places in other planes. You're one of the most famous humans, and I understand that I use the term loosely, to ever exist in the supernatural world. They're going to recognize you. The only way it doesn't devolve into a fight three seconds after you walk into a room is if Faustus goes with you."

"You really think Faustus being with me will stop a fight from breaking out?" I asked. He's the demon, but it's often hard to tell which of us has worse impulse control.

"Not for long, but I also think he's smart enough to stay out of the fight for ten seconds to text for backup. You aren't." Glory just stood there giving me her best judgmental look, which she's practiced for millennia so it's pretty good, until I nodded. I left her and Sara down there with virtual Harrison trying to translate other bits of the spell that was used, not that it should have been a problem for the angel.

That was one of the problems with having a Guardian Angel. Aside from the whole thing about not being sure if she was guarding me from the world, or the world from me, or both. There were things she wasn't allowed to tell me, and if she couldn't tell me, she literally *couldn't* say it. I was starting to see more and more why Lucifer wanted to overthrow Heaven. Living forever but not having agency would be a pretty shitty gig.

I stepped out of the lair and looked up the hill. Faustus was leaning against the monument with his phone out, so I shouted up at him. He held up a finger, turned his attention back to his phone for about a minute, then slipped it into his pocket and started toward me. "Bring the keys!" I shouted, and he turned to Becks.

Where are you going? she asked.

I need to do some research with the local demonic element. We need to find out if Albemerich has been recruiting helpers on this side of the portal for his murders, and we need to see if there's any info floating around about a possible invasion. If this portal really does go both ways, and he can come and go as he pleases, this would be the perfect place for demons to establish a beachhead for an invasion.

Wouldn't they have done that at some point in the past five hundred years if they were going to do it? Becks asked.

Probably, but I just want a little more info before I decide if we're going to lure Albemerich here to kick his ass, or if we have to go downstairs and beat the shit out of him on his home turf.

And the rich assholes up here pissed you off so you want to go beat someone's head in.

It is frighteningly difficult to keep your motives disguised from someone who is literally in your head. *Yeah, that too. It's been a rough couple days, and I'd kinda like to punch somebody. I think The Reaper showing up at the local demon bar probably ensures a certain amount of punching.*

Try not to die.

Always the goal. Love you. I mentally signed off before she could add "don't kill anybody" to her list of instructions. I mean, trying not to die made a lot of sense. I died once. It sucked, and I was informed that I'd used my Get Out of Hell Free card and if I wound up back in front of any eternal judgement tribunal, it would not go well for me. So I definitely was in favor of not dying.

But not killing anybody? In a demon bar?

Let's not be silly.

CHAPTER TWENTY-EIGHT

Apparently demon bars in vacation spots use the same decorator as the human bars, because this place had the same wicker furniture as the last bar we went to, just with a few touches designed to make the place feel less welcoming to human visitors. Like the massive Hieronymuous Bosch mural on the wall behind the bar and the huge goat head hanging over the pool tables in the back. The clientele were all wearing their human suits, but it was pretty obvious that most of them were from way farther south than the Carolina coast, and that was without me using my Sight.

"What are you doing back, Faustus?" the bartender asked. He was a big man, probably some type of mid-Circle Enforcer demon or something like that. His human guise was a solid six-and-a-half feet tall with a long black ponytail, long handlebar mustache trailing into his goatee, and a t-shirt a size too small that said "I support single moms" with a silhouette of a woman spinning around a pole. There's a certain level of class in dive bar staff that you just can't get away from, no matter what species they are. The only incongruous thing about him was the pair of round wire-rimmed glasses. Demons don't need glasses. Ever.

Faustus and I walked up to the bar and took a pair of empty stools, leaving space between us and the other four demons there. Three of them looked us up and down as if appraising a threat, while the fourth had his head down and was snoring softly into his umbrella drink. Either he was a very minor demon or this place had some hellacious drink recipes. Pun definitely intended. "I need some information," Faustus said, leaning on the bar. "And a couple of beers."

"You, no problem," the barkeep said. "But we don't serve his kind in here."

"You got a problem with humans?" I asked, putting on a fake belligerence. I mean, I'm generally pretty belligerent, but I didn't give a shit if I got a drink or not. I just wanted to know if he knew who I was. I'd stopped in the parking lot to cast a glamour on myself in an attempt to hide my identity, so to all appearances, I should've looked like I was five foot eight, pudgy, and balding. So either the bartender had a thing against humans, or he saw through my spell. One of those was way more worrisome than the other.

"I don't have a problem with humans, but you ain't human. I don't know what you are, but your aura is *fucked*." He adjusted his glasses, and I caught a flicker of rainbow reflecting across the lenses.

Glimmerglass. That explained it. There are certain types of glass that can be ensorcelled to reveal the true nature of a being. It won't pierce a glamour, per se, but it will allow the wearer to see a subject's aura. And mine is certainly...interesting. Let's leave it at "interesting."

"I don't want any trouble. I just want a drink. And maybe some information," I said, sliding a hundred-dollar bill across the polished wood of the bar.

My photo of Benji Franklin vanished quicker than a virgin at a West Virginia family reunion, and the bartender put two plain brown bottles in front of us. "Drink up," he said. "I'll be back in ten minutes. If you're still standing and those bottles are empty, you can ask me a question. One. Question. Then you get the fuck out of my bar and don't ever darken my door again. I don't know who or what you are, but I know I don't like mysteries. So get drinking, then get gone."

He turned and stomped off toward the far end of the bar, and I picked up my bottle. Faustus reached out and put a hand on my wrist.

"Are you sure you want to do that?" he asked.

"Dude, I have rarely wanted a beer more than I do tonight."

"Yeah, but that's demon beer. It's...not what you're used to."

"Faustus, I've drank fermented yak milk on the steppes of East Asia. I've drank rainwater out of the gutter in Rio the morning after Carnival. I've partied with The Rolling Stones and snorted coke of a drag queen's ass on the center stage at Studio 54. I think I can handle one demonic beer." I took a big swallow and doubled over, trying desperately not to spew my drink all over the bar, Faustus, and myself.

"What the fuck is that?!?" I asked, glaring at my friend.

"I warned you," he said, trying and failing to stifle a laugh. "It's demon beer. There's a pretty high sulfur content, and if he went for the good stuff, there's probably the blood of more than one innocent mythical creature mixed in for flavor. Does it have a slight hint of cotton candy?"

I noticed he hadn't touched his drink yet. "No, it doesn't taste like cotton candy, you obsidian-faced prick. It tastes like licking a match then using kerosene as mouthwash. No, scratch that. Kerosene probably tastes better."

"Then it's probably just fermented imp piss mixed with lemon juice and cod liver oil. If you manage to drink the whole thing, you'll be regular as clockwork for a month."

"If I drink a whole bottle of that shit, I'll be puking up my goddamned toenails," I said.

"Well, better get a quick pedicure because you're gonna have to down the whole thing to get any answers out of Horace," Faustus said.

"Horace? I just got poisoned by a demon named *Horace*?"

"Technically his name has like seventeen syllables and only eight of them can be formed by a human voice box, but Horace is close enough."

"I don't give a fuck if his name is Beyoncé, I'm not drinking that shit."

"Well, if you're not drinking, then I'm not answering," Horace the demon bartender said, returning to stand in front of us. "You know the rules, Faustus. Everything has a price, and if you don't pay, you don't get what you're after."

"I bet there's another way I can convince you to give us the information we're after," I said, glowering at the demon across the bar.

"Oh," Horace said. "And what way is that?"

"Well," I said. "You couldn't tell who or what I was with your little glimmerglass specs, so why don't I introduce myself?" I let my glamour fall away, revealing my full height and moderately familiar visage in most demonic circles. I held out a hand. "Quincy Harker. But you can call me Reaper."

You know those moments in movies when everything goes completely silent and you know in your heart of hearts that a big fight is about to break out? Yeah, that happens around me a lot. I've learned to recognize those moments, and this was definitely one of them. Horace's eyes got round, and I was afraid for a second he was going to go full Tex Avery and they were gonna pop right out of his head, but instead, he whipped his head from side to side and just yelled "Reaper!" at the top of his lungs.

"So much for keeping a low profile," Faustus said. "What did that take, three minutes? That's gotta be some kind of a record, even for you."

"Not even close," I replied. "You keep Horace from jumping me from behind. I'll take care of the rest of the..." I was going to say that I'd handle the rest of the bar, but when I turned around, I began to rethink my strategy. Or my lack of strategy. Because there were a *lot* of demons in the bar. A lot more than I would have expected in a human resort town in the wee hours of the morning. There were a pair of Reaver demons already shredding out of their human suits to free up their long slashing arms, a Torment demon who had just Incredible Hulked right out of the skin he'd been wearing, a succubus whose wings had sprouted right through the Hooters crop tank top she was wearing, and a bunch of random low-level Hellspawn showing claws or grabbing pool cues to come after me.

I held up my right hand, wreathed in purple flame, then thought about my conversation with Glory earlier about looking like a book cover and changed the flame to my bright white flaming soulblade. Never too early to start revamping my image. "You all know who I am, right?" I asked, barely audible over the Scandinavian death metal blaring from the jukebox. I pointed my sword at the noise, and power streaked out, melting the jukebox into a heap of metal and plastic.

"Now," I said into the much quieter room. "You all know who I am?" There were a lot of nods. "You know what they call me?" More nods. "So that means you either think my reputation is bullshit and you can probably take down the famous Reaper, or you want a one-way trip home, courtesy of my murdering your ass."

I spun on my heels, slashing my sword across right about five feet and a few inches above the ground. Faustus, having seen this move before, dropped to one knee, and my blade whizzed right over his head. Horace had not seen me do this trick, so he didn't duck. His head hit the bar, and a second or two later, his body thumped to the floor. Both parts began to melt into a foul-smelling black sludge that would itself dissolve in a few hours, but not before ruining the finish on the bar.

"My reputation is, I guaran-fucking-tee you, not bullshit. Just ask Horace." To further illustrate, I dismissed my magical sword and picked Horace's severed head up by his hair.

"Horace, is The Reaper just a myth?" I asked the head.

I reached over and moved Horace's jaw, made a bit more difficult by the rate at which he was melting. "No, Quincy Harker is a bad—"

"Shut yo mouth, Horace," I said. Then I dropped the head over the bar onto the floor. Might as well save a little cleanup for the next guy who runs the place. I turned back to the demons. "Well? Who wants to dance?"

I expected them to run. Really, I did. Okay, probably not the Reavers, because those guys are just stone psychopaths. But I figured the rest of them would head for the hills. They didn't.

Nope, they charged me, a dozen demons of various shapes and sizes running right at Faustus and me with claws, fangs, and whatever the fuck else they could swing at us. I looked at Faustus and shrugged. "I told Becks having you with me wouldn't stop me getting in a fight."

"I fucking hate it when you're right," he replied, manifesting his very own soulblade. That was a trick I hadn't seen from him before, and I was so surprised that the first demon actually got a lucky shot in with a pool cue before I focused on the problems at hand. But me and Faustus were definitely going to talk about his newfound, or at least new-shared, powers after we got done slaughtering an entire bar full of demons.

CHAPTER TWENTY-NINE

The pool cue across my ribs definitely refocused my attention on the matter at hand, namely a dozen demons who wanted to rip my head off and mount it on the wall, probably after taking a crap down my neck. I wrapped an arm around the stick and held it tight to my body as the demon tried to pull it back for another swing, then I went all Three Stooges on his ass. And by that, I mean I poked him in both eyes. Except Larry never channeled pure kinetic force through his index finger, blowing a hole straight through Moe's skull. He dropped like a sack of potatoes, and I swung the abandoned pool cue around my head before jamming it through the throat of another onrushing demon. That one dropped, too, and the rest hesitated for a few seconds before a deep voice rumbled, "Outta the way!"

Demons of all shapes scattered as a truly massive pile of red-skinned corpulent nastiness stomped toward me. Demons, in their natural forms, are not typically attractive, but this dude had hit every branch on the ugly tree when he fell into Hell. He was a solid seven feet tall, bald, and must have had at least six hundred pounds of flesh and fat wrapped up in his crimson hide. Huge tufts of black hair stuck out of his shoulders and odd spots on his face, and a pair of small tusks curled up from his lower jaw to protrude past his thick, rubbery lips. He looked kinda like Squidward mated with a warthog, only angrier. He lashed out at me with a fist the size of my head, and I had to duck the surprisingly fast strike.

I wasn't putting my hands anywhere near that thing if I had a choice, because not only was he oozing slime from his every pore, I was also a little bit worried that he'd eat my hand. But that didn't mean I was defenseless. Nah, I do my best work with no physical contact. I aimed both palms up at the center of the demon's mass and shouted, "*Infernos!*"

Twin streams of magical fire leapt from my hands, slamming into the demon's massive belly and wrapping the whole immense body in fire. The demon looked down at me in confusion for a second, then its face split in the most disgusting grin I've ever seen and it started rubbing its chest and smiling.

"Yummy! That feels *goooood*, Reaper. Keep going and I might not kill you right away," the demon said, smiling down at me. Then I experienced the most revolting thing I've seen in over a century and a quarter of life. The quarter ton of ruby-fleshed fun reached up and tweaked both his nipples while he grinned at me.

Yeah, fire probably wasn't the way to go with these assholes. They did grow up in literal lakes of the stuff. I let my flames peter out, trying not to look directly into the awfulness above me, and summoned my soulblade. The demon's eyes widened, and the grin fell away from his face as he stumbled backward away from me, but I just straightened, bringing the blade slicing up through the corpulent fucker and cutting him from his nuts to his nose. Green and yellow ichor exploded from the gash I made up the demon's torso, and it let out a high-pitched squeal of pain. I slashed again, this time across the upper part of its torso, and it fell to the floor on its back, innards gushing from its belly and chest to land beside the creature's body with a *splat*.

Trying not to slip in dissolving demon guts, I advanced on the remaining demons, my soulblade blazing white in the dim light of the bar. I heard grunts from my right and glanced over to see Faustus struggling with a much larger demon who held a meat cleaver in one hand. I flicked a little bubble of energy toward the bad guy's ear, distracting it just long enough for Faustus to shove his soulblade through the demon's skull. He gave me a nod, then pointed over my shoulder, and I turned my attention back to my own fight.

The demons in front of me were way more reluctant to engage than they had been a few seconds earlier, except for the pair of Reavers, who had gone all the way across the room to build up a running start as they charged me with their razor-sharp blade arms. I mentioned those guys were all psychopaths, right? Because this pair were coming at me like a

Ginsu commercial on steroids, all high-pitched squealing and blade arms whirling around like a walking food processor. I channeled my inner Harrison Ford, dismissed my sword, and drew my Glock. I fired four shots into the center mass on the first Reaver, then adjusted my aim and did the same on the second. With seven rounds remaining, I spread the love around, putting two rounds in the face of three more demons.

They all dropped to the floor, where they would dissolve into stinky black ooze before that dissolved as well. The only demon in front of me that looked like it still had an ounce of fight left in it was the massive Torment demon, every inch of eight feet tall, heavily muscled, and of course impervious to damage from mundane weapons. I holstered my pistol, summoned my soulblade again, and made a "come at me" wave with my left hand.

The demon took one step before a crash came from my left and the sheriff rushed in with a twelve-gauge shotgun and a pair of deputies. "*Palarand gat imronis!*" he shouted, and the demon froze in place.

It glared over at the sheriff and snarled, "*Bitrumis fasitim al wotarus.*"

Sheriff French walked right up to the Torment demon, stuck the barrel of his shotgun under the creature's chin, and said, in a slow, clear voice, "You know I've got holy water rounds in this thing, right? They'll turn your face to jelly, and you'll be stuck wearing those scars for the rest of eternity, unless Lucifer decides you're such a fucking embarrassment for getting your ticket punched by a human that he just flosses his teeth with your soul for kicks. Now get your fucking human suit back on and get the fuck out of this bar. If I see you again before the harvest is complete, I'll send you back to the Fifth Circle in a pizza box." The scariest thing about that speech wasn't the words, it was the fact that he hadn't spoken English, or any human language. This fucker spoke *Enochian*.

The Torment demon held up both hands and backed away, shrinking and transforming into a large, but human-sized, trucker-looking guy in the process. He waved to the rest of the demons, all of whom were shifting into their human disguises, and said, "Come on. Let's go. The sheriff will deal with The Reaper."

And just like that, the fight was over.

Well, one fight, anyway. I now had a corrupt sheriff who was fluent in the language of angels and demons on my hands. I'm pretty sure I was in better shape fighting the demons. I looked over at Faustus, except my resident demon sidekick was nowhere to be seen. Great. Every time I thought I was starting to trust the yellow-eyed bastard, he vanished on me when I needed backup. That's what I get for trusting demons.

The sheriff and I locked eyes, and I took a second to consider the man. I obviously needed to reevaluate every idea in our heads about the sheriff. At first meeting, he was a typical territorial redneck lawman who didn't want any federal agents poking around his town. Then he seemed to be a perfectly reasonable cop in over his head with a murder investigation. Then earlier tonight he came across as the territorial prick again, but this time maybe as someone involved in the coverup of whatever sinister shit was going on around Manteo.

But now he comes charging into the middle of a horde of demons loaded with holy water in his shotgun and shouting orders in an ancient divine language. This dude was way more than met the eye, and not in a fun *Transformers* kind of way. Definitely more like a *Supernatural* meets *Criminal Minds* kinda way, and I was nowhere near smart enough to profile this guy. I looked at him, taking a moment to glance at the shotgun that was pointing in my general direction, and said, "Hello again, Sheriff. Long time, no see."

"Not long enough, Harker," he said, his voice barely more than a growl. "How about you come with me and I'll make sure none of these boys start any more trouble."

"Pretty sure I wasn't the one in trouble," I said with a little smile.

"Pretty sure you are now," he replied, raising the shotgun a little. Now it was definitely pointed at my midsection. "So come along with me and let's go have a little chat."

"If this chat involves you shooting me, I think I'm good right here," I said, calling up power and channeling it into a shield that I could snap into place in an instant. I just hoped my reflexes were faster than Sheriff French's trigger finger.

"I don't intend to shoot you," he said, lowering the gun maybe an inch. Not enough to make me relax, but it was something. "Just come with me and we can discuss what you've seen tonight. I may have some answers for you."

Dammit. I hate it when the bad guys promise answers. It's like catnip. No way was I not going with him to try and find out all I could about what was going on between the town fathers and Albemerich. "Okay, but I'll drive."

"Not a chance," the sheriff said. "You'll ride in the back of the patrol car just like a normal perp, so we can make it look like I'm taking you in."

"Besides," one of the deputies chimed in, "all the tires on your Suburban are flat. Somebody must not like you very much."

There are a lot of people who don't like me. Some of them are even in Manteo. But the folks I would most suspect of slashing my tires in front of this particular dive bar all left through the back door after the cops arrived. So the only way he'd know my tires were slashed is if he did the slashing. I walked over to the deputy, a skinny man in his late twenties with a mustache made for seventies porn films, and looked down at him. "I'll expect four brand new tires on that Suburban when I get back from wherever I'm going with your boss. If they aren't there, I know where the first place I'm heading will be, Deputy..." I looked down at the gold name tag on the opposite side of his shirt from his badge. "McKeown. And trust me when I say that I am not someone you want showing up on your doorstep in a bad mood."

He gave me a shaky nod, then as I walked past him, I heard the skinny little shit mutter something about me not coming back, so I took a little sliver of the power I was holding, spun it into a sphere of pure kinetic energy, and flicked it at him. A globe of force about the size of a softball slammed into his solar plexus, and he dropped to the floor, curled up gasping in a little ball. I nodded to the sheriff. "Okay, hoss. Let's ride."

I turned around, presenting my wrists to him behind my back, and just as I heard the metallic *click-click* of the cuffs, I felt a barrier slam down between me and my magic, cutting me off from the energy around me. I tried to call power to shatter the cuffs, but my connection to magic had been severed. I reached for Flynn through our mental link, but there was nothing there. It was like there was a wall all around me, keeping me from any contact with the well of power I could normally draw from to power my spells.

I was handcuffed, surrounded by bad guys, and now I had no magic. This was very, very bad.

CHAPTER THIRTY

I gave no hint of my alarm as one of the deputies grabbed me by my left elbow and perp walked me out the door, down the front steps, and to the back of a waiting squad car. Someone had certainly alerted the media because there were a handful of reporters and photographers forming a very short corridor of people between us and the car. I saw Faustus lurking in the shadows near a Channel 12 news van and gave him a nod to let him know I saw him. So he hadn't completely abandoned me. I guess I should have more faith in people, even demons. But most people suck, and Faustus is kinda famous for screwing humans in shitty deals, so he's even harder to trust than most folks. But he was still here to back me up, and hopefully he'd catch on to the fact that I was sans magic at the moment, and he'd go get some help. I reached out to Becks again through our mental link, but the cuffs blocking my magic were screwing up our connection, too, so all I got was static.

But for the moment, I ducked my head and got into the back of the police car like a good little criminal, wondering if we were even going to pretend like we were going to the station, or if he was just going to rendition my ass right out here in the open. I got my answer less than a minute later when Sheriff French sent his deputies back to the station to start processing me, then turned his car in the opposite direction out of the parking lot.

"Don't I actually need to be there for them to process me?" I asked from the back seat.

"Not really," Sheriff French replied. "You'd be amazed what we can falsify using a little bit of Photoshop these days."

I really wouldn't. I worked for the U.S. government. We employed some of the best hackers and unscrupulous nerds in the world, and I called on them to falsify documents for me on the regular. I was pretty sure the level of criminal talent in the Outer Banks was going to lag a little behind DC's, but with demon money behind them, they were probably more than capable of falsifying records showing that I was killed trying to escape. I wracked my brain for the best way to get out of this mess without magic but kept coming up empty.

"You know, you keep thinking so hard, you're gonna strain something," French said from the front seat. "Those cuffs were designed to be strong enough to imprison an Archangel, so there's no way you're going to be able to draw on your magic while you've got them on."

I've met Archangels, and if this dipshit thought he was ever going to be able to get handcuffs on one, he was sadly mistaken. But he was correct that I couldn't feel even a trickle of magic while I had them on. So I just tried to get as comfortable as possible and watched the scenery. If I could at least keep track of where we were going, I'd have a better chance of getting back after I killed this prick. "Why didn't you just shoot me in the bar?" I asked. "Would have been pretty easy to fake the paperwork to show I resisted."

"Boss wants to talk to you," French replied. "He's concerned that you and your people might know too much, so he wants to have a chat and figure out if we just have to kill you, or if we've gotta go all scorched earth on you, your girl, and your pals, too."

"What about my cat?" I asked.

"What?"

"If you have to kill me and all my friends, will you at least make sure somebody takes care of Nameless? I'm pretty fond of him."

"I just told you that you'll be dead before sunrise, and you're worried about your *cat*?" Wow. And here I thought bad guys all loved cats. Dr. Evil had certainly led me astray on this one.

"Do you have any idea how many times somebody has told me they're going to kill me? It happens at least once a week. And at least once every other week, some dingus threatens everyone I care about. So that's nothing new. But I haven't had the cat very long, so he's not used to the inherent dangers of being around Quincy Harker."

"You might be the craziest bastard I've ever met, and I'm literally taking you to meet a guy who summons demons," the sheriff said, disbelief coloring his every word.

I guess it's good to be the best. More to the point, the more he talked, the less he watched me in the mirror, so he couldn't see me bunching my shoulders and trying to get leverage on the cuffs. My ability to cast spells was blocked, and I couldn't communicate with Becks and direct backup to my location, but I was still Quincy Fucking Harker, legendary demon-killing badass, nephew to Count Fucking Dracula, and the motherfucker that demon mommies tell stories about to scare their kids into night terrors. I've also led quite a…fascinating life and have ended up in the back of more than one police car in my time. As a matter of fact, it's happened enough that I have my belts specially made with a small zipper pocket in the center of my back. I fidgeted around enough to unzip said pocket and remove the small aluminum lock picks I kept tucked there. I didn't pop the cuffs completely, just enough that I could slip one hand free quickly if I felt the need.

I still couldn't cast spells, but unless the sheriff planned to just haul me out of the car and put a couple bullets right in my forehead, I had faith in my ability to take his gun away and shove it up his ass before he could kill me. So when he turned off the main road and pulled up to a gated driveway, I got ready to pounce. I paused as he rolled down the window, spoke into the intercom, and then drove through the gate. It might be better to just chill for a bit and gather more intel, then kill this son of a bitch a little later.

He pulled up in front of a sprawling mansion with a circular driveway, lowering the property value by at least a hundred grand just by parking an American-made car in front of the place. The house was massive, at least three stories with a pair of broad wings spreading out from the central entranceway. It was a huge brick edifice, with carefully cultivated shrubbery and tasteful exterior lighting. The whole thing looked like the kind of place you see on the cover of a decorating magazine, except there was a sense of age and decay hanging over the whole place like a fog. I couldn't put my finger on it, but something about the place felt *wrong*. I tried to open my Sight, but all I got for my troubles was a stabbing pain in my head. Oh yeah, cut off from my magic. Right. Definitely killing this guy.

On the bright side, rich people don't generally commit bloody murder inside their expensive homes. Not before putting down plastic, at least. So as long as the floors were uncovered, I could go along with this little kidnapping, meet the boss, and figure out exactly who in this town I had to kill. And maybe figure out the demon's endgame in hundreds of years of dicking around on the Carolina coast, but that wasn't my top priority. No, that spot went to "staying alive." Everything else would have to fall in line behind survival for the next little while.

The door creaked open as we approached, and a trim white man in a tux nodded to the sheriff as we entered the grand foyer. It was somewhere in the neighborhood of four in the morning, and this dude's butler was still on duty? Even Luke wasn't that much of a dick to his employees.

"Sheriff French," the man intoned as we passed.

"Stevenson," the sheriff replied.

"Harker," I said, nodding. "Nice to meet you. I'd shake your hand, but Sheriff Dillhole here has me at a bit of a disadvantage." French slapped me across the back of my head and gave me a shove between my shoulder blades. I faked a stumble, and when he moved in to catch my arm, I yanked my hand free, spun around, and punched him right between the eyes. He slumped, but I caught him by the gunbelt, relieved him of his service pistol, and turned back to the butler, who stood there wide-eyed.

"You might want to take the rest of the night off," I said. "Maybe even the rest of forever. I don't think your boss is gonna have much need of your services after the conversation we're about to have." I didn't point the gun at the butler. He hadn't done anything yet except open the door, so he was just asshole-adjacent at this point. But it wouldn't take much to move him over onto my naughty list, so I kept a keen watch on his hands as he considered my proposal. After a tense few seconds, he nodded and walked past me through the front door and out into the night.

Well, he was either going to go get backup for the sheriff, which wouldn't arrive for quite some time given how remote the location was and how few cops vacation towns usually have working the graveyard shift, or he was heading for the hills, in which case I probably would never see him again. Either way was fine with me. I hauled the sheriff over to one of the massive, curved staircases and set him down. He was still unconscious, which made it a lot easier to relieve him of his backup piece, his gunbelt, and the keys to my handcuffs. I threaded used his mundane cuffs to secure his hands, then tossed his cell phone and radio through the open front door into the driveway.

As soon as I got the cuff off my left wrist, I was slammed to one knee under the frantic mental assault of a distraught Becks calling for me over our mental link. *Harker! Where the fuck are you?!? Nobody can find you. Goddammit Harker, if you're dead I'm going to find a fucking necromancer, get your skinny ass resurrected, then beat you to death my damn self! Where ARE you?*

I'm here, I said, interrupting her stream of panicked thoughts.

Quincy? Her mental voice was soft, as though she almost couldn't believe it was really me. *Harker? You're...*

Not dead, I replied. *Not even close. I'm fine. The sheriff put some kind of magic dampening cuffs on me, and he must have tossed my phone, too.*

When we get home, I am reinstituting subdermal tracker implants for all our agents. I am tired of you vanishing on me, Harker.

Good to hear your voice, too. I could feel the relief flooding through her, quickly followed by a white-hot anger.

Where's that fucking sheriff? I'm going to kick his balls up through his eye sockets for this. It's bad enough I just had to deal with a bunch of low-rent Amity Island politicians who expect me to give a flying fuck at a rolling doughnut how many shitty used car lots they own or how many goddamn strip malls they've built, but not he kidnaps my man? Oh, HELL no. That shit will not stand.

Well, right now neither can the sheriff. I punched him a little and he's resting for a while.

Did you kill him?

You know I don't kill everybody that pisses me off, right?

Yeah, but did you kill this guy that pissed you off?

No, I did not kill the sheriff. He's lying in the floor, knocked out cold. I think he was bringing me to meet the Big Bad. I might have picked the cuffs and punched him. But just a little, I promise.

Good. Not that you're in the bad guy's lair without backup. Good that Sheriff Dickhead is still alive. When we get done with this shit, I'm going to rendition him into the deepest cells under fucking Gitmo.

There are cells under Gitmo? I thought it was in Cuba. You know, the island?

Cells, shark cages, what's the difference to domestic terrorists or assholes who consort with demons and piss off high-ranking deputy directors of clandestine government agencies?

Sometimes my fiancée scares the shit out of me. I was formulating the perfect witty response about not killing any local law enforcement when I heard a door open at the top of the stairs. I looked up to a broad landing where an ancient man stood smiling down upon me.

"Quincy Harker, I presume?" the old man said. "Please, do come in. Let's have a chat."

I suddenly felt dangerously like the fly about to sit down for tea with the spider.

CHAPTER THIRTY-ONE

Now, when I say this guy was old, I'm not talking "might need a cane now and then and definitely gets the discount at Golden Corral" old. I'm talking "holy shit I'm over a century old and hang out with Count Friggin' Dracula and this motherfucker looks ancient" old. I know, comparing anyone to Luke as a measure of apparent age is silly, because he died about the time Gutenberg was really dialing in that whole movable type thing, but this motherfucker was *old*. He was almost completely bald, with a few Riff-Raff style wisps of white hair sprouting from the sides of his gleaming pate, and he had more wrinkles than a shar pei. He was dressed formally, in a tweed jacket and red tie, leading me to wonder what these people were doing fully dressed at this godforsaken hour, and as I climbed the stairs to meet him, he smiled, showing off a mouth full of gleaming dentures.

"Mr. Harker, welcome to my humble abode. Please, join me in my study. I would have met you at the door myself, but stairs have become somewhat challenging in recent years." He turned and toddled off through a heavy mahogany door into a massive room filled with dark wood furniture, dark wood paneling, and burgundy leather furniture. Luke would have loved this shit. I thought it was depressing. Nice, but depressing.

Uncomfortable, too, as I discovered upon taking a seat in an armchair that looked like it should have swallowed me whole in massive fluffy cushions. Except the leather seat was so overstuffed as to be rock-hard, so I didn't so much collapse into the chair as perch awkwardly on a cushion that felt like it was made of plywood. "You have me at a disadvantage, Mr...." I let the thought trail off, hoping for some flavor of introduction.

No, I didn't give a fuck who this old fart was. I knew that odds were better than even I'd have to kill him before the sun came up, because if the sheriff thought this guy was important enough to cuff me with spell-dampeners and drag me out here, he was probably the source of a lot of our demon problems. I only know one real way to solve demon problems, and that's with excessive amounts of bloodshed. Assuming the desiccated husk of humanity in front of me had any blood left to shed.

"My name is Drew Greene, and I am, to the best of my knowledge, the sole surviving member of the original Roanoke Colony. I would say that it is a pleasure to meet you, but I fear that the results of our meeting may be very unpleasant," the old man said.

There was a lot to unpack there, not the least of which was that he said he was the surviving member of the Roanoke Colony. Had this wrinkled old fuck really been murdering people in a tourist trap for *centuries?* He certainly had one thing right. If I had anything to say about it, our meeting was going to be unpleasant as fuck. For him.

"Well, then I won't bullshit you and say that it's nice to meet you," I replied. "Why don't we cut right to the chase? What the fuck are you doing and why are you feeding innocent people to a demon?"

He sighed, and it wasn't even one of those bad guy sighs where they're pretending to be so misunderstood, except they're really just evil fucks. No, this sigh felt sincere, like there was something about what he was about to confess that he really did feel bad about. I leaned forward a little, wondering exactly what a sociopath who'd survived five centuries by sacrificing people to never-ending torment could feel bad about.

"It was never supposed to go on this long," he said. "What I did was horrible, and it cost the lives of so many of the people who put their trust in me, but it was only supposed to be one time."

"You only meant to feed people to a demon once?" I asked. "That's the defense you're going with? I'm no Johnny Cochran, but I think even Judge Judy would call bullshit on that one."

He looked confused. "I don't know what any of that means, but yes, it was only supposed to happen one time. You have to understand, Mr.

Harker. We were starving. There had been no supplies from home for many months, and our crops had not been nearly as successful as we needed them to be. So when the demon Albemerich came to me with an offer that would save the lives of most of the colony, I felt I had no choice. The needs of the entire colony outweighed those of the few we would have to sacrifice."

"How very Vulcan of you," I muttered, assuming he wouldn't get that reference either. "How did you decide who you were going to feed to the demon? And how many?"

"Albemerich decreed that for every person I sacrificed, he would save ten. There were over a hundred people living on Roanoke Island at the time, so if I sacrificed ten percent of the colony, the rest would be saved. So I drew lots."

"Only there was no lot with your name on it, was there? Or anyone in your family, I bet." This son of a bitch. He was trying to justify his selfish bullshit by acting like it was random, but I knew damn well he was saving his own ass, and those of his family, and he was offering up his neighbors to do so.

"No, there wasn't. I left out the names of all the leaders of the colony, and all the young people. I selected ten of the oldest settlers, older men typically, but a few women, and one by one, I lured them into the forest where I gave them over to Albemerich. And he held up his end of the bargain. He provided enough food for all of us to survive. Barely, and with very tight belts by the time the ground thawed, but those of us who avoided illness or accidents through the winter saw spring, and I thought it was over."

"But it wasn't," I said. I wanted to keep him monologuing so Becks could hear what was going on, and to give her a chance to arrive with backup. This guy needed killing as much as anyone I'd ever met, but I was really working on my restraint, so if I could keep myself in check until the cavalry arrived, not only would I score points with my fiancée/boss for doing things at least somewhat by the book, I might even learn a little more about the demon behind all this *before* I had to fight him. Now, *the demon* I could murder without getting any shit from Becks over it, so the more intel I had on Albemerich, the better.

"No, it wasn't over. I learned soon that it never ends with demons. Never. We planted crops in the spring, hunted as best we could, and I watched as people continued to fall ill, or worse, intermingle with the savages surrounding us, abandoning their Christian values to live in the woods naked like animals."

Wow. Five centuries later and still a racist piece of shit. This guy was the epitome of class. Old, wrinkled, racist, murderous class. "And the rest? The people who didn't join the local tribes and didn't know you'd murdered one out of every ten people living in the colony?"

He flushed slightly. "I murdered no one. Albemerich killed them. I just..."

Served them up on a platter, I thought. I kept my mouth shut, hoping that I could get some kind of hint about a weakness in the demon. So far, this guy was just a piece of shit, without even the redeeming quality of being an informative piece of shit.

"Regardless, we put away what we thought would be enough food, but it wasn't. Some of our stores went bad, and the harvest didn't yield near what we needed, so when Albemerich returned that autumn with news that the supply ships from England had been sunk in a storm off the coast, I had no choice. I took another ten percent of the colony, only eight this time due to death and defections, and gave them to the demon. In exchange, he helped us through the winter."

"Helped," I said, my tone bitter and judgmental.

"This time he did. He gave us far more food than the previous year, and when spring came, we were prosperous. We were healthy, and two more babies had been born. All was going far better than we could have hoped. Until..."

"Until what?" Seemed like Albemerich had played this moron perfectly. Give them just enough to make it through one winter, then sabotage the crops and food so he has to come back the next year for more help, then give them unexpected bounty so they come out of the dark and the cold feeling flush and confident, so when he pulled the rug out from under them again, they'd be even more desperate than they had been in the first place. Pretty smart, which didn't thrill me. If given a choice, I'll always fight the stupid demons. Way easier.

"Until sickness struck the colony. Men and women fell deathly ill, unable to keep food down and so weak they could barely stand. Within a few weeks, half the colony was abed with illness, and the other half was frantically trying to keep them alive and keep up with the planting. The local tribes, who had been so helpful in the early years of the colony, now left us stranded and alone, refusing to come near any of us out of fear of growing ill."

That made sense. A mysterious illness befalls a group of strangers, and no fucking way would I be going inside their walls and helping them empty bedpans. And I'd read a bit about how the locals were treated by the colonists. It fluctuated between acceptance and loathing, depending on how desperate for food the colonists were. I wouldn't have saved their asses, either.

"So what did you do? Give everyone but your family to Albemerich?" I asked, expecting some kind of desperate denial.

Instead, I got a bowed head and an almost whispered, "Yes."

"What?"

"That's exactly what I did. I bartered the lives of the entire colony to Albemerich in order to save my wife and daughter. He took them all, all at once, and we were placed in some type of strange slumber, awakening many hundreds of years later when the island was settled in earnest. It wasn't until I came out of that mysterious sleep that I learned that no ships had been wrecked, and that supply ships landed just a few months after I gave us all into Albemerich's gentle care." His lips curled into a sneer at the word "gentle."

"That was too much for my poor wife Elizabeth to bear. She hadn't known anything of my dealings with the demon, and the moment she learned I had consorted with dark forces to save her and our darling Esther, she hung herself. I begged Albemerich to bring her back to me, but he refused, saying that she was beyond his reach now. I was grief-stricken, disconsolate, and angry. The demon had lied to me, deceived me, and tricked me into betraying everything I had ever loved. He cost me my wife, my community, and my faith in God. If God was so powerful, how did he let me do these horrible things?"

I started to explain exactly what "free will" meant but decided he was still pontificating and rationalizing. I've never been able to watch first-hand someone justify themselves into being the hero of their story, but this prick was trying his damnedest to do exactly that. He'd given a hundred or more people to a demon, then kept doing it over and over again for centuries, and here he was rationalizing it into not being his fault.

Fuck it, I thought. *Babe, are you hearing this shit?*

Becks's voice in my head was heavy with scorn and loathing. *Every disgusting word.*

Good. Because I'm killing this motherfucker, then I'm killing every son of a bitch in his little dark coven, then I'm going to kill Albemerich, even if I have to go to the lowest Circle of Hell to do it.

Part of me expected her to object, but all that came across our mental link was a sense of satisfaction. *Go get 'em, babe. And make it hurt. This prick deserves everything he gets.*

CHAPTER THIRTY-TWO

One thing I don't understand," I said to the demon-dealing prick standing in front of me. "How did all these other assholes get involved? You said you took a nap for centuries and woke up... when? After the Revolutionary War? The Civil War? Last month? How did this go from you selling out the entire Roanoke Colony to now feeding tourists to demons five hundred years later?"

He had the good grace to look a little ashamed, at least. "We were awakened after the Civil War, when the Freedmen's Colony was disbanded. There were a lot of white landowners returning after the war, and much of the area was in turmoil and disarray. It made it very simple for me to assume the identity of one of the men who was killed in battle and lay claim to his former property. Albemerich must have sensed opportunity in this turmoil, as he wasted little time in reasserting the terms of our agreement. I tried to stop him, telling him that without Elizabeth, I didn't care what happened to me, but he reminded me that I still had a daughter. He told me that if I didn't provide him with adequate tribute, she would suffer the consequences. So I killed for him again. And again. And again. I lured unsuspecting freed slaves into the swamps and drowned them. I caught travelers unawares on the roads outside of town and cut their throats as they slept. I shed more blood with these hands than the foulest war criminals, and still he wanted more. It wasn't until I was discovered in the commission of my foul deeds that I enlisted the aid of town leaders."

"So...what? The chief of police caught you and you bribed him to be another one of your demon flunkies?" I asked.

"In essence, yes," he said. "An ambitious young deputy happened across me as I disposed of a body in the caves beneath Kill Devil Hill, and I told him that if he aided me in my mission, Albemerich would ensure the prosperity of his family as well as mine. The demon appeared when I called to him, and we added the deputy to our pact. Not long after that, the sheriff died and my deputy friend became the new sheriff."

"What a coincidence," I said, the sarcasm heavy on my tongue.

"I thought as much," said the magician. "But it was not a coincidence, of course. It was Albemerich. And his power was seductive. The more prominent the sheriff became in the community, the more prominent he wanted to become. So eventually he needed money and went to the president of the local bank for a loan. Albemerich persuaded him to not only provide the sheriff with the funds for his campaign, but to join our union as well. The bank's investments quadrupled in value within a matter of months."

"So you kept bringing in new members to your Asshole of the Month Club, and eventually every influential prick in the area was working together to feed innocent victims to a demon, and you all just sat back and collected the dividends."

"It wasn't like that! We never took the innocent. We chose women of low moral standing, vagrants, criminals, and migrant laborers. We didn't take people who would be missed."

"So you preyed on the most vulnerable, because they were morally inferior to you fine, upstanding pillars of the community," I said.

"We did what we had to do!" the old man bellowed, a thick vein pulsing along his temple. "I made a mistake, but it was for the greater good! I didn't want anyone to get hurt, but if I could save my colony from certain death, it was worth the sacrifice of a few to do so."

"And when you kept going? I'm dying to hear how you rationalized centuries of murder. Couldn't have been you trying to save more people because you'd already given the entire fucking colony to him!"

"I had a family to protect!"

"A wife that would rather die than live in a world with you, and a daughter who...what? Stood by you the whole way?"

All the steam went out of him in a rush, like I'd deflated him with my words. "She left when her mother passed. I haven't seen her since 1866."

"So you have no idea if she's still alive or not," I said. "But she's not just standing on the sidelines cheering while you stack corpses like firewood." Suddenly I started to feel a little bad for this idiot. He didn't know what he was getting into; he just made a bad deal and kept getting further and further upside down. Then I felt the mental equivalent of a slap upside my head as Becks brought me back to reality.

He lured freed slaves into the swamp and murdered them. People born in chains who had just tasted freedom, and this son of a bitch snuffed out their lives so he and his cronies could stay rich and healthy. Wake up, Harker!

Fuck, I replied. *You're right. There's nothing else to learn from this prick. Time to open up the can.*

The can?

Of Whoop-Ass.

"Hey, Shithead?" I locked eyes with the old wizard. "You got any useful information before I roast your nuts in their sack, like the names of everyone you're working with, or should we just cut straight to the part where I fuck you up and send you off to finally meet your fate?"

His eyes widened, then narrowed. "Surely you can't mean to end our arrangement with Albemerich now. I can have you added to our pact. It shouldn't cost much. Just the life of that Negress you've been seen around town with. Then you can be rich and powerful beyond your wildest imaginings."

Negress? I don't think I'm even offended by that one. It's like when your uncle with dementia uses antisemitic slurs at Thanksgiving. He's just too fucking addled to get pissed at. I mean, still kill his ass, but you don't have to kill him any deader for the "Negress" thing, Becks said in my head.

I blew out a snort of laughter, both at the lame-ass offer and at her response. "You stupid bag of dicks," I said to the wizard. "You did enough research to see that I'm marrying a Black woman, but not enough to figure out who the fuck I am. I'm Quincy Fucking Harker, you twat. I've been around since the dawn of the twentieth century, and I stopped aging around World War One. I throw fireballs for fun, and my uncle is Count Goddamn Dracula, and he's been *very* careful with his investments. I'm *already* richer than fuck, and I have all the power I need right at my fingertips." To demonstrate, I summoned two small orbs of purple energy and flung them in his direction.

I wasn't aiming directly at him; rather, I sent one blasting into each side of the banister he was leaning over, raining splinters down into the grand foyer and sending him scurrying away from the edge of the balcony. He slipped out of sight for a moment until I sprinted up the stairs to find him opening a tiny Gate right there in his house.

Great. This asshat had enough power stored to call demons right here on the balcony. This might turn into a real fight. I smiled a little when I saw the size of the Gate. Barely six feet tall and less than four feet across, the narrow oval wouldn't let anything really terrible through. Don't get me wrong, little demons are as bad as those little dinosaurs in the *Jurassic Park* movies and can totally swarm somebody and tear them to pieces. But I've dealt with a lot worse than a compy swarm of demons, so as soon as the first one stepped through, I called up a spike of pure energy and shoved it through the demon's head. Then I planted a boot in its chest and sent it careening back through the Gate, a dying message to its buddies back home. Too bad I didn't have time to write a note.

Then I coiled my legs under me and leapt, straight up over the Gate in an arcing dive that I turned into a front roll as I came down in front of the wizard. I sprang to my feet and punched him in the jaw, spinning him completely around before he dropped flat on his ass on his expensive carpet. I could feel the Gate close behind me, and a thin wail of demonic rage trickled through, then I grinned down at the man who'd wrought so much death and destruction for so many years.

"Names," I said, my smile a grim rictus.

"W-what?"

"I want the names of everyone involved in this shit, from the sheriff to the real estate asshole, to every single one percenter motherfucker you've been enriching off the blood of this community. You bastards call my Uncle Luke a fucking vampire? You're the parasites. And the buffet is fucking *closed*. Now talk."

Spoiler alert—he talked. Twenty minutes later, I had a list of eight names, a busted knuckle from punching the old man in the mouth, and a deep-seated loathing for all the local business leaders. The list included the sheriff, which I expected, the mayor (also not a surprise), one county council member, the real estate prick I'd met at the recent crime scene, the editor of the local paper, which explained not only the weak coverage of a string of murders but also how the local print rag managed to stay in business in this day and age, and two names that really pissed me off—the senior priest of the local Methodist church, and the principal of the high school.

Now look, I'm not all that religious, despite hanging out with a literal angel. But church is supposed to be where people go for succor and safety when they're running bad. It's not supposed to be where demons get their takeout. And the school? Kids are fucking sacred, man. Even shithead high school kids deserve a chance to grow up and be less shitty. They don't deserve to get fed to demons.

But first on my personal hit list was my buddy the sheriff. The gay lawman bringing progress and equality to the yokels, all the while cherry picking people to be fed to a fucking demon. He was also the one tied to this plot for the longest, through his family history, so if there was more to learn about Albemerich before I kicked his flaming ass back to Hell, Sheriff French would be the person to tell me. Unfortunately, at some point during my conversation with Drew the Dickhead Wizard, Sheriff French had woken up and driven away. *Good,* I thought. *The chase makes it more fun.*

I felt that evil grin stretch across my face again as I walked out the front door of the mansion, the wizard's corpse hanging from his massive crystal chandelier like some kind of Hannibal Lector sculpture. Time to hunt.

CHAPTER THIRTY-THREE

Y ou can't do this to me! Don't you know who I am?" That was the most common refrain for the rest of my night, stretching into the early morning hours. The mayor said it when I kicked in his bedroom door and blasted him through the sliding glass door of his bedroom halfway down the beachfront his estate opened up onto. He didn't say anything else after I kicked him so hard in the balls that he lifted several feet up into the air before collapsing in a heap on the sand. I channeled power through my hands into his body and blasted so much fire through his worthless carcass that it turned the patch of sand he'd been lying on into smoked glass.

The county commissioner said it when I threw him out of his bed onto the bedroom floor, ignoring the two college-aged young men that went running naked out into the night. He said it again when I planted one of my black Doc Martens in his side, snapping three ribs like pretzels. He tried to say it after I punched him in the face, but it's really hard to talk with a broken jaw. He didn't say anything after I jammed his head in the toilet and slammed the lid down hard enough to shatter the bowl. He just lay in the floor, water gushing around him and washing the blood from his severed carotid across the formerly gleaming white tiles.

The principal didn't say anything, just nodded when I burst through the double doors of her bedroom. She sat up against a stack of pillows with the ugly boxlike shape of a Glock pistol in her hand. I readied a shield, but she pressed the gun to her temple and pulled the trigger, jolting her sleeping husband awake as blood and gray matter splashed through his Ambien-fueled dreams.

The minister dropped to his knees and started reciting the twenty-third psalm, but when he got to the point about fearing no evil, I leaned over and whispered in his ear, "I am the baddest motherfucker in the valley, bitch," and twisted his neck around so hard he was looking at his own asshole when he breathed his last. I got a little more creative with the newspaper editor, since there was an antique printing press in the back of his office. I set it up so when I was finished with him, he was shoved halfway inside the machinery with "murderer" stamped on every inch of his visible skin. And it was all pretty visible, since I flayed him, stamped his flesh, and nailed it to the wall before I let him die.

The real estate douchebag went full circle back to where the mayor started—he tried to bribe me. I didn't bother explaining myself to him, I just set his ass on fire, then burned his house down around him. I did carry his dog outside, though, and chained it to a tree far away from the burning structure. No point in punishing the Lab for the shitty stuff his owner did. Some firefighter's kid was going to wake up to a new companion.

Sheriff French was the first emergency vehicle on the scene, which made my life a little easier. Now I wouldn't have to hunt his sorry ass down. I would have to make sure none of the innocent members of the department were around to see me kill his sorry ass, but that was a fairly simple affair. There were a whole lot of brand-new dead bodies and an arson to deal with, a heavy load for four hours in most any jurisdiction, much less a sleepy tourist town in North Carolina. I walked up to his car as soon as he parked.

"Hi, Sheriff," I said, hopping up to sit on the hood.

He exited the car with his riot gun in hand, racked a shell, and leveled the twelve-gauge at me. "Don't move!" he yelled. He reached for the radio clipped to his shoulder, and I held up my right index finger to stop him.

"I wouldn't do that," I said. "Trust me, it's going to go a lot better for you if you just take your lumps from me and don't involve any of your deputies. Besides, I think they're probably responding to burglar alarms at the homes of some of your most prominent citizens, aren't they?"

His face was a stone mask, giving nothing away. "Quincy Harker, you are under arrest—"

"If I had a nickel for every time I've heard those words, I'd be a millionaire," I said, then thought about it. I was probably already a millionaire. I did own a really big building right outside of uptown Charlotte. I bought it with Luke's money, but it was my building. That alone probably left me stupid rich, and that's before I start hocking Luke's antiques and art. Or looking into any of my dad's accounts. Stoker set him up to get a piece of royalties and licensing when he wrote my parents' story, but we kinda got screwed when he messed up the copyright documents. That cost me millions, but I was definitely never hurting for money. But I returned my focus to the problem at hand, namely how to kill the sheriff without getting arrested for it. I still had a few names on my list before I went deepest South to kill Albemerich and get some justice for Milton and the other victims.

"You...killed them," Sheriff French said.

"I did."

"Are you planning to kill me, too?"

"No."

"You're not?"

"No. I'm not *planning* to kill you. I'm fucking *going* to kill you. I'm going to kill your worthless ass, and my only regret in killing you will be that I don't have magic enough to resurrect you and kill you over and over again, once for every death you've been responsible for. You've been playing in deep water, Sheriff, and now something has come up from the depths to drag you down."

"So what are you? An avenging angel?"

"Oh, I am no angel, Sheriff. Angels have rules. Angels have a code. Angels have a sense of what is too far. I have none of those things. I'm not an angel, Sheriff. I am justice fucking personified, and you're a piece of shit tin star motherfucker who's been using his position of power and trust to lure people to their death so you and your asshole friends could get rich and stay rich. All on the backs of people you think are less than yourselves. And this from a gay man in the South? After all the shit you've had to put up with, you take the first hint of power and use it against other people? Other marginalized people? How many gay people have you fed to the demon? How many Black people? How many undocumented immigrants? Or did you just prey on poor people, drug addicts, sex workers, and travelers? Seasonal workers and tourists? What made somebody worthless enough for you to murder, Sheriff?"

"They just weren't me," he said simply. "I didn't give a shit who they were, as long as they weren't me. And you're not me, either, but I know who you are. You're The Reaper. You're the one they tell stories about in whispers, around campfires, and in the dark corners of the worst bars on the planet. You've killed more people than the plague, Harker, so don't fucking lecture me on taking lives. I bet you can't even remember half the people you've slaughtered. Name them, Reaper. Go ahead, tell me the names of the people you've killed. I bet you can't remember any of them."

He's right and wrong all at the same time. I have left behind me a swath of bodies wider than an interstate highway, and I don't know all their names, much less remember them. But there are a lot of them who haunt me. A lot of voices that come to whisper in my ear in the middle of the night, or scream in the predawn hours, jolting me awake in a cold sweat. There's a roll call every night after I close my eyes, but those aren't the names of the people I've killed. No, the ones that make it hard for me to sleep are the ones I couldn't save. The ones who died because of me, but not at my hand. The ones whose lives weren't cut short because of something I did, but because of who I am. The deaths that haunt me aren't the ones I caused with magic, or a gun, or even my bare hands. The ones that haunt me are the ones that I caused just by being close to them. Just by loving them. Those are the deaths that keep me awake at night.

"You're right, Sheriff. I am The Reaper. And you're just another piece of shit with a gun who's stepped to the wrong magic-wielding mother-fucker." I channeled power down the barrel of his shotgun with my right hand while I wrapped myself in a shield with my left. The energy flowed into the gun and ignited all the shells in the magazine, exploding the gun and sending a ridiculous number of double-ought buckshot pellets whizzing around the sheriff's car. A fair number of them blew right through the sheriff, and no small number of them slammed into the car as well. I heard the spatter of liquid on pavement, smelled the telltale scent of gasoline, and started walking away, leaving Sheriff French writhing and moaning on the driveway. He'd bleed out within minutes, but I knew there were already more first responders on the way. Just to make sure he didn't find someone, human or demon, to come to his rescue, I flicked a little fireball over my shoulder at the car, hearing a satisfying *whoosh* as it burst into flames.

I walked down the driveway, illuminated by the burning house, car, and pair of demon flunkies as I did my badass movie no-look-back exit. Just one more name on my list, and it was the woman they called The Key. Time to go unlock some shit and take the slaughter to Albemerich for a change.

CHAPTER THIRTY-FOUR

The last name on my list was, according to Dead Wizard Drew, the owner of the town's lone New Age bookstore, incense shop, chandlery, and general purveyor of magical trinkets, most of which were completely useless and mundane. Except for the ones that weren't. I could smell the power from a block away, and when I peered at the entrance to Aunt Jayel's Emporium of the Mystical Arts, it glowed with wards covering the front door and windows. I wasn't even quite sure I could get through them without dying to the backlash of disrupted power. Fortunately for me, I'm usually only about fifty-fifty on doors.

Most people have good doors. Smart people use heavy-duty impact-resistant glass in their plate-glass windows and reinforce the doorframe as well. Not nearly enough people do much to shore up the walls, and a determined, or in my case righteously pissed off, magic user can blast through them like the Kool-Aid man, only way less fun for the people on the other side of the wall. Aunt Jayel's Emporium shared a wall with Happy Harry's House of Haste, an alliterative bike shop specializing in renting beach cruisers to families. Happy Harry was going to lose his adjective when he got the call from the surviving members of the sheriff's department, because I kicked his plate glass window in, stepped through the falling shards, and blew out the wall between his bicycle showroom and Aunt Jayel's magic shop.

Aunt Jayel stood behind her counter, elbows on the glass and a grim scowl on her face. "You shouldn't be here, Reaper."

"You shouldn't be murdering tourists and feeding them to demons, Auntie," I replied. "Now that we've gotten that out of the way, are we doing this the easy way or the hard way?"

"What, pray tell, is the easy way?" she asked, her hair falling in pink-dyed waves across her shoulders. She was an older woman, mid-sixties maybe, with a few extra pounds here and there and lines around her eyes that gave the impression of general mirth. But there were no crinkly smiles tonight. No, she was flitting back and forth between angry and scared shitless, with the needle dipping a little more heavily into "scared shitless" than I'm sure she wanted.

"The easy way is you give me the ritual to open Albemerich's Gate, I shoot you in the face, and then I go to Hell and beat up your pet demon before you finish shuffling off this mortal coil."

"That doesn't sound very easy."

"I've been killing people for a very long time," I replied. "It gets easier with experience."

"I meant easy for me."

"Nah," I said. "Dying's easy. Almost everybody does it."

"Then let's see how you do with it," she said, then flung a handful of red dust in my direction. "*Rend!*" she shouted, channeling power into the dust. The flecks of crimson sand elongated into slivers of blood-toned glass, all flying at my face.

I called up a shield around my left arm and held it in front of me, smiling through the glimmering purple aura as the slivers shattered back into sand as they met my defenses. "Not bad," I said. "Haven't seen that one before. *Infernos!*" I dropped my shield and flung my right hand out straight from my chest, sending a basketball-sized orb of white-hot flame streaking toward her face.

She ducked, and the fireball slammed into the shelves of books and potions behind her, shattering the bottles and jars and setting the display ablaze. I thought for a second that she should probably be careful breathing that stuff in, then remembered that I was going to kill her ass, so I didn't care if she suffocated or if I burned her from the inside out. Dead's dead, and it didn't matter to me how she got there, just *that* she got there.

"*Grapple,*" she hissed, pointing at the tiles beneath my feet. The floor started to writhe and roil, and vines split the concrete slab and punched their way up to twine around my legs. In seconds, I was held fast from the knees down, completely immobile.

From the knees down. Which did nothing to keep me from manifesting my soulblade and slicing through the magical bonds like overcooked spaghetti. Aunt Jayel staggered back as the magic she'd poured into the vines slammed back into her, and she shrieked in pain as her shirt began to smolder.

"Careful, Auntie," I said. "Polyester melts like a motherfucker."

"Don't use that coarse language around me, young man! *Agony!*" She pointed at me again, and I felt her magic batter my mental defenses, trying to hammer pure power straight into my brain. And people say *I* lack subtlety? This woman was nothing more than a mystical hammer with legs. And not a terribly strong hammer, at that.

I waved my hand in front of my face, dispelling the power she called. "You get by on the fact that nobody around here has any talent, don't you?" My tone was light, mocking, pushing on the idea that I wasn't even breathing hard and I was thwarting her every move. Because I wasn't. She was a middling power at best, not even really strong enough to brew most of the potions she had on her shelves. Shelves which were still burning and getting more and more engulfed in flames by the second. I wasn't in any danger from her magic, but if I spent too much time fucking around in here with her, I was definitely in danger of having the building fall in on my head. Time to get serious.

"Just tell me how to open Albemerich's Gate and I'll end this quick," I offered.

"Just go fuck off into the ocean and I won't curse you and that Black bitch you're screwing," Auntie replied, shocking me a little.

"Wow," I said, feigning surprise. "Consorting with demons and casual racism. Wanna throw in a little homophobia and antisemitism while you're at it? And what happened to not using coarse language, *Auntie?*"

"Fuck you, Harker." Her face twisted in an ugly snarl. "Lord Albemerich will flay you alive and pick his teeth with your bones." She called up power around her left hand, a sickening yellow-green ball of vile energy that she flung in my direction.

I ducked it easily, but that was just a feint. The real attack was a beam of crimson energy that came streaking toward me from a ring on her right fist, power that slammed into my gut and dropped me to one knee, wracked with pain. It felt like every nerve in my body had been plugged into a live electrical circuit and turned up to eleven. I tried to lift my head, struggling against the pain, but Auntie threw another ball of yellow nastiness at me, and this one I couldn't avoid. My head was wreathed in the stench of sulfur, bile, and excrement—a seething ball of grossness that swirled around me, clouding my vision and making my eyes and nose stream. Seemed I might have underestimated Auntie.

Would you quit dancing with this old biddy and do your damn job?!? Becks's mental voice jarred me loose from my pain and Auntie's magical disorientation. I sent power streaming out from me in every direction, searing away her spells and dissolving the globe of piss-power around my face. I opened my eyes to see that Aunt Jayel had taken advantage of my distraction to extinguish the flames, and she turned back to me with a wicked grin on her face.

"Looks like the little old lady might have some power after all, huh, Reaper?" she said, her tone mocking me.

"Yeah, you've got a little power," I said. "But only a little. *Forzare!*" I channeled pure kinetic energy at her, slamming her back into the smoldering bookshelves and jostling loose a half-dozen jars of esoteric ingredients.

I walked toward the counter, my steps slow, measured, implacable. "I'm going to ask you again, just this one last time. Where is the ritual?"

"I'm going to tell you one last time. Go fuck yourself."

I waved a finger at her like a disapproving substitute teacher. "Tsk, tsk. Language." Then I pointed my index finger at her mouth and sent a laser-tight beam of power streaking in her direction. Magic wrapped around her head, clamping her jaw shut, then power arced across her face, welding her lips together with mystical flame. She screamed, but the sound was muffled. She clutched at her mouth, but there wasn't really a mouth there anymore, just a pair of lips, forever sealed. She looked at me, terror filling her face as it began to dawn on her that I really was going to kill her and there wasn't a goddamned thing she could do to stop it.

She turned pleading eyes in my direction, and I could almost hear the begging. My resolve faltered for the briefest instant, and I saw hope blossom on her face as she read my expression. Then I thought about Milton, and how she and her friends fed him to a demon just because he did his job. And I thought of all the others these assholes had given over to Albemerich's tender mercies for centuries, just to keep themselves healthy and wealthy.

All that flashed through my head, and in an instant, I reached a decision. I could spend the rest of the night sorting through her books and papers to find the ritual for Albemerich's Gate. Because I had that kind of time. But she didn't. Her time was up. Right. Fucking. Now.

She read it in my eyes, and I watched the terror return to hers as she realized that the end wasn't nigh, it was right in front of her. "You called me Reaper, Auntie? Well, guess what? It's harvest time." At least with her lips sewn shut she didn't scream as much.

CHAPTER THIRTY-FIVE

No fucking way," Becks said, and I was surprised that for once, the first f-bomb wasn't mine.

"Sorry, babe. You know this is how it's gotta go. The only ones that can go to Hell without some serious protective mojo are me and Glory."

The angel looked a little abashed. "Um...about that, Harker..."

I turned to her. I'd seen Glory in all kinds of states. Furious, disappointed, grieving, furious again, joyful...but I'd never seen her...embarrassed. She saw *me* embarrassed all the fucking time, thanks to her annoying tendency to pop into my bedroom when I was absolutely bare-assed, but I'd never seen the emotion on her. I figured it probably didn't bode well for me. "What's the deal, Glory?"

"I can't go."

"What?" Becks and I asked simultaneously.

"I can't go to Hell. I'm not allowed."

"But you went last time," Becks argued. And she was right. When I went into Hell to keep Lucifer from ascending and becoming an Archangel again, Glory was the only member of Team Harker who could accompany me, because passing into a Divine or Demonic plane wouldn't tear her to shreds or leave her severed from her body like it would Luke or Flynn.

"I wasn't fully an angel again at that point, nor was I fully human. I didn't know if I'd be allowed to pass through with you, and I definitely didn't know if I'd be allowed to come back, but we...got lucky."

"Got lucky?" I asked. "We *got lucky?* We went to *Hell*, Glory! And we came back! We didn't get lucky, we're fucking badasses! We waltzed into Hell, gave Lucifer the middle finger, and waltzed right back out again. And now you're telling me you can't do it again? Of course you can! You're all you again now! You've got your groove back. Nothing can stop us!"

"Ahem," Faustus said from where he stood by the bar in our Airbnb. I don't know what he thought was going to materialize in the time since we left and now, since he'd already cleaned me out of anything but cheap gin before we left the house last night. "One, I think you may be glossing over the contributions of the member of the party who dragged you out of the deepest Circle, thereby guaranteeing that no matter how many millennia he'd faithfully served the Lords of Hell, he would never be allowed back in his home again."

He had a point. We never would have gotten home if Faustus hadn't come down to save us, and he'd given up any hope of being able to return to his former life in the process. If the demon underground news network was to be believed, my glossy black friend sat only a step or two below me on Lucifer's People I Most Want to Anally Penetrate with a Rotating Pitchfork list. "You're right," I said. "We never would have made it home without you. Sorry for not mentioning that. But I know you can't go with me. Every demon within three Circles would be on us like a dog on a bone the second word got out that you were there. I'm betting the bounty on your head is pretty substantial."

"At last reporting, I was good for a Two-Circle promotion. That's the kind of thing you only see awarded for a major service to the boss. So yeah, he wants to see to my punishment personally. I'd be flattered if the idea didn't turn my bowels to water."

"Do you have bowels?" I asked.

"Depends on how I build the meat suit," he replied. "If I want to eat, I have to poop. Everybody poops, Harker. There's even a book about it."

"People!" Becks clapped her hands. "Can we focus? Harker is not going alone into the Fifth Circle of Hell to fight a demon. That's suicide."

"You're right," I said. She whirled around, her mouth hanging open. I held up a finger before she could draw in a breath to keep yelling at me.

"And if I was going down there to fight him, that would be a problem. But I'm not. I don't want to fight Albemerich. Especially not in his house. That's a losing proposition whether I have you all with me or not. I just need to get down there and destroy the side of the Gate that is anchored in his lair. Then he can't just pop up to the Carolina coast to chomp on vacationers whenever he's feeling peckish."

"You're going to destroy the Gate?" Becks asked.

"That's the plan."

"While you're on the other side of it?" Her eyebrow kept climbing and the question dripped with sarcasm.

"I'm not going to close the Gate," I said. "Not until I'm home, at any rate. I just need to destroy the anchor. Then it'll be just like any other temporary passage between dimensions—*temporary*. Then I hop back through, where you lot are waiting with sledgehammers and holy water, and we break up the anchor point on this side, closing the Gate and cutting off Albemerich's expressway to the mortal plane."

Becks's face relaxed a little, but she still looked dubious. "You're sure this will work?"

"Not even a little bit." Pro tip—don't bother trying to lie to someone who is inside your head. It doesn't go well. So I just told her the truth. "I hope it works, but I'm not sure of anything. Hell, at this point I'm barely convinced that the sun rises in the east."

"It does," Luke said from his spot on the couch. Nameless was sprawled on the vampire's lap, allowing belly rubs. I swear, that was the weirdest damn cat. He followed Luke around like a guard dog, even curling up on top of the bed when Luke slept under it, but he wouldn't let Faustus anywhere near him and tolerated the rest of our existence in typical cat-like fashion. Except Glory. Furry little bastard just *loved* my Guardian Angel. "Trust me, Quincy. I am all too aware of where the sun is at every moment of the day."

Well, he did have a vested interest in that very fact. "Okay, so the sun rises in the east, and Harker's going to Hell alone. Anything else we need to get sorted?"

"Tell me again why Glory can't go?" Becks said.

"I was able to go last time because I was only partly an angel at the time, and because the remaining Archangels were there and approving. This time they are…less so," Glory replied.

"The Archangels won't let you go to Hell with Harker?" Becks asked. "Why not?"

"Because it's not their fucking problem, and they figure if I'm stupid enough to go to Hell, I can figure out my own way out," I said. "That basically it?"

Glory's cheeks flamed red. "Pretty much. Michael's phrasing included something about arrogant mortal pricks overreaching, but you got the gist of it."

"I should have punched him when I had the chance," I said.

"Before he had his memories back and knew he was the strongest warrior angel in the Host, you mean," Glory said.

"Yeah, that was implied," I agreed. I turned back to Flynn, who was fuming and looking from one person to the other. "Sorry, babe. It's got to be a solo flight. Wish it was different, because I could sure use the backup, but it's gotta be me. Otherwise, if we just destabilize the Gate from this side, he could move the anchor and continue to pass through at will."

Then I had an idea. "Hey, Nameless," I said to the cat. "Wanna go on an adventure?"

Luke scowled at me as the cat just gave me a flat stare. "Quincy, you are not taking my cat to Hell."

"*Your* cat?" I asked. "Who brought him home?"

"Whose lap is he currently purring on?" Luke replied. "I believe I heard somewhere that a cat purring because he loves you is a form of karma. So since he is currently very contented in my lap, I feel that is an endorsement of my moral fiber and proof that I am worthy. Also, it's a law that I can't move while a cat is on me. I saw that on the internet."

"I think the world's most famous bloodsucking fiend just admitted to being a Taylor Swift fan," I said. "I think anywhere I go now will be less foreign to me than this world is right now."

"Quincy, it's the twenty-first century. Everyone is a Taylor Swift fan," Luke said, petting Nameless's belly.

My worldview completely twisted, I gathered up my bag of supplies and headed for the door. "I'm gonna head back over to Kill Devil Hill and...well, kill a devil, I suppose."

"I'm driving," Becks said.

"Shotgun!" Faustus called.

"You don't get shotgun when someone else in the car is literally going to Hell to fight a demon in his lair," I said.

"Harker, I helped create the concept of 'shotgun,' you cannot try to confuse me about the rules," Faustus said.

"You're full of shit," I said. "You didn't have anything to do with creating the concept of 'shotgun."

"No," he admitted. "But admit it. You bought it for half a second, didn't you?"

Goddammit. No way was I admitting that. "Get in the car, demon. I'm going to Hell to pick a fight."

CHAPTER THIRTY-SIX

The ritual to open the Gate was simple. A little of my blood, a Latin incantation, enough power to sink an aircraft carrier channeled through the design inscribed in the floor, and a rip in the fabric of the universe opened up in front of me. I turned to Becks. "I'll be back soon. I love you."

"You'd better come back, you prick. We have a wedding to plan. And if you think you can escape picking out the paper for invitations just by getting trapped in Hell, you've got another think coming."

"Well...I *had* considered just staying down there so I wouldn't have to fuck around with the seating chart for the reception. I mean, Stoker has a nephew, so I guess we have to invite him, but I can't put him anywhere too close to Luke or he'll hear my uncle's opinion of his uncle's writing, and then there's the question of how many plus ones does Bubba get, and what fae we can put next to which cryptids. You gotta admit, Hell seems preferable."

She put her arms around my neck and kissed me, a soul-searing kiss that climbed inside my mouth and danced around, touching every part of me, body and soul. I wrapped my arms around her and straightened, leaving her legs dangling in midair and kissed her back, pouring every bit of love and devotion I had into it. After a kiss that lasted either seconds or hours, I put her down, looked her in the eyes, and said, "I'll be right back. I promise."

"You better," she said, wiping a lone tear from her eye. "I love you, asshole."

I gave her my very best sideways half-smile and said, "I know." Then I turned and stepped through the Gate, sealing it behind me with a gesture. I always wanted to have the cool Han Solo line, and that was as close as I was going to get.

I looked around, getting the lay of the land. I'm not all that familiar with the landscape of Hell, having only made the one trip through. Albemerich was a Fifth Circle demon, and the Fifth is the Circle of Wrath, so I expected a horde of screaming war demons to come rushing at me the second I appeared. That was what happened the last time I popped into this level, anyway. But it was quiet. Eerily so, in a *High Plains Drifter* kind of way, where I expected to see tumbleweeds blowing down the streets of a deserted Western town.

Except there were no tumbleweeds. No town, either. Just a blasted red-tinged landscape covered in sharp rocks. The whole place looked a lot like pictures I'd seen from Mars, all desolate and unforgiving. I didn't expect an oasis, but I did expect a welcoming party of sorts. Here I was, all dressed up and nobody to kill. How did I end up in the one section of Hell where there were no demons around?

Until there were. In a blink, my surroundings went from deserted to horrifyingly crowded as a literal horde of demons appeared out of nowhere. Now, normally when someone says "out of nowhere," they mean that someone snuck up on them, or popped out of a hidey hole, or maybe jumped down from a tree. Nope. These assholes literally came *out of nowhere*, complete with the "pop" sound of displaced air that teleportation causes. One second I was alone, the next second I was surrounded.

And directly in front of me was a massive Torment demon, heavily muscled, eight feet tall, and grinning like a kid on Christmas. "I remember you," he said.

Well, fuck. This was not going to be good. If a demon remembers you, it's *never* good. They only remember people they strike deals with and people they really want to kill. This is even more true with Torment demons. They are brutally stupid. Like, a demon from the Seventh Circle invented Velcro so Torment demons could wear shoes in their meat suits because they never managed to grasp the concept of tying shoes. Or even magically manifesting shoes that were already tied. *That* level of stupid. But they know how to hold a grudge.

So if this Torment demon remembered me, it was almost certainly because I'd killed him at least once back in the mortal realm. But the longer I kept him talking (grunting, really), the more time I had to formulate a plan to get out of the mess I was in. I'd come in expecting a fight, but I thought I'd be able to see them coming. The teleportation thing was a shocker, and I needed a few extra seconds to adjust. Time to keep the demon confused. Not a huge task, given the demon in question. "Oh?" I asked. "Where did we meet? Tijuana? There are a lot of TJ nights I don't remember."

The demon scrunched his brow, then said, "No. You threw me off the big wheel thing. I fell down. Hurt my head." He rubbed his ass when he mentioned hurting his head, and I somehow managed to still take him seriously as a threat.

I mean, he literally didn't know his head from his ass, but he could rip my head off and shit down my neck if I couldn't stay out of his grip. So I didn't laugh. I coughed a couple times but didn't laugh. Then I remembered. He must have been one of the Torment demons I tossed off the Ferris wheel in Atlanta a few years back. Yeah, that woulda hurt. Okay, not apologizing for that one, so time to cheat.

Torment demons are huge, pushing eight feet tall most of the time, and when they're on our plane of existence, they're almost invulnerable to physical harm. I was really hoping that wouldn't be the case here, so I reared back and kicked him in the nuts as hard as I could, summoning my soulblade at the same time.

Unfortunately, I was ignoring a very important point in demonic and angelic anatomy. Torment demons don't have balls. They're neuter, so there are no reproductive organs. So while I kicked the big bastard right between the legs, and it was obviously painful, it wasn't the crippling blow it would have been to a human. And it gave away any element of surprise I might have had. Well, shit.

"That wasn't very nice, Reaper," the demon said, a smile stretching its crimson face. A pair of small white fangs protruded slightly from its upper lip. "I think I eat your spleen now."

"I think go fuck yourself," I said, slashing through its chest with my soulblade. The Torment demon screeched in pain and fell backward, black blood spraying from the wound. I spun, taking the head off a scrawny pit demon in the process. There were demons surrounding me, leaving a small circle in the middle of their mob where they weren't quite sure they wanted to take on The Reaper, but the second they realized exactly how much of a numbers advantage they had, I was fucked.

Unless I struck first. So I did. I struck first, and I struck *hard*. I called power and blasted a wave of force in a circle around me, throwing demons ass over teakettle back in a wave. I saw a slight opening and sprinted for a rocky outcropping. If I could get to high ground, or at least put my back to a solid wall or boulder so I couldn't be surrounded, I'd be in a lot better shape. A Reaver demon leapt out in front of me, but I vaulted over it, kicking the nasty little shit right in the face as I did so. Even though I was nothing but a soul here, that's all the demons were, too, so any damage I did was just like it would be in the physical plane.

I got to the rocks, more a few shards of some reddish stone than a real wall, but at least it limited the lines of attack from the horde. Several pit demons came at me, but I was able to keep them at bay with my soulblade. But there were so many of them. I slashed and cut and hacked and killed, but for every nasty little bastard I cut down, two stepped in to fill the gap. I felt a set of claws grab my shield, and I channeled more power through it, blasting the demon to pieces and sending several others scattering back, giving me a few seconds' reprieve.

This wasn't working. There were too many of them. And if I stood here with my back to a wall, every demon in the Fifth Circle could just waltz over and take a shot at me. It might take hours, it might take days, but even here where magic was stronger and I wasn't burdened by the weight of a physical body, I couldn't fight forever. Eventually I'd get tired and slip, or just miss an attack, and that would be the end of Quincy Fucking Harker.

So it was time to change the game. Standing there waiting for them to come to me wasn't working, so I decided to take the fight to Albemerich himself. I charged forward, wreathing myself in a cocoon of power and bowling demons over as I ran into them. I stomped on heads, leapt over fallen bodies, and barreled through the horde, leaving a trail of beaten and broken bodies in my wake.

"ALBEMERICH!" I bellowed, slicing the head off a pit demon as I sprinted past. "Get your chickenshit ass out here and fight me, you cowardly bag of pus!"

No response from the boss demon, but another Torment demon stepped into my path and grinned at me. "Hello, Reaper. Time to die." He rubbed his palms together and grinned a wicked smile, but I just sprang high into the air and turned around, bringing my sword down on the side of his neck as I landed. My soulblade sliced deep into his neck and buried itself in his chest, carving a massive chunk out of the demon's torso. He fell forward and I banished the blade, summoning it again in an instant. One of the great things about magically manifesting a sliver of your soul as a magical weapon—you can't really drop it, and nobody else can *ever* pick it up and use it against you.

One of the downsides is that, at least in my case, it's locked into one form. So when a massive demon in a suit of thick plate armor steps up and whips a flail at your head, a longsword isn't very useful. All I could do was duck and slash at his legs, but his greaves deflected my blow with barely a *clang* of impact. He lashed out with his massive shield and caught me in the face, flinging me backward onto my ass. I rolled to the side, avoiding the flail that slammed down with ground-shaking force, and sprang to my feet.

I channeled power through the blade and shouted, *"Frigore!"* A stream of biting cold energy shot from the tip of my sword, slamming into the demon's chest and driving it back a couple feet. Ice enveloped the big bastard, immobilizing it for just a few seconds. But a few seconds was all I needed. I sprang forward, raising the sword high overhead, and brought it down right on the demon's forehead.

Or I would have if there had still been a demon standing there wrapped in ice like he was supposed to be. But no, it couldn't be that easy. This big fucker flexed his arms, shredded the icy bonds like they were tissue paper, and slid two feet to the left, making me miss entirely and overbalance, staggering forward to try and keep from falling on my face. Which is exactly what I did half a second later as a massive flail slammed into my kidneys.

I flew at least five feet and landed on my stomach, all the wind knocked out of me. I know I didn't really *need* to breathe, but fighting in immaterial planes is all wrapped up in what you expect to happen and what actually happens, so landing on my face knocked the wind out of me, just like it would if I were in my body. And it sucked at least as much. I lay there gasping for half a second, then felt the ground quiver beneath me under the armored demon's heavy footsteps. I rolled over onto my back without sliding sideways, aimed both hands straight up at its head, and channeled power through my palms.

"Cultro!" I shouted, and hundreds of little blades crafted of pure energy streaked from my hands. Most bounced off the demon's armor, but they were tiny little magical flechettes, so some lodged in joints of its armor, and some found the holes in its visor or the gaps where flesh was exposed. It let out an ear-splitting shriek, clutching its eyes and falling

backward. I got to my feet, called up my soulblade, and shoved the tip right through the hollow of the demon's throat, cutting off its cries of agony.

"Albemerich!" I shouted again. "Get your cowardly ass out here before I carve my way through every horned motherfucker in this Circle!"

A low voice came from behind me. "Alright, Reaper. I'm here."

I turned to see a massive demon standing twenty feet away, a pair of foot-long daggers in its hands. Albemerich. The demon was a good nine feet tall, bigger than even the Torment demons, with long black horns curling up from a thick bony ridge above its eyes. Its skin was crimson, with thick black eyebrows and a shaggy black beard. It wore no armor, bare to the waist with its muscular form on full display. Its chest and arms were crisscrossed with hundreds of black lines that I realized were scars. This dude had seen some combat. Probably started off its existence as your basic pit demon and fought, scratched, and slaughtered its way into demonic hierarchy. Great. Not only was he powerful, but with that kind of background, he'd be crafty as fuck, too. I wasn't getting any simple tricks over on this fucker.

But it didn't matter. This was the son of a bitch I'd come here to kill, so it was time to get to killing. I looked up at the massive demon, manifested my shield and soulblade, and grinned. "Let's dance, bitch."

CHAPTER THIRTY-SEVEN

Albemerich grinned down at me, showing off a double row of pointed teeth. "Nice of my earthbound minions to send me a snack. It does get tiresome going upstairs to fetch my meals."

"I'm afraid meat, and everything else, is off the menu, dickhead," I replied. "Every single one of your little friends topside is deader than fuck."

"I know, Harker. I'm a demon. You don't think we get a memo when one of our earthly associates makes their way into this domain? I knew you were coming before you even set foot in my shrine at Kill Devil Hill. Ironic name, isn't it? Since that's where I did so much killing." He grinned again, then swung a meaty hand in my direction, long black talons tipping all six of his elongated fingers.

I stepped back, then felt a presence behind me. I whirled around and sliced the head off a pit demon sneaking up on me. I whirled around again, but Albemerich just stood there, smiling at me. "You gonna fight like a real demon, or are you just going to have your passant little hench-horns do your dirty work?"

The big demon chuckled. "Fighting dirty is kind of our thing, isn't it? We're the bad guys, Harker. We don't play by the rules. But I do want to kill you myself. It'll score me points with the bosses if I bring your head to them myself. My boys can eat the rest of you, so long as Lucifer gets your soul. And your head. I think he said something about manifesting a penis just so he could fuck both your eye sockets."

"Descriptive, isn't he?" I said. "But there's one problem with that plan, Al."

"What's that?"

"You gotta kill me first." I launched myself at him, channeling power behind me to add a speed boost to my charge. I slashed at his face with my soulblade, but he got an arm up in time to block. My sword slammed into his forearm, and it felt like I'd hit a brick wall. Then the rest of me smacked into Albemerich, and *I* felt like I'd hit a brick wall. I bounced off him and landed flat on my back, staring up at the demon.

"Nice try, but you don't have the power here, Harker. This is *my* domain, *my* home, and the rules, such as they are, are in *my* favor. You should have tried to bring me to your world. You might have had a chance there. At least you would have had backup." He reached down and snatched me up into the air by the front of my shirt. I dangled from his grip, helpless. I battered his wrist with punches and kicks. I threw power at his face and at his body. I kicked him on the point of his jaw and slammed a heel into his ear.

Nothing. It was like I was punching a statue. Only statues have more give in them. Albemerich stood tall, holding me three feet off the ground like I weighed nothing, and laughed in my face. "You have no power here, mortal! This is not where you belong, and no matter how much power you draw, it pales in comparison to what I can control. You thought to face me in my seat of power? You are a fool, Quincy Harker. And you are soon to be a dead fool. Then I will take your head to Lucifer and become the Ruler of the Sixth Circle!"

"Well, you're partially right," came a dry voice from behind me. "Harker is a fool. The rest, though? Not so much. See, I won't let you kill him, which means you won't be taking his head anywhere, and I stopped in for a visit with Vasariole on the way up to see you, and he's not ready to give up his throne in the Sixth Circle yet, so there's probably going to be a little bit of resistance to your planned takeover. Oh, and by the way... put my fucking friend down before I rip your arm off and beat you to death with it."

Albemerich actually did put me down, although dropped me would be more precise. I slammed to the ground, air rushing out of me in a *whoof.* I scrambled to my feet, turning to see who was coming to my rescue. I thought I recognized the voice, but it couldn't be. Could it?

Oh, it could. It very much could. Standing all alone in a sea of demon corpses, bodies of pit dwellers and Torment demons alike piled all around like cordwood, was Faustus. Not the silly Hawaiian-shirt wearing Faustus who raided my liquor cabinet at every opportunity. No, this was Faustus the motherfucking *demon*. He stood nearly as tall as Albemerich and looked more imposing than I'd ever seen him, even in all the battles we'd fought together. He was clad in armor head to toe, with jet-black metal wrapping every inch of him, save his face, and he held a massive soulblade wreathed in crimson flame. This wasn't the crazy trickster who made so many deals with mortals that bargains were named after him. This was the Faustus who stormed the Gate of Heaven at Lucifer's side, a General in the Armies of the Fallen, one of the most powerful demons to ever step out of Hell.

And now, thanks to coming to my rescue, he'd never be able to leave. "What the fuck are you doing here?" I asked. "You know Lucifer is never going to let you leave. You turned on him. He's going to do to you everything he wants to do to me, only worse!"

"That's a problem for Future Faustus," he said with a wicked grin. "Present Faustus is focused on whether or not he's cutting Albemerich in half lengthwise or across the gut. Come on, Fifth Circle," he mocked. "Time to play with the varsity team."

"Faustus?" Albemerich said, taking a step back. "I've got no beef with you. I just want to murder Harker and move up in the ranks. You know how it is, right?"

Faustus's voice was cold. "No, Al. I don't know how it is. I know that I stood by Lucifer's side when we stormed the Gates, and I know that you weren't there. I know that I've sent more souls to Hell than every war mankind has ever waged, and I know that all you've ever done is murder a bunch of colonists and fuck up a bunch of people's vacation plans. I know that I'm a motherfucking Seventh Circle General and you're barely a middle management flunkie. So why don't you just fuck off back into the pit you spawned from and let me take my friend home."

Albemerich smiled then, a vicious thing that made his face even more hideous. "Oh no, Faustus. You're not taking anyone anywhere. You might kill me, and I might have to respawn in the pit and slaughter my way back to power. But Lucifer knows you're here by now, and there's not a snowball's chance in, well...*here* that you *or* Harker are getting out. So if you're going to kill me, go for it. But I don't have to make it easy on you." He manifested his own soulblade, this one red and rimmed in black flame, and charged us.

Spoiler alert—he did not make it easy on us. Albemerich was a big, powerful demon with a very large sword, and he knew how to use it. He started with a big, looping slash that would have decapitated both of us had it connected. Faustus and I ducked it easily and stepped in to stab the big bastard in the guts, thinking we'd finally gotten an easy fight.

Except we hadn't. As soon as I ducked, Al snapped out a quick front kick and slammed his big foot into my jaw. I flopped onto my back, sword vanishing with my wind. Faustus ran into a massive left fist as Al took one hand off his blade to drop my demonic savior with an open-handed slap that spun Faustus clean around before he flopped onto his belly. Al reversed the stroke of his sword into a big loop and grabbed the hilt with both hands again, aiming his strike downward at Faustus's throat.

I was on my feet by this point and manifested my soulblade again, knocking Albemerich's aside. I pushed off my feet, ramming a shoulder into the massive demon's chest, trying to knock him back and give Faustus enough space to regain his feet. Al staggered a couple steps backward, but didn't go down, and knocked me half-silly with a huge left to the jaw. I took three steps sideways to catch my balance, and barely deflected a sideways slash that would have cut me in half. But Faustus had regained his feet, and with a nod to me, pressed in on Albemerich's left while I attacked from the right.

The tandem offense staggered the big demon, and as Faustus and I grew more coordinated with our attacks, he had a harder and harder time blocking us. If there are two attackers who haven't fought together much or trained in two-on-one offense, the defender actually has a little bit of an advantage. And with Al's size and strength edge on each of us, it could have gone very badly. Except we *had* trained together, and fought together, and nearly died together. This wasn't the first time Faustus and I had taken on opponents who were bigger, stronger, or faster than us. Frankly, it was kinda the norm. So after a few seconds of trying not to step on each other's feet, we fell into a rhythm with our attacks and slowly took the upper hand from the murderous demon.

Albemerich was a stout opponent, and he fended off our attacks for a lot longer than most could, but eventually he bit on a high feint I made toward his throat, and Faustus slashed him across the back of one knee. The demon let out a high-pitched screech and dropped to the ground, his soulblade vanishing. He dragged himself up to his uninjured knee, but I kicked him in the temple, and he sprawled in the dirt.

I stepped over him, flaming sword held high, and he glared up at me, defiant to the end. I drove the blade down into his chest, and he let out a howl of agony. Then he looked up at me, and with his dying breath, said, "You'll never find the Lost Colony now, Reaper. They'll be here forever."

Then he faded from the ground before me, his essence absorbed back into the pit that spawned him. I knew that even as I stood there staring at the patch of dirt where he'd been seconds ago, he was already being reborn from a lake of fire somewhere in the First Circle. It would take him many years, maybe even eons, but eventually Albemerich would regain his power and be a pain in humanity's ass again. Just not today.

"What did he mean with that last bit?" I asked Faustus, who looked surprisingly concerned.

"There have been rumors for centuries about a mid-tier demon trapping a bunch of humans in a pocket dimension and keeping them for his own amusement, like an ant farm. I thought it was bullshit, but now..."

"You think this motherfucker didn't kill the Lost Colony, but he kidnapped them and stuck them in Hell for five hundred years?" I asked.

"Kinda sounds like it," Faustus agreed.

"And I just slaughtered the only person on any plane who knows exactly where they are and how to rescue them?"

"Not to sound like a broken record, but it kinda sounds like it."

"Fuck." Now I not only had to figure out how to get out of Hell without Lucifer noticing I was there, I had to figure out how to get *Faustus* out of Hell without Lucifer noticing, *and* I needed to find and rescue a hundred sixteenth-century colonists and return them to a world that would be all but unrecognizable to them.

This vacation was really making me need a vacation.

CHAPTER THIRTY-EIGHT

S o...now what?" I asked Faustus. We stood in the middle of a desolate patch of the Fifth Circle of Hell, dedicated to wrath, rage, and all sorts of other pissed-off emotions that coursed through my veins like lightning. I was pissed at myself for not digging deeper into Albemerich, for not considering the possibility that he lied to Dead Wizard Drew and the colonists were still alive, and for not even trying to interrogate the prick before slaughtering him. Admittedly, we'd thought we were finishing the boss fight, not dealing with a next-to-boss fight, but that didn't make me feel any better.

"Well, there's nobody on the Fifth that will give a shit about us or be willing to give me any kind of help," the demon replied. "Everybody here is just pissed off all the time and usually kinda sucks at quid pro quo."

"And there are demons in other Circles that don't hate you and might be willing to wheel and deal a little?" I asked.

"Hell runs on the barter system, and I have spent literal millennia stockpiling favors from assholes in half the Circles down here," he replied.

"Why only half?"

"Because the First Circle jerks don't have enough juice to be useful, and neither do the Second Circle assclowns. They're all either weak, or stupid. Or both. I mentioned that this Circle is useless because everybody's so goddamned angry all the time, and the Eighth and Ninth Circle types don't need anything I could provide. Plus, those guys are scary as fuck, so I try to stay away from them. That leaves us Three, Four, Six, or Seven to find someone useful, and then we need to find access to whatever Circle Albie stashed the colonists on."

"Don't you think they'll be here on Five?"

"Probably not. This Circle is pretty fucking inhospitable, and changing the nature of a plane gets harder the further you want to change it from its natural state. So turning a piece of this Circle into something that looks like Roanoke Island would be really difficult. I'm guessing they'll be stashed somewhere on Four. That's the Circle dedicated to greed, and there are a lot of areas that look like Earth. Easier to make people suffer for their greed if you can remind them what they coveted, and since most of the people here are from your plane, most of Four looks like Earth."

"You're saying that like there are people in Hell who didn't come from Earth," I mentioned, keeping my tone faux casual. I had the sense that he was saying something really important without actually saying it, and I really wanted to dig a little deeper into this.

"Angels, Harker. Angels. Not aliens. Stop watching conspiracy theory videos on YouTube and get with the program," he said, his tone flat. "The angels that fell are here, too, and they aren't all Lucifer or Generals. Some are just lame-ass angels who are suffering through the same bullshit humans have to suffer through. And some of them are greedy fucks, so they end up on Four."

"Oh." I'll admit, I was a little disappointed. I didn't come to Hell specifically to meet aliens, but if it happened, I wasn't going to complain. "So we need to get to the Fourth Circle and find the colonists. But how do we do that?"

"When we're on Earth and you need to find information, where do you go?" Faustus asked.

"A bar."

"Same thing down here. And there's one bar in particular that not only has brokers in all sorts of substances, vices, and information, but it also had doors that open to every Circle. Buckle up, Reaper. You're going to Jerry's Place."

~

Jerry's Place turned out to be close, although in a purely spiritual plane distance is even more relative than in a physical one. But it only took us about fifteen minutes of walking to get to an unmarked door standing completely alone in the middle of a scorched chunk of desert. And I'm not saying there was an unmarked door set into a stone wall of some sort. Nope, this was a door, standing all on its own, with no structure around it at all. I walked around it, and it looked exactly the same from both sides— just a plan red door with a glittery black "J" in cursive right at eye level.

Faustus walked up to the door and knocked three times. He waited a moment, then knocked three times again. As he raised his hand to knock for a third time, it swung open and a massive demon of a type I'd never seen before stuck its head out.

"The fuck you want, Faustus?" the demon asked, its voice sounding like boulders scraping together. This thing was butt-ugly, if your butt looked like someone took an octopus, slapped it on Arnold Schwarzenegger's head, added a spiral horn coming out of the center of its forehead, and then painted the whole thing piss yellow. It looked like Cthulhu had sex with a bodybuilder and shit out a weird noodle-faced unicorn baby.

"I want to see Jerry, Hy," Faustus replied. "Now get out of the way before my friend gets impatient." Faustus motioned in my direction.

I gave a little wave. "Hi."

"Oh, fuck," the demon called Hy said, drawing back through the door and trying to slam it shut behind him. Faustus had his foot wedged in, though, so he didn't get very far.

I stepped forward, calling up my soulblade. It was a little dimmer than normal on account of me calling power again and again this far from home, but still blazed with enough fire to put the fear of me into this spaghetti-mouthed monstrosity. "You know who I am."

It wasn't a question, but I paused anyway. Noodleface nodded. "You know what I'm said to do."

Another nod.

"Well, Hy. Is it alright if I call you Hy?" He opened his mouth to answer, which I could only really see because the tentacles on the lower half of his face moved, and I snapped my sword up to rest right under his chin. "I don't give a fuck if it's alright or not. Now we need information. And Faustus seems to think that we can find that information inside that door. You're between me and the information I want, which is generally a very bad place to be. Bad things happen to people, and demons, who are in my way. I don't like doing bad things, and I'm going to guess that you don't like it when people do bad things to you. Do you, Hy?"

He shook his head very gently. Wise, given the flaming magical sword at his throat. "Since you don't want me to bad things to you, and I don't *want* to do bad things, you're going to get the fuck out of our way and pretend you never saw us, aren't you?"

Hy nodded, his tentacles dripping saliva onto the sword. His spit sizzled as it came into contact with the flames. That resonated with Hy, who obviously didn't want any of that sizzle to come from his flesh, so he let go of the door and stepped back, leaving us to enter the demonic equivalent of the Mos Eisley cantina. Truly a "wretched hive of scum and villainy" if ever there was one.

It was dark, lit by sconces and braziers full of burning things, some of which were also screaming, adding to the general ambience. If I had to name the decor, I'd probably land somewhere around "vampire cosplay BDSM dungeon" if outfitted by someone who'd never actually had sex with another person, just watched *50 Shades of Grey* seventeen times on repeat. All the lighting was red or flame, and all the demons wandering around carrying trays were dressed in black leather, if at all. The patrons were demons of all stripe, from pissant little pit dwellers to Reavers, Torment demons, and even some that were obviously officers in Hell's Legions.

"How are we supposed to find anyone in here?" I asked, leaning down to Faustus's ear.

"*You* aren't," he said. "You aren't supposed to even know this place exists, much less ever darken the door. But those of us who are mostly native to this shithole of a plane understand the hierarchy of the building." He pointed to a massive spiral staircase that dominated the center of the room, all black wrought iron and dripping crimson candles. "That leads between floors, and each floor corresponds to a Circle. You don't have to reside in a Circle to go there inside Jerry's, but if you're going to a deeper Circle than your own, you'd better be invited, powerful as fuck, or a fast talker."

"So we came in on the Fifth Circle level," I said. "And what Circle did you live on when you were last here?"

"I lived on Seven, but most of my work was on Four. Greed and all, remember? So as long as I don't try to go any higher than Seven, we should be fine."

"Higher?" I asked. "Don't you mean lower?"

"No," Faustus replied. "In Jerry's, the more powerful demons are on the top floors, the better to lord their superiority over everyone else. The higher we go, the more danger we're in."

"Can they kill us in here? Isn't there some kind of Sanctuary thing going on?"

"Harker, we're in Hell. Sanctuary can be found in a lot of places, but this isn't one of them. There are no repercussions for murder in Jerry's, other than having to split the reward with the ownership if there's a bounty on whoever you kill. And trust me, the bounty on us is big enough that it's worth the split. So look sharp, there will be a *lot* of demons in this place willing to take on The Reaper for a two-level advancement."

"Is that before or after the split with the bar owners?" I asked. I was kinda curious to see how big a reward there was for killing me. That kind of thing can be flattering, you know.

"After. So if this asshole heading our way claims your head, he gets to jump two Circles even after Jerry takes their cut." Sure enough, there was a Reaver walking toward us, his scythe-like arms quivering with what I took to be anticipation for the upcoming scrap.

"And I can kill him without any problems, too?" I asked. I was going to murder this shithead either way, I just needed to know if a shitstorm was going to immediately land on my head, or if it was going to hold off for a few minutes.

"Yeah, he's just a Reaver. Nobody will give a shit."

That's what I wanted to hear. The Reaver got about eight feet away, and I brought up my hands, palms out. "You should fuck off now, pal," I said, giving him one last chance to walk on by.

The Reaver raised his blade-arms into the air and charged me, or tried to. The second he opened his mouth to let out what I assumed would be some kind of war cry, I channeled pure force through my palms and blew a hole right through his chest. I shot a hole through the middle of that little bastard big enough to stick my head through, and he dropped, already dissolving before he hit the floor.

The bar fell silent for an interminable set of heartbeats as every demon on our level turned to stare at us, and more than a few from higher levels looked down at the mess I'd made. Then, like nothing out of the ordinary happened, the conversation snapped back to its former level and everyone turned back to exactly what they'd been doing before I blasted the Reaver to bits.

"Well, that was anticlimactic," I said.

"But effective," Faustus replied, pointing up one level. A thick-shouldered demon with curling black horns set into an obsidian forehead stared down at us. When he saw me take notice, he crooked a finger at me. "That's Chuck. He's one of the demons I wanted to try and find. Good job, Harker. You do know how to make friends, no matter what plane of existence we're on. Now let's go talk to a Seventh-Circle Colonel."

Can't think of anything I'd rather do. Oh wait, yes I can. But I did it anyway.

CHAPTER THIRTY-NINE

Chuck was a very large demon. Not General-sized, but definitely Torment Demon-sized, or maybe even a little bigger. Nobody I'd want to run into in a dark alley, that's for sure. Even sitting down, it was obvious that he was pushing eight feet tall, with muscles bulging through a tight-fitting black shirt with "CBGB" written in white letters. Demons in punk rock merchandising? Rock n' roll really has gone to Hell these days. A wide grin split his jet-black face as we walked up the stairs.

"Faustus, old friend! Welcome home! I thought you'd never show your ugly face in Hell again after Lucifer's decree. You are either very brave or very, very stupid," the big demon said in a vaguely Middle Eastern accent, which confused me a little, since demons don't usually have accents. I guessed it was affectation.

Faustus looked a little crestfallen. "Probably very stupid," he said. "My friend here was in trouble, so I came to help him out. I don't know that it's going to end well for either of us. But maybe you can do a favor for an old buddy? One that's probably going to be buggered by the boss's pitchfork for the next couple thousand years?"

Chuck stood and opened his arms wide. "Of course, my friend! Anything I can do for you, as always. If the price is right."

"What happened to doing a favor for a friend?" I asked.

The demon wasn't smiling when he turned his gaze to me, and I instantly regretted bearding the dragon in its lair, as it were. I was sitting in this guy's private lounge area in a bar that spanned all nine Circles of Hell. I probably should have thought about that before opening my very mortal mouth, but I was tired, annoyed, and getting strangely hungry for a disembodied soul. I wished I'd brought some ethereal granola bars or something.

"Everything has a price, Reaper," Chuck said. "And for traitors who choose to side with human scum against our lord and master Lucifer, that price is very high indeed. Our long friendship is the only reason I'm speaking with Faustus at all, much less entertaining whatever stupid request he's going to make of me. He knows how this world works. That's why he's not whining about my price. You aren't from around here, so why don't you step back and shut the fuck up while your betters are speaking? Or would you like me to call Asmodeus and let him know you've delivered yourself up to his tender fucking mercies?"

In a move that would have completely stunned Becks had she been there to see it, I shut the fuck up. I held up my hands, took a step back, and motioned zipping my lips closed.

"Good," Chuck said, turning back to Faustus. He waved his minions away and made a gesture, forming a translucent bubble of light around the three of us. As soon as we were obscured from view a little, and presumably shielded from eavesdroppers, his entire demeanor changed. His shoulders relaxed, his posture sagged, and he just generally looked more like a regular guy, albeit huge and with horns, than a Demon Colonel. "Dude, you know the heat on you is ridiculously high, right? Even talking to you can get me busted down a Circle or two. What the fuck were you thinking, man? I mean, look, I miss having you around. You livened shit up in a big way with your schemes and your tricks, but the boss is seriously pissed about you helping this prick get away." He gestured at me, just in case there was any question about the prick he meant.

"I wasn't kidding," Faustus said. "Harker's my friend, and if I didn't come help him out, he'd be a Reaper-skin rug in Albemerich's lair right now and his head would be decorating one of Lucifer's bedposts. I didn't have a lot of choice."

"Jesus, Faustus. You put your ass on the line for a mortal? A *friend*? I've got lots of friends, Faustus."

Faustus slipped into a picture-perfect imitation of Val Kilmer in *Tombstone* and replied, very simply, "I don't."

That was when I really realized exactly what he'd put on the line for me. I knew we were in trouble, and that Lucifer totally had it in for the both of us, but I didn't grasp until this meeting that Lucifer was at least as pissed at Faustus as he was at me, and that by coming down here to save my butt, he'd probably guaranteed himself the same level torture as I'd endure when I died, if not worse. I gazed at the scheming little demon with newfound respect.

Faustus took a breath, then passed over a small polished white stone to Chuck. "That's the ward stone for my place on Six. There's plenty of loot there, should be more than enough to cover the costs of any favor I need you to do for me."

"Is that including the statue? You know the one I mean," Chuck asked.

"Yes, the statue is in there. Yes, you can have it. I just need some information, an internal Gate, and maybe a little power boost for a few hours. You good for that?" Faustus asked.

"Depends on what information, where you want to go, and how much power I'm loaning. And am I expected to provide passage for this asshole, too?" Chuck gestured at me.

"Yes," I said, stepping forward. "And a little power boost for me as well. We're probably going to get into a fight, and I need to at least be able to hold my own."

Chuck sneered at me, a black lip curling up to reveal a pointed yellow fang. "If I channeled even one percent of my power into your human carcass, you'd explode like a sausage in a microwave. But I can do the rest."

"Thanks," Faustus said, then looked over at me. "Okay, Harker, ask him what you want to know."

Time's weird in Hell, so I don't know if it was five minutes or five hours later that we stood outside a glowing bubble of force on the Fourth Circle, looking in through a portal in the magical barrier at a set of sixteenth-century colonists trying desperately to gather nuts and scattered winter berries for food.

"This is pretty fucking ingenious," Chuck said, looking at the glowing barricade before us. "I can't believe Albemerich came up with this all on his own. It's way smarter than his usual shit."

It did seem to be a pretty clever setup. We were in a valley in the

Fourth Circle, nestled between massive mountain peaks. The area was pretty, in a Hellscape sort of way, and extremely isolated. This being the Circle dedicated to Lust, an area with few or no souls wasn't all that interesting to the demons or the condemned, so almost no one would wander by Albemerich's little kidnapping project on their own, and there were signs all around the barrier warning of the consequences of tampering with his torment of the souls within.

No Fourth Circle demon that wanted to stay corporeal would dare fuck with a more powerful demon, so just Albemerich's name on a sign would be enough to have the succubi and incubi that made up most of the Fourth Circle's denizens shitting themselves, and even the most adventurous wouldn't have the power to pass through the barrier. And more powerful demons almost never venture higher in the Circles than their own, worried about losing face if anyone saw them fraternizing with lower powered beings. So no one who lived on this Circle would be able to fuck with Al's little ant farm, and no one more powerful would be caught dead in a low-rent Circle like the Fourth, so the colonists had been undisturbed for the past six centuries, living out the same terrifying season of starvation and desperation for Albemerich's amusement for eternity. I was really glad I'd killed that motherfucker.

"So…now what?" I asked, looking between Chuck and Faustus. "How do we get them out and get them home?"

Chuck raised his hands in the air and took a couple steps back. "Nope," he said, smiling at us. "I held up my end. I got you here. Getting through the barrier, and anything even resembling getting out of Hell is on you. Besides, I think there's somebody over there that might have something to say about you leaving." He gestured to the left, where a massive form was stomping in our direction, a flaming black soulblade already manifested.

You see, that's the problem with demons. You kill on one Earth, it just reconstitutes in Hell and comes back to be a pain in your ass on Earth again. But you've probably bought yourself at least a couple years before the piece of shit manages to get back topside. But you kill one in *Hell*, and they're supposed to be reborn in the Pits and have to fight their way back to their former prominence and power.

Unfortunately and surprising literally no one, Hell is full of schemers, cheats, and backstabbers, so when I killed Albemerich back on the Fifth Circle, he found some way to come back at full strength almost immediately, and now he was running across the valley of the Fourth Circle at us, screaming like a maniac with a horde of lesser demons following behind, all looking to take a bite out of our asses. And Chuck, our extremely powerful Seventh-Circle Colonel in the Armies of Hell, had already noped right the fuck out and vanished, presumable back to his bottle service at Jerry's Hellside Bar & Grill.

I looked at Faustus, who looked at me and shrugged. "Well, buddy. We found the colonists. Problem is, the demons found us finding them. So now what do we do?"

I grinned back at him. "We do what we do best, pal. We fuck shit up." I turned to face the onrushing horde of demons, called up my own soul-blade, then split the weapon into two shorter, curved blades. "Hey, assholes!" I yelled, feeling a psychotic grin split my face.

"Come get some."

CHAPTER FORTY

And fuck shit up we did, in colossal fashion. Faustus and I stationed ourselves shoulder to shoulder with our backs to the barrier keeping the colonists trapped in their own little Hell-bubble, limiting the number of demons we'd have to handle at one time. Even with that, the number was pretty high, since they could come at us from three sides.

The Reavers struck first, whirling dervishes of rage and bloodlust, all slashing razor-sharp forearm ridges and hunger for Reaper meat. But I wasn't on the menu today, at least not for those little shits. I sliced off any arm that reached for me, making a pile of Reaver limbs in front of me that looked like an all-you-can-eat crab leg buffet in Vegas. Faustus was more precise in his slaughter, lunging for throats, eyes, guts—basically every strike of mine left an appendage lying on the ground, while every cut of Faustus's blade left a demon screeching out its death throes at his feet.

The pile of corpses and severed limbs grew for several minutes, and not for the first time did I think how happy I was that soul blades don't have physical weight. Not that I had a physical body, but it was still some-thing I thought about as I hacked and slashed my way through the first wave of demons. When the Reavers had fallen, there was a moment to breathe before an absolute tidal wave of pit dwellers crashed down on top of us, almost smothering Faustus and me with their sheer numbers. I cut as many as I could to ribbons, but when monsters are diving at you a dozen at a time and literally vaulting over the corpses of their fellows to get at you, a sword, or even three swords, isn't enough.

"Grab on to my belt!" I yelled at Faustus.

"A little busy here!" he shouted back.

"And you're gonna be a little dead if you don't quit fucking around with these little turds and do as I say!"

I could feel his eyes on me, then saw his soulblade wink out in the corner of my eye. I let my blades vanish as well, throwing up a small shield with my left hand as I felt Faustus latch onto my midsection. Then I called up energy from the seemingly boundless well of power that surrounded us, and channeled it outward from me in every direction, just a supernova of magical energy blasting out on all sides. The power that shot out behind me struck the colonist's enclosure and rebounded, adding its energy to the rest of the blast. A massive wave of pure kinetic force emanated from me as I yelled *"FORZARE!"* at the top of my lungs.

Demons flew through the air, some landing more than fifty feet away. It looked like someone dropped a boulder in the middle of a bowling pin collection, the way they flew out in all directions. Some tumbled to a stop and got up, shaking their heads in confusion, but most were slammed to the ground so hard they just disintegrated on the spot, headed back to the pits where they'd respawn. The ones that weren't destroyed on impact still weren't interested in coming at us again, no matter how much Al and the pair of big nasty brutes he had with him flogged them with barbed whips.

I leaned against the barrier to catch my breath for a second, looking around at the suddenly very clean ground around us. There were no more Reaver parts scattered in a semicircle in front of us. There was barely even dirt in the vicinity of our feet, I'd thrown so much power out from my core. Faustus let go of my belt and gave me a nod of thanks, then called forth his soulblade and stepped in front of me.

"Take a second to regroup. I can hold these dickheads for a few seconds." The obvious unstated truth was that a few seconds was all he'd be able to hold them. Albemerich was probably no match for Faustus in a one-on-one fight, but the bruisers flanking him looked at least as powerful as Al, which meant that Faustus was way outgunned against the three of them. I wasn't quite sure I would be able to go heads-up against *any* of the three baddies, but I didn't really plan to. I figured I'd cheat somehow and pull out a win that way.

Now I just needed to figure out exactly *how* to cheat. I was in Hell, facing off against a trio of powerful demons on their home turf, and I had exactly one ally fighting beside me. My magic was supercharged on account of being in a plane that was nothing *but* magic, but that still might not be enough to take out these guys. Not to mention that I was still throwing enough power around to be a little worried about burning myself out. And I wasn't sure what their vulnerabilities were. Reavers and pit dwellers were simple, but these guys were all higher-ups in Hell's legions, probably even tougher than Torment Demons, who were mostly immune to mortal magic.

"You aren't getting out of this alive, Reaper," Albemerich taunted, a grin stretching his hideous face. Seriously, this dude was butt-ugly, and smiling didn't make it any less terrible.

"As long as I can die without finding out if your breath is as bad as your face, I'm okay with that," I called back. I might not know how to fight these bastards, but the longer we bantered, the longer I had to come up with a plan. And I can talk shit for a *loooong* time when I need to.

"Kill this fucking human so I can go back to playing with my pets!" Al roared, and the demons beside him manifested soulblades of their own and charged. Shit. I really needed more time to think, and I *really* needed these guys to not be powerful enough to conjure weapons out of thin air.

"Left," I called to Faustus, and launched myself at the demon on that side. He charged the demon coming in on the right, and after he took his first step, I was in the fight of my life and didn't have time to pay attention to Faustus. I leapt high into the air, vaulting over the demon, spinning in midair, and coming down with a devastating slash across his back. My hope was that it would be enough to kill or incapacitate the demon, but you don't get to be that big or that strong without winning a few fights, so when I landed, my blade found a block waiting for it, sending shockwaves up both my arms. A massive foot slammed into my chest, and I flew back several feet to land flat on my ass, dropping my soulblade in the process.

It winked out of existence the moment I lost contact with it, and I brought my fists together in front of me. Like I expected, the demon was in a full charge, his sword raised high above his head in a strike that would have split me from nose to nuts if it had connected. So I made sure it didn't connect, channeling power through my hands and blasting energy right into the demon. This was the same trick I'd used to blow holes through demons earlier, but I knew this jackass was way too powerful for that to work.

So I shot him in the knees instead. Just like Sam Elliott said in *Road House*: you smash a motherfucker's knees, he's going down. I don't think Sam was talking about demons in that film, but the principle holds. I cut loose with a narrow band of power blasting horizontally from my outstretched arms, slamming into the demon's legs just below the knees and dropping it to the dirt face-first. I sprang to my feet, called up my soulblade, and drove it through the demon's skull, pinning its dying carcass to the ground as it dissolved back into the primordial shit-soup from whence it came.

Faustus stepped up to my shoulder, his sword glowing with red flames along the black blade. I still didn't have any great ideas on how to save us and take out Albemerich, and I was out of time. "This would be a great time to tell me you're stronger than this asshole," I muttered. "You're from a lower Circle, right?"

Faustus shook his head beside me. "Before I betrayed Lucifer to save your ass, I probably had more stroke in Hell's hierarchy than Al, but I was never stronger. I'm more of a 'talk people into punching themselves in the face' kind of guy than a 'do the punching myself' kind of guy. So...no, I'm not stronger than he is, especially when he has this lovely little cornucopia of innocent suffering to draw from right behind us."

Well, shit. We couldn't beat him straight up, and there was nothing around to use as a surprise weapon, so I had no idea how we were getting out of this mess. It was really starting to look like this trip to Hell might not have come with a round-trip ticket. "Okay, so we fight, and we try to get lucky?" I asked.

"There are two of us," Faustus replied. "And we are pretty good at the whole killing thing."

"Yep," I said, trying to cram as much unfelt and unearned confidence into my voice as I could. We were about to die, and it wasn't even going to be a cool death, like defenestration. No, I was going to die because I had finally run headlong into a fight I couldn't win, and this time nobody could come save my ass. At least Becks was still on Earth, so she was insulated from my bad decisions this time.

"Then fuck it," I said. I looked at Faustus, tapped my magical energy sword to his, and gave him a nod. "Let's do this."

"Hey shithead!" Faustus shouted at Albemerich. The big demon stopped and stared at us. "We who are about to die salute you!" Then we both held up the middle finger of our left hand and sprang toward what was almost certainly our last fight. Time to make it a good one.

CHAPTER FORTY-ONE

Albemerich had the good grace to look startled, at least. I guess it wasn't every day that a con artist demon and a human wizard charged him on the field of battle with their swords blazing. He stared at us dumbfounded for the span of three running steps, then summoned a pair of massive soulblades and took a defensive stance. Faustus reached him half a step before me and took a running slash at Al's throat. The demon blocked easily, then turned to meet my sword as it rushed at his knees.

We kept up a high-low attack pattern, each alternating whether we struck for the head or the legs. About every fourth slash, I pivoted into a lunging shot at his guts, but Albemerich knocked those away without missing a beat. This guy was *good*. But we'd beaten him once, and we could do it again, even if he did seem to come back stronger than before. Even if we were exhausted from fighting our way through hundreds of pit dwellers and a shitload of Reavers to face the same nasty bastard we'd killed just a few hours ago. Or was it days? Hell Time is more confusing than Daylight Savings Time, I swear to God.

Faustus shifted away from me, widening the distance between us, and I followed suit. The farther apart we were, the harder it would be for Albemerich to see both of us coming, and when he spun to face a feint from Faustus, I took one short hop forward and drove my sword through his back, skewering the massive demon and fixing him in place for Faustus to start slicing parts off.

At least that was the plan. What really happened was that Faustus feinted a high strike to Al's neck, but this time, instead of biting on the feint like he'd done before, Al dropped to one knee and spun around, knocking aside my thrust with his blade and letting go of his sword with his left hand so he could backhand me across the jaw.

Now, getting the absolute taste slapped out of your mouth hurts bad enough when a human does it, and if they're wearing jewelry, it can actually slice you up pretty bad. But that's nothing compared to getting slugged by an open hand the size of a goddamned tennis racket with massive bony spurs sticking out of the knuckles. Al's shot spun me around and opened up five parallel lines of bloody slashes down my cheeks, one for each finger. I decided as I wiped blood out of my mouth that the son of a bitch had an extra finger just to be a bigger dick when he hit people. He was a big deal on the rage plane, so I totally wouldn't put it past him. I dropped to one knee, my head spinning, and felt pain explode inside my chest as a huge foot caught me in the ribs and lifted me six inches into the air. I collapsed to the dirt, wheezing for air. How the fuck can getting kicked in the guts hurt so bad when I'm incorporeal?

That was the main thought running through my head as I struggled to my feet, along with a running chorus of *Oh shit, don't die don't die don't die.* A flicker of movement out of the corner of my eye was the only warning I got before the next strike came, and this time I managed to get a shield up around my left arm before Al's soulblade slammed into it, driving me back to my knees as a sickening *crack* rang through the air. Funny, in all the years I've lived, and all the injuries I've somehow survived, how little a broken arm actually hurts. Until you try to move it. Or touch it. Or breathe. Or think clearly. As long as you don't do any of those things, a broken arm isn't really a big deal. Good thing, because I also had at least one cracked rib to deal with, not to mention what felt like a busted orbital socket. If I lived through this shit, I was going to need a serious vacation. Hopefully without serial murder and ghostly visitations next time.

"You're going to look good with your skull spinning around on Lucifer's dick like a set of overpriced hubcaps, Harker," Albemerich said with a grin.

"You'll look good when you turn back into pit sludge and a First Circle demon is wiping you off the bottom of his hoof," I slurred, struggling to my feet. I tried to manifest my soulblade, but the broken bones in my face were making it hard to concentrate. Or maybe it was the rib. Or the arm. Whatever. Something hurt like a motherfucker, and I couldn't focus enough to get my power to hold the form of a sword. I wreathed my fists in purple energy and raised them in front of my face. "Come on, chicken-shit. Let's dance."

Al smiled for real now, a nasty thing that let his gross yellow teeth show. He raised his sword and stepped toward me, starting his attack with a big, looping strike that would have taken my head off had it connected. I ducked it easily, stepping in to deliver a magically fueled punch to the big demon's midsection. Nothing. Even after dying, resurrecting, and fighting off me and Faustus, my hardest punch didn't even register on this fucker's radar.

But his return shot definitely registered on mine. He didn't even punch me, just slipped a little to the side and raised a knee up into my midsection. I felt something else crack in my ribcage, and another little dagger of pain jabbed into my middle. A couple more of those and he wouldn't have to stab me. The broken pieces of bone in my chest would take care of that for him.

I staggered back, my head whipping around for Faustus. The last I'd seen, he took a hard elbow to the side of his head and was laid out on the ground, but now he was nowhere to be seen. Fuck. I couldn't beat this son of a bitch with help, how was I supposed to do it on my own?

Despair started to creep in. The sense of being abandoned in my darkest fucking hour rose up in me, my greatest fear manifesting right here in the bowels of Hell. It was somehow fitting that the guy who always talks a big game about going his own way and not needing anybody's help was going to die alone because he trusted a demon to save him. I hoped Faustus was negotiating a better deal with Lucifer while I fought my last fight, maybe spinning it so he was responsible for bringing me here. If anybody could make the Lord of Hell buy his bullshit and get himself a lighter sentence, it was Faustus. I didn't blame him, either. He was a demon, and even coming down here to help me in the first place was way more self-sacrifice than I expected. Well, if Lucifer didn't believe whatever bullshit Faustus was spinning, at least I wouldn't be suffering alone for all eternity.

I looked back to Albemerich, who was grinning down at me. He opened his hands and his soulblade winked out of existence. "I don't think I'll be needing that, do you?" he asked. He took a step forward and slapped me again, this time with his massive palm. He just reached right past my upraised fists and slapped me to the ground like I was a naughty toddler. "Faustus is gone, Harker. Your pet angel can't save you here. Your dear uncle is too afraid of what might happen if Skiffrax gets loose to come down to my neighborhood, and that delicious-looking human of yours can't come down here unless she really wants to spend time with you. A lot of time. Like an eternity. Too bad. She might have wanted to meet her great-great-great-auntie." He gestured to the shimmering dome behind me.

"What the fuck are you talking about?" I asked. I didn't know or care what he meant, but the more I kept him talking, the longer I had to think up a plan. Any plan. Other than "stand still and die," which was the plan I was currently working on.

"Your lovely Rebecca is a descendant of one of the colonists I have in my own little recreation of *Under the Dome*," he said. "Her great-times a bunch grandmother along one spindly branch of her family tree was one of the colonists here. She became friendly with, and eventually married, one of the local tribe members and had a baby who lived out a normal life as one of them. There were a dozen or so colonists who decided to live with the local tribe rather than trying to wait for help from the Old Country. Help that was never going to arrive in time, of course. Then through the vagaries of time, travel, and the presence of a freedmen's colony on the island, her great-something uncle, who was an escaped slave, married a woman who was from the local tribe, and when the freedmen's colony was disbanded after the Civil War, they moved west toward the middle of the state. Over the decades, they migrated to Charlotte, until finally she ended up with you. All while her great-grandmother's many times removed brother stayed here, under my loving care and attention. I expect that's why she's had such unpleasant dreams since coming to Manteo. Although not nearly as unpleasant as the ones she'll have when you never make it home, of course."

He grinned at me, then planted a foot in the center of my chest and shoved. He didn't even really kick me, just pushed me over using his foot. He laughed like a schoolyard bully, throwing his head back and cackling as I struggled to my feet. My ribs were killing me, my face hurt like a motherfucker, and my arm, while still the least of my worries, was starting to throb and lose strength. "You aren't in my league, Harker. You couldn't kill me with the help of your little turncoat friend, and you certainly can't do it without him. You're going to die in Hell, Harker, which is convenient, because you'll be here for a very, *very* long time."

Then he punched me, and this wasn't some little love tap like he'd been blessing me with. No, this was a swing from the hips, throw your whole weight into it kind of blow, and his massive left fist slammed into the side of my face like a sledgehammer. Worse, actually, because I've been hit by sledgehammers that didn't hurt as much. Don't ask. When you spend as much of your life pissing people off as I have, you get hit with a lot of different shit. He nailed me in the jaw, and I spun around to meet his right coming from the opposite direction, and when he made contact, so did I. Only difference is I made contact with the ground.

I lay there wishing for unconsciousness, but this was not the kind of place where wishes are often granted, so I just writhed in pain, trying to focus my mind enough to call up even the tiniest sliver of power. Nothing. I couldn't even pull enough juice to light a match, much less throw a fireball at a demon. Which is a terrible idea in its own right, but that's beside the point. I couldn't defend myself, I couldn't strike back, and I couldn't run. So I did the only thing I could think to do.

I dragged myself to my feet, spit a gobbet of blood on the ground at Albemerich's feet, and gave him my most psychotic grin. "Come on, motherfucker," I said. "Like the man said in the movies, I can do this shit all day."

Al's grin grew even wider as he summoned his soulblade and raised it over his head. "Language, Reaper. Language." Then he raised his sword high and brought it slamming down—

Right into the gleaming black blade held by the single most beautiful sight I'd laid eyes on in maybe forever. Faustus deflected Al's crushing blow down into the turf and launched a blinding flurry of slashes, lunges, and cuts at the big demon. His soulblade moved in a blur of crimson fire, a burning brand of death and destruction that was as glorious as anything I'd ever seen. The demon turned friend went after Albemerich with the kind of vigor and determination I'd only ever seen him use when decimating a liquor cabinet. He cut, he feinted, he parried, and he slashed. He stabbed and sliced, he blocked and battered, and he kept pushing Albemerich back with every stroke of his blade.

"You came back," I said, spitting out another mouthful of blood.

"Like I said, I don't have many friends. Can't go letting Al chop the few I do have into kibble, now can I?"

"Thanks," I said, trying to take the moment's respite to get my head centered and draw on some power, both to heal my injuries and to lend a hand. Not that Faustus looked like he needed it. He was kicking *ass*.

Until he wasn't. "Faustus!" Al roared, throwing his arms wide and letting out a primal scream of rage. The massive demon just stepped inside Faustus's next looping slash, putting his left shoulder into the path of Faustus's arm and keeping his sword far enough away to be useless. Al wrapped both massive hands around Faustus's throat and started to squeeze, then he started to head butt the smaller demon, his horns opening huge bloody furrows along Faustus's forehead. He'd told me once that he decided to forego horns when he fell in love with hats, but at the moment, it looked like that fashion decision was going to cost him. Dearly.

I tried to call power, but the only thing emanating from my fists were drops of blood and puny purple sparks. I still couldn't focus, probably on account of the concussion I was pretty sure I had. Again. I tried to call up my soulblade, but my arm hurt too bad to wield it, and the thing flickered out as soon as I tried even the feeblest swipe. I finally sucked in a deep breath and maneuvered around behind Albemerich, thinking that if I could jump up onto the demon's back, maybe it would distract him enough for Faustus to stab him in the guts or come up with something equally underhanded.

I gathered my feet under me to pounce as Al let go of Faustus with his right hand, holding his limp form off the ground with his left wrapped around my buddy's throat. He called up his massive soulblade, and just as he was about to shove it through Faustus's chest, I leapt for him.

Only to be slammed back to the ground by a gleaming white missile that shot out of the sky between us and crashed to the ground, leveling me, Faustus, and Albemerich.

"Leave. My friends. *Alone*." I knew that voice. It was a voice that *really* wasn't supposed to be there. I lifted my head despite the protestations of most of my body and got a good look at the slender blond woman clad in brilliant white plate armor and holding a six-foot sword wreathed in fire. Not magical flame that's some kind of manifestation of emotion, but real, no shit *fire*.

"Glory," I whispered. "How?"

"Long story, Q," my Guardian Angel replied, then straightened up. She'd dropped to a perfect superhero landing with one leg bent and the other extended straight out to the side, all Natasha Romanoff in white with wings, but when she stood, there wasn't even a hint of levity in her expression.

"Albemerich," she said, her tone formal and her words precise. "You have overstepped your bounds. You may not lay hands upon one of The Host, upon penalty of permanent dissolution. It has been decided that as you have performed your duties faithfully for many millennia, that you shall not be exterminated if you quit the field immediately. This is your only opportunity to do so."

She looked at Al for a long moment before she relaxed a little and leaned forward. "This is the part where you run, dickhead."

Al ran. He waved his hands in front of himself, carved a small Gate in the air, and stepped through. From what I could see through the portal, he teleported himself right back to the Fifth Circle. I turned to Glory, who was still wrapped in her plate armor holding a soulblade that didn't look like hers but was still unsettlingly familiar.

"Thanks for the save, Glory," I said. "I thought we were gonna have to sign a long-term lease down here. But how are you here? I thought you couldn't come down here with me unless somebody way up the celestial food chain okayed it."

Her stony expression never changed; she just pointed the flaming blade at Faustus. "I'm not here to rescue you, Harker. I'm here for him."

Faustus turned to her, confusion all over his face. "What are you talking about, G? As much as I hate to admit it and as shitty as the scenery is, I'm right where I'm supposed to be."

She smiled at the demon, and a warmth filled me at the gentle, even loving, expression on her face. "Father sent me for you. This is no longer your place, Fautinir. It's time to come home." She looked at me. "Harker, you should probably hold on tight."

Then she swung her borrowed soulblade in a huge X, cutting a massive tear in the very fabric of reality around us. She reached out, grabbed Faustus's wrist in one hand, and as I latched onto his other one with all my remaining strength, we stepped through the brand-new Gate and went home.

EPILOGUE

A nd by "home" I mean we crashed to the turf in the cemetery surrounded by Heavenly ward stones, where I proceeded to puke up what felt like everything I'd eaten for the past week, making my cracked ribs send even more stabbing pain through my chest. "That sucked," I croaked. "Who the fuck taught you how to build Gates?"

"That wasn't a Gate, jackass. That was a rip in the fabric of the planes, and it's not meant to be comfortable. If it was, every asshole with a magic sword would be carving up the fabric of reality, and we have like five seasons of *The Flash* and fourteen Spider-man movies to show us what a terrible idea that is," Glory replied. "Here." She held out a bottle of water. I took it, not asking where she kept bottled water in her plate armor, which had been replaced by her more standard look of faded blue jeans and a t-shirt featuring the big dude from *Hawaii 5-0* advertising Kamekona's Shrimp Truck.

"Pretty sure Barry Allen was fucking around with time, not inter-dimensional travel, sis," Faustus chimed in. "But the question is valid. How *did* you do that, and more importantly...whose sword is that?" He sounded suspicious, but I guess if someone had just chased me into Hell and yanked me out of a fight for my survival while telling me that my name and basically everything about myself were changing.

"That belongs to me," came a deep voice from a tombstone the next row over. I rolled over and there he was, douchebag-in-chief of the Heavenly Host, the Archangel Michael. I shoulda known. I'd already gotten my face kicked in once tonight, why not go for two with the biggest asshat of an angel I'd ever met. This dude had a stick so far up his ass that someone could screw a shifter knob onto the top of his head. He was *the* Archangel, Glory's penultimate boss, second only to God in the hierarchy of Heaven, so far as I knew. And with the Big Guy on walkabout for most of humanity's existence, he was the final arbiter of what happened in Heaven and whether or not Glory could interfere with whatever shit we got into down on Earth. Or elsewhere.

Michael was wearing his human suit, except instead of looking like a battered amnesiac cage fighter like the last time he'd been bumming around dirtside, he was dressed in a pair of crisp khakis and a white dress shirt. I looked for the Rainbow flip-flops but couldn't see his feet to know if he'd gone full Beach Douche or was just in his Business Casual Douche uniform. He stepped forward and held out his hand to Glory, who surrendered the flaming sword. The flames went out, and with a flick of his wrist, the sword was gone.

"That's…not a soulblade," I said.

"No, it is not," Michael agreed. "Hello again, Harker. I see you have not made even the slightest effort at staying out of trouble since last we met."

"Gotta go with what you're good at, Mikey," I replied. "You're a colossal dickwhistle; I'm a force for chaos in the universe. We gotta do what we gotta do."

He ignored me. I was grateful for that small kindness, because I can't go one-on-one with an Archangel when I'm at my best, and given that I hadn't managed to stand up yet, I was a long way from my best. "Fautinir, welcome home. In the eons since The Fall, very few of your kind have managed to return to The Host, and none within the last millennium. We are glad you have earned your way back to us, not only because it deprives Lucifer of one of his most effective weapons against humanity, but also because our hearts grieve for all who Fell, even Lucifer."

I didn't openly call bullshit on that one, but only because I didn't want Michael to decide he still wanted to smite me into oblivion. He hated Lucifer with the blazing passion of a thousand suns, because Lucky Luce was Daddy's favorite, until he made humans. Then Lucifer fell out of fashion, leading him to storm the Gates of Heaven in a weird metaphysical example of a teenager acting out to get a parent's attention. What it got Lucifer was sent to his room, only the room was Hell, and instead of being sent there without his dinner, he was sent there for all eternity to play warden to all the souls of the humans he hated so much.

Which led to a promotion for Michael, who would never, under any circumstances, want to give up his spot as Daddy's Loyalest Archangel. So he probably spent about one nanosecond per century grieving about his poor Fallen brother Lucy.

"What did I do to deserve this?" Faustus asked.

"You went down there after Harker," Glory said. "You knew Lucifer would never let you escape again, and that there was a very good chance you would both be trapped suffering the worst torments every demon in Hell could dream up for you, and you went anyway. That level of self-sacrifice, combined with the good works you've done on Earth the past few years, was enough to convince The Host that you were ready to Return."

Michael swirled his hand through the air again, and his sword reappeared. "Come forward, Fautinir."

Faustus took a step toward Michael, who raised the flaming blade high into the air. That didn't look good. I dragged myself to my feet and called power into my fists. "You don't fucking touch him, Mikey."

Michael turned to me, his eyes wide. "What are you doing, Harker?"

"You're holding a flaming sword over the head of somebody who just literally rescued me from Hell. You think I'm gonna just stand here and let you chop him in half? Fuck you, pal. He risked Hell for me. The least I can do is beat the shit out of a douchebag Archangel for him."

My words lacked a little in the way of threat given that I couldn't really stand without holding on to a headstone, but the sentiment was real. He was *not* hurting my friend. Not without going through me first. Which realistically meant that he was going to hurt me real quick, *then* hurt Faustus. But at least I'd go back to Hell knowing that I tried.

Harker, chill. The voice in my head rang with command, and I whirled around, almost losing my feet as I saw Becks striding across the dew-soaked cemetery. Luke was with her, but he kept looking to the east where the sky was rapidly lightening. *Glory told us what was up. He's not going to hurt Faustus. Fautinir. Whatever his fucking name is now. Oh, and welcome home. You ever leave me behind like that again, no matter where you're going, and I'm going to inflict the kind of suffering on you that Lucifer and his little buddies can only imagine.*

Yes, ma'am. And there are people who claim that I can't learn. "Okay, Mikey. Do your deal. Becks says it's okay."

Glory looked a little hurt. "You needed Becks to tell you it was alright? You didn't trust my judgement?"

"Not with this asshole anywhere in the vicinity," I replied with a gesture to Michael. "You can't disobey his orders, and I wouldn't put it past him to order you to tell me it was all going to be fine, when it very much was not going to be fine."

She looked at Michael, who gave a little "he's right, what you gonna do?" shrug. "Fair," she said. *Thanks, Becks.* Sometimes I forget that Glory can butt into our mental link. Sometimes I try really hard to forget that my Guardian Angel can essentially read my mind. It's not always the kind of place where I want visitors.

Michael looked around the assemblage, which now included Luke and Becks. "May I continue?" We nodded, and he raised his sword again. "Kneel, Fautinir."

Faustus hit his knees, looking up with no small trepidation at the blade and the stony-faced Archangel. "I haven't answered to that name in eons. I don't know if I even remember what Fautinir feels like."

"He feels like someone who will sacrifice himself for one he loves. He feels like someone who will risk eternity for a friend. He feels like someone who will defy Lucifer himself for what he feels is right. He feels like an angel, Faustus. No matter what name he uses." With those words, Glory leaned forward and kissed him on his obsidian forehead, then stepped back out of Michael's way. The muscular angel lowered the blade, edge-first, onto the tip of Faustus...Fautinir's head, and as the blade passed through him, he started to change. The obsidian shell of his skin cracked like an egg, falling away from his face in chunks. His yellow eyes flashed a blinding white, then settled to a mercurial hazel color, and with a deafening *SNAP*, a pair of catlike wings extended from his shoulders, only to immediately catch fire as they were enveloped in a blazing white light so bright we mortals and mostly-mortals had to avert our eyes.

When I was able to look at him again, Faustus was gone. Standing in front of me, decked out in silver chain mail with a white tabard, was a motherfucking *angel*. He was tall, even taller than me, built like a diver with lean muscle on display everywhere, holding a blazing white soul-blade and sporting a gleaming pair of eight-foot white feathered wings that seemed to glow from within. Or maybe it was just Fautinir glowing, because he *definitely* was. And smiling, and crying, and then Glory was crying and hugging him and telling him welcome home and that so many of his family had missed him.

That's when it hit me. The Fall wasn't just a betrayal, and it wasn't just a war. It was the world's longest and nastiest family feud. Glory and Faustus had been *family* since the beginning of time, and when Lucifer led his rebellion, it wasn't just angels versus demons, it was brothers against sisters. I knew a little about that, I thought ruefully. Watching Glory and Fautinir embrace, tears rolling down both their faces, I couldn't help but find a little hope that maybe my long-lost sister and I could someday reconcile. If she didn't kill me first.

Putting thoughts of my own family drama aside, I limped over to Michael and held out a hand. "Thank you," I said. "You could have let me die down there and just saved Faust—Fautinir. I appreciate you letting me hitch a ride home with him."

"I was not given a choice, Quincy Harker. I was told to rescue everyone in that Circle who didn't belong there. I do not disobey orders." He gave me a level stare, as if trying to drive a point home, then I got it.

"Oh." I didn't have anything else to say. I didn't know what else *to* say. "Well, thanks anyway. Even if it wasn't your idea, I still appreciate it." Michael didn't say anything, just gave me a nod, turned around, and vanished.

Not much on long goodbyes, is he? Becks asked in my head.

Nope. Still a dick.

What was that about him not being given a choice? Isn't he like the head Archangel?

Yeah, I replied. *He is. There's only one being in the universe that can tell Michael what to do. And before this weekend, nobody had heard from him in a very long time.*

Who's that?

I didn't reply.

Harker? Who is it?

Wait for it…

Wait…you mean…oh! Oh, shit!

In-fucking-deed, I said. "Hey, Glory?" I asked.

"Yeah, Q?" She pulled away from Fautinir, and they both wiped away their tears, which glistened like quicksilver in the glow from the streetlights.

"What happened to the colonists? Michael said he was told to rescue everyone from the Circle, so I assume that meant them, too."

A shadow flickered across her face. "There was…some debate about them, but eventually they all ascended."

"All of them?" Becks asked.

"Yeah," Glory said. "Michael was just going to drop them back where they came from, but we can't really fuck with time like that. Then some of the other Archangels wanted to just let them appear in the middle of downtown Manteo, but cooler heads were able to convince them that dropping a hundred sixteenth-century British citizens in twenty-first century America wouldn't be a good thing, either."

"So you…killed them?" I asked.

"Harker, they were trapped in Hell for four hundred years. Without even knowing it. We couldn't leave them in the Fourth Circle, and we couldn't put them back where they came from, so all we could do was let them go. Some of our people are working on assimilating them into Heaven as we speak."

I guess that was about as good as it was going to get for them. And for us, we started this case with a demon sidekick, and now we had a brand-new angel on our side. I hobbled over to Fautinir and stuck out a hand. "Fautinir, good to meet you. I'm Harker."

He pulled me into a tight hug, and I'm pretty sure I heard another rib pop when he did. But it was worth it. "My name is Faustus, you twat. And if you think I'm going to run around saying stupid shit like holy forking shirtballs, you've got another think coming. I might be officially a good guy now, but I'm still the same motherfucker that pulled you out of Hell, and don't you forget it."

"Twice," I corrected. "You're the motherfucker that pulled me out of Hell twice. And there's no way I'll ever forget it. You went down there after me knowing full well that even if you got me out, you were gonna be stuck. That's divine shit, brother, and you deserve the upgrade in wings for it." I pulled back out of our hug and looked him in the eyes. "Thank you. I don't know if I deserve a friend like you, but I know I'll keep trying to."

"We all will," Luke said, stepping forward and putting a hand on Faustus's shoulder. "Thank you for bringing him back to us."

"Yeah," Becks said, wrapping her arms around the newly minted angel. "Thanks, bud." Then she turned to Glory, and I held my breath for a second. "You too, Wings," she said. "Thanks for bringing them both home. Now get over here."

Glory stepped in, joined the pile, and we stood there in the predawn light with our arms wrapped around each other, my pile of misfit toys all hugging and crying and laughing.

My family.

THE END

ACKNOWLEDGEMENTS AND A NOTE ABOUT A CAT

What do you say in the acknowledgements of a book that you've kept readers waiting way too long for? All I can really say is thank you for being patient (mostly) with me. It's been a rough few years, and the past two just caught up with me and I didn't write much. I spent a lot of time trying to keep a publishing company afloat through a pandemic and the new post-pandemic economy, as well as working on a few other projects and dealing with some health issues of my own and among my family. But we're all doing pretty well now, and hopefully we won't be waiting nearly as long for the next Harker adventure.

I have to thank the amazing Natania Barron for her work on the cover, Melissa McArthur for her editorial help, Theresa Glover for being a great right hand on our convention outings, and K.E. Mair for helping get the word out about this and all our Falstaff Books titles. It really does take a village to make a book, and I really appreciate everyone who reads any of this stuff, and everyone who gives their time, energy, and effort to bring these books to life.

Now…about the cat.

Yes, Quincy Harker now has a cat. Yes, the cat bears a striking resemblance to one of my cats, Gandalf. Yes, I am the nerd with a Magic: the Gathering tattoo who named his gray cat Gandalf. Yes, my characters are less nerdy than I am.

I created Nameless for the Instinct anthology edited by L.J. Hachmeister, and he is also featured in the upcoming Feisty Felines and Other Fantastical Familiars anthology coming from Wordfire Press, edited by Kevin J. Anderson and Alysson Longuiera. Nameless is Luke's new Renfield, although he doesn't quite know that yet. No, I am not turning the Harker series into some Lillian Jackson Braun knockoff, I was just happy to be invited into an animal rescue anthology, and another edited by my friend Kevin, and I like the dynamic of Harker having to deal with another sentient being who is even more a force for chaos in the universe than he is. So Team Harker has a cat now. It's gotta be at least a little less weird than having a digital rainbow unicorn hacker hanging around.

So I hope you like Nameless, because I plan on having him stick around for a while. Hell, I might even get Bubba a dog (yes, it would be a bulldog) and then do a short story where the pets hunt a monster. As long as I'm having fun writing it, you'll get the chance to read it.

Thanks for being patient, and for coming back. I really appreciate it.

ABOUT THE AUTHOR

John G. Hartness is a teller of tales, a righter of wrong, defender of ladies' virtues, and some people call him Maurice, for he speaks of the pompatus of love. He is also the award-winning author of the urban fantasy series *The Black Knight Chronicles*, the Bubba the Monster Hunter comedic horror series, the Quincy Harker, Demon Hunter dark fantasy series, and many other projects.

In 2016, John teamed up with several other publishing industry professionals to create Falstaff Books, a small press dedicated to publishing the best of genre fiction's "misfit toys." Falstaff Books has since published over 300 titles with authors ranging from first-timers to NY Times bestsellers, with no signs of slowing down any time soon. He is also the founder of the SAGA Genre Fiction Writers' Conference, where students hone their business and craft skills to write better books and make more money.

In his copious free time John enjoys long walks on the beach, rescuing kittens from trees and playing *Magic: the Gathering*. John's pronouns are he/him.

ALSO BY JOHN G. HARTNESS

Zombies Ate My Homework: Shingles Book 5

Slow Ride: Shingles Book 12

Carnival of Psychos: Shingles Book 19

Jingle My Balls: Shingles Book 24

Snatched: Grandma Annie and the Cooter of Doom: Shingles Book 29

Deader than Hell: Shingles Book 40

NSFW - The Shingles Collection

OTHER WORK

The True Confessions of Fandingo the Fantastical (with EM Kaplan)

Queen of Kats

Fireheart

Amazing Grace: A Dead Old Ladies Detective Agency Mystery

From the Stone

The Chosen

Genesis

Hazard Pay and Other Tales

Have Spacecat, Will Travel

Identity Theft

STAY IN TOUCH!

If you enjoyed this book, please leave a review on Amazon, Goodreads, or wherever you like.

If you'd like to hear more about or from the author, please join my mailing list at https://www.subscribepage.com/g8d0a9.

You can get some free short stories just for signing up, and whenever a book gets 50 reviews, the author gets a unicorn. I need another unicorn. The ones I have are getting lonely. So please leave a review and get me another unicorn!

FRIENDS OF FALSTAFF

Thank You to All our Falstaff Books Patrons, who get extra digital content each month! To be featured here and see what other great rewards we offer, go to www.patreon.com/falstaffbooks.

PATRONS

Dino Hicks
John Hooks
John Kilgallon
Larissa Lichty
Travis & Casey Schilling
Staci-Leigh Santore
Sheryl R. Hayes
Scott Norris
Samuel Montgomery-Blinn
Junkle